P9-ECK-990

# Praise for *New York Times* bestselling author

## Leslie Kelly

"Sexy, funny and a little outrageous, Leslie Kelly is a must read!"
—*New York Times* bestselling author Carly Phillips

"Ms. Kelly has sent her readers into the heat with this one. The perfect blend of romance and lust... This is a great story with passion and complications that make it hard to put down and easy to read."
—*Harlequin Junkie* on *Oh, Naughty Night*

"*Oh, Naughty Night* is a fun, erotic story...also a thoroughly modern story... I'll be looking out for [Kelly's books] from now on, given her sexy tales of well-drawn characters in awkward situations."
—*Fresh Fiction*

"Kelly employs a great deal of heart and humor to achieve balance with this incendiary romance."
—*The Romance Reader's Connection* on *Overexposed*

"Kelly is a top writer."
—*RT Book Reviews*

Dear Reader,

When I wrote my November 2014 Blaze, *Oh, Naughty Night*, I didn't really envision making a heroine out of sassy, sexy Viv Callahan. But sometimes when you're writing, a character will just spring off the page, demanding that you tell their story. Viv, with all her brassy self-confidence, was someone I wanted to explore, to try to figure out who she really was and what made her tick.

Coming up with the appropriate hero for this very bad girl wasn't much of a problem. Ever since the release of my Blaze novella *Triple Play*, I've heard from readers who wanted more of superrich, supersexy bad boy Damien Black. Who better to tame the wild ways of a naughty seductress than an equally naughty billionaire? Their romance sears the pages, but also touches the heart.

Honestly, I love every story as I write it, but I have to say Viv and Damien's now holds a place in my personal top five of all my books. I love their relationship—the heat and the emotion—and for the first time have found myself wishing I could write a sequel just about this pair.

I so hope you enjoy reading about them, too!

Best wishes—

*Leslie Kelly*

# Leslie Kelly

—

## Insatiable

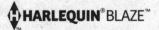

If you purchased this book without a cover you should be aware that this book is stolen property. It was reported as "unsold and destroyed" to the publisher, and neither the author nor the publisher has received any payment for this "stripped book."

Recycling programs
for this product may
not exist in your area.

ISBN-13: 978-0-373-79866-7

Insatiable

Copyright © 2015 by Leslie A. Kelly

The publisher acknowledges the copyright
holder of the additional work:

Hard Knocks

Copyright © 2014 by Lori Foster

All rights reserved. Except for use in any review, the reproduction or utilization of this work in whole or in part in any form by any electronic, mechanical or other means, now known or hereinafter invented, including xerography, photocopying and recording, or in any information storage or retrieval system, is forbidden without the written permission of the publisher, Harlequin Enterprises Limited, 225 Duncan Mill Road, Don Mills, Ontario M3B 3K9, Canada.

This is a work of fiction. Names, characters, places and incidents are either the product of the author's imagination or are used fictitiously, and any resemblance to actual persons, living or dead, business establishments, events or locales is entirely coincidental.

This edition published by arrangement with Harlequin Books S.A.

For questions and comments about the quality of this book, please contact us at CustomerService@Harlequin.com.

® and TM are trademarks of Harlequin Enterprises Limited or its corporate affiliates. Trademarks indicated with ® are registered in the United States Patent and Trademark Office, the Canadian Intellectual Property Office and in other countries.

HARLEQUIN®
™ www.Harlequin.com

**Printed in U.S.A.**

# CONTENTS

*New York Times* bestselling author **Leslie Kelly** has written dozens of books and novellas for the Harlequin Blaze, Temptation and HQN lines. Known for her sparkling dialogue, fun characters and steamy sensuality, she has been honored with numerous awards, including a National Readers' Choice Award, a Colorado Award of Excellence, a Golden Quill and an *RT Book Reviews* Career Achievement Award in Series Romance. Leslie has also been nominated four times for the highest award in romance fiction, the RWA RITA® Award. Leslie lives in Maryland with her own romantic hero, Bruce, and their daughters.

Visit her online at lesliekelly.com or at her blog, plotmonkeys.com.

### Books by Leslie Kelly
### HARLEQUIN BLAZE

*Another Wild Wedding Night*
*Terms of Surrender*
*It Happened One Christmas*
"Sleeping with a Beauty" in *Once Upon a Valentine*
*Blazing Midsummer Nights*
"The Prince Who Stole Christmas" in *Let It Snow...*
*Waking Up to You*
*Lying in Your Arms*
"I'll Be Home for Christmas" in *A Soldier's Christmas*
*Double Take*
*Oh, Naughty Night*

To get the inside scoop on Harlequin Blaze and its talented writers, be sure to check out BlazeAuthors.com.

All backlist available in ebook format.

Visit the Author Profile page at Harlequin.com for more titles.

# INSATIABLE

## Leslie Kelly

Dedicated with love to Kim Abod.

I'm the one who writes about dreams coming true. You're the one who helped make that happen for my baby.

I can never thank you enough.

# 1

"It was the slap heard 'round the wide world of sports. For a nanosecond, I felt the thrill of victory. Then when I realized what I'd done—and in front of whom—I felt the pure agony of defeat."

After making that pronouncement, Viv Callahan lifted her glass of wine and gulped a mouthful. Her two best friends, Lulu and Amelia, didn't touch theirs. Both of them looked shocked by what Viv had just told them.

"Seriously?" asked Lulu, her big brown eyes round. "You slapped hockey star Bruno Neeley across the face, in front of the other players, the press and your own boss?"

"I'm afraid so." Viv rubbed her hand. It had been red for a half hour after she'd whacked the jerk, and it was still sore now, hours later. "Every hockey fan knows the creep's head is harder than a rock. But I never realized his face was just as hard."

Maybe it was because his entire skull—including whatever excuse he'd once had for a brain—had calcified.

"I'm so sorry," said Amelia, the gentlest of their trio. Proving she could also be feisty, she added, "What a prick."

"Thanks. You know I can put up with a lot. But when he shoved his tongue down my throat and tried to get his hand between my legs—in a room full of people—I went straight to DEFCON One."

She couldn't recall a moment in her life when she'd been more shocked. Surrounded by coworkers at a publicity party she'd helped coordinate, she'd been sitting quietly in the back. Viv had been caught totally off-guard when Neeley had bent over from behind her chair. Grabbing her upper thigh—and trying to go higher—he'd yanked her face up for a kiss, wrenching her neck. As soon as she'd been able to extricate herself, she'd launched out of the chair, swung around and slapped him with all her might.

Of course the cameras had focused on *that*. There'd been no reason for anybody to notice what had precipitated the slap; all attention had been on the team's general manager who'd been speaking at the time, at the front of the room. Ouch.

"You shoulda kicked him in the balls," Lulu snapped.

"I've been tempted to in recent weeks. Working for the team has certainly torn the blinders off my eyes about pro athletes."

"I don't understand how anybody could have blinders about pro athletes," Amelia pointed out with a small moue of distaste.

"I guess I thought they were like my brothers. Strong, a bit goofy, but with big hearts and tender souls."

"Bruno Neeley's as tender as a rhino," Lulu said.

Viv ran a weary hand through her hair, pulling it out of the conservative bun she was totally sick of wearing. One good thing about potentially losing her job—at least she could stop dressing so frumpily, something her boss had advised her to do after she'd started complaining about the unwanted attention she was getting from some players on the team. And that advice had come from the head of PR, who actually liked her. She could only imagine what the general manager had said—probably something along the lines of "Get rid of her."

"I swear, it's as though a few of the players intentionally set out to be pigs," she admitted. "No matter how often I politely refused, they just wouldn't stop trying to pick me up."

"That's probably why," Lulu said with a sneer. "They're not used to hearing 'no' and when they realized you wouldn't go out with any of them, you became some kind of challenge."

"You might be right." Viv reached again for her wine. "For the first time in my life, I try for the straight and narrow, act like a nun, and look where it gets me."

Fired. Not officially yet, that would happen tomorrow. But one second after the impulsive swing, when she'd heard the clicking of cameras and seen the shock of the reporters gathered for this afternoon's press reception, she'd had a mental flash of homelessness. Just because she couldn't control her temper. And Bruno Neeley couldn't control his libido.

It sucked. She loved her job with the Virginia Vanguard, happy to have a chance to blend her event-planning background with her knowledge of sports. With five brothers, how could she not be knowledgeable? Since childhood, she'd sat through hundreds of games, dozens of tournaments. She'd been enlisted as scorekeeper, batboy, snack runner, uniform washer, locker-room cleaner. At twelve, the smell of sweat and jockstraps had been more familiar to Viv than the latest Britney Spears perfume.

It was kind of funny in comparison to how she lived her life now. She wouldn't go so far as to call herself a tramp, but she had a reputation. One she'd earned. Having spent the first eighteen years of her life wearing a brotherly chastity belt, she'd let loose once she'd gotten out on her own.

Deep inside, though, she was still the sister of all those jocks, and still knew her way around a locker room better than a fashion show. And that meant she was perfect for her job.

Certainly, her siblings had been thrilled when she'd been hired a little over two months ago as a special-events coordinator for the Vanguard. They'd been talking about visits and season passes before the team had played their first game.

*So much for that.*

It wasn't just that she liked the job, and that her family was so enthusiastic—she was also proud of the work she'd done to build support for the new team, which was part of a brand-new international hockey league. She'd done well, if she did say so herself, and didn't relish going back to the unemployment line, especially in the metro DC area, where the job market was notoriously tight.

"If they do fire you, you march right out and get a lawyer to sue them for sexual harassment," Lulu insisted.

"I could, I guess, but I doubt it would work."

Her boss, Tim, would back her up. But *his* boss, Fred Stoker, definitely wouldn't. As the general manager had reminded her when she'd complained one too many times about the behavior of some of the players, she was a probationary employee.

"When they hired me, I signed a contract saying I can be let go without cause during my first six months."

"That doesn't matter. You were sexually harassed almost nonstop. A good attorney can get around whatever you signed."

"Maybe. But who can afford a good attorney? Besides, Stoker has been building a case, finding reasons to criticize me," Viv admitted. "Little stuff, ridiculous, really. But it started right after he warned me to stop being a 'distraction' to the players. I'm sure he's got a file full of excuses to fire me."

"God, this pisses me off!" Lulu exclaimed. "You get the shaft because you wouldn't go out with some spoiled athletes, and there's nothing you can do about it? I can't believe you're not throwing bricks through their office windows."

"Maybe I'm just tired of fighting," Viv said, more to herself than the others. She'd always been tough, a fighter—her dad said she was as ballsy as her brothers.

But the past few months had taken their toll. And it wasn't just her job, but also what had happened last spring with Dale, the guy she'd been dating.

She was weary. And more than a little heartsick.

Making eye contact with the waiter, Viv pointed to her already half-empty glass. Lulu, and even Amelia, nodded for more, too, out of solidarity, though it was a weeknight. Viv appreciated them meeting her at their favorite bar. Lulu was a newlywed, and Amelia engaged, so their girls' nights were few and far between. It was good to know her friends always had her back, even if the team's management did not.

"Can you go over his head, to the team's owner?" asked Lulu.

"I'm not sure who the owner is—some big corporation, I think."

"That's not unusual," Amelia interjected. "Often a few millionaires pool their money, start up a corporation to shield their other assets and buy a team."

Viv and Lulu eyed their completely unathletic friend.

Amelia explained. "You don't suppose I can be engaged to a sports reporter and not pick up some stuff, do you?"

Viv sighed. "Lex is a good one. You are both so lucky."

"You will be, too," Amelia said. "There are other nice guys out there."

"I'd be happy with one who didn't believe he had the right to grab my crotch because he makes millions playing a damn game." Running a weary hand over her brow, she added, "To be honest, I'm kinda burned out on the whole male species right now."

Lulu waggled her brows suggestively.

"Not that I'm suddenly into girls," Viv said with a chuckle, understanding what her friend was implying. "You know I love cock. If only I could get it without a bunch of strings."

Amelia stuck her fingers into her ears and feigned shocked innocence. Considering she was shacking up with Lex, who was a Hottie McHottentot, it would take a lot more than that to singe her pretty ears.

"There's always your dildo," said Lulu.

Amelia coughed into her fist. Viv and Lulu both smirked.

"Yeah," Viv replied, "but it's not the same as real, genuine man meat. Unfortunately, lately, all that meat has been attached to asshole jerks." And not just at work, either.

"The perfect guy is out there waiting to nudge his way into your heart," said Amelia, skipping the man-meat comment.

Viv almost retorted that she only wanted one to nudge his face between her thighs, but figured she'd shocked the other woman enough for one evening. "I can't look for one now. I have to get a new job and straighten myself out before I can even think about letting any man near my heart." Her vagina was a different matter, but she didn't mention that, either.

"Neeley ought to be shot for making you feel that way. Or at least arrested for assault," said Lulu.

She laughed bitterly. "Oh, *that* would go over well."

Talk about bad publicity for the new team, and she wouldn't do herself any favors in the long run. She needed to look toward the future, toward landing another job, and fast. She lived in an expensive high-rise in Arlington, and only had enough in reserve to cover two months' rent. Filing charges against a huge sports star—the most popular guy in the state right now—would not win her any friends among hiring officials, or anybody else.

Heck, her five brothers—all of them hockey nuts—might even be annoyed at her. Of course, they all also might want to kill Neeley. She honestly didn't know how her family would react, and didn't want to find out. She only prayed that the story wouldn't go national, and her family wouldn't see any coverage of it in the tiny Pennsylvania town where they all lived.

"I hate it, and it goes against everything I believe in, but I have to just let it go," she said. "Gotta hope karma takes care of this one for me and Neeley gets what he deserves."

"If there's anything Lex can do, I'm sure he would," said Amelia. "He's no fan of Neeley's. He thinks he's a fathead."

"Well, he's certainly a hardhead. And thanks, I appreciate it," Viv said, meaning it. Amelia's fiancé was a popular DC sports reporter. If worse came to worst, it might not be bad to have him on her side. "But I guess I just want to get the firing over with and move on."

"Don't give up," said Lulu. "Somebody in that room had to have seen what Neeley did. Or you can explain to the general manager. He might be so worried about bad publicity that he'll let you stay."

It was possible, she supposed, and she allowed her friend's words to cheer her up momentarily.

But they proved to be overly optimistic.

Because about eighteen hours later, after a meeting with the team's general manager that left her humiliated and angry, Viv was cleaning out her desk.

Fired.

WHAT DAMIEN BLACK knew about cars would probably fit on the inside cover of a matchbook. But as he watched a shapely blonde lift the hood of her sedan and stare with a complete lack of comprehension at the inner workings of the engine, he found himself wishing he was an ace mechanic.

One thing he did know how to do, however, was spell AAA. So without even hesitating, he changed direction, heading not toward the exit and the adjoining office building that he owned, but to the woman with the car trouble.

"Problems?"

The blonde had been mumbling some colorful words under her breath as he walked up behind her, and obviously hadn't heard him approach. His words startled her. She jerked her head, glancing at him over her shoulder, giving him his first real look at her.

Damien's lips parted in a small, surprised inhalation, but he quickly schooled his features. He was used to not giving anything away, and he definitely didn't want to let this gorgeous female know he'd been briefly rendered speechless by how stunning she was.

He'd seen the golden-blond hair confined in a tight bun, and the tall body clad in a somewhat baggy gray suit as he'd approached her. But nothing had prepared him for the big baby blues, surrounded by long, thick lashes. The heart-shaped face was flawless, the mouth wide, the lips lush, the cheekbones high.

But her makeup wasn't exactly perfect—in fact, some dark smudges under her eyes hinted that she'd either cried or wiped off some mascara in the recent past. The thin streaks on her cheeks suggested tears.

*Who made you cry? And how can I hurt him for you?*

"Do you know anything about cars?" she asked, her voice shaking.

He didn't even try to lie, though he also didn't admit that he had a driver most of the time. "I'm afraid not. But I do have a cell phone and can call you a tow truck."

She blew out a frustrated breath. "I can't afford that. Not anymore, anyway."

Curious, he raised a brow.

"I just got fired."

Damien frowned, hearing the hurt in her voice that she tried to disguise with a harsh laugh.

"Can you beat it? Lose my job and have a breakdown

all within the same hour. This day's just stellar. Hell, this whole week's going to be one for the record books."

"That's too bad," he said, meaning it. "Where did you work?"

"It doesn't matter." She slammed down the hood of her car, giving up on even trying to figure out what was wrong with it. "It's their loss, anyway."

Swinging around to face him, he saw her eyes widen, much as his just had. He was used to having an effect on women, though he didn't necessarily try to. Part of it was his money, some of which he'd inherited from his father, but most he'd earned on his own. But he'd also been gifted with his late father's tall, lean build, black hair and dark brown eyes. He knew when women became aware of him as a man...and this one just had.

But instead of smiling flirtatiously, as he expected, she instead jabbed an index finger toward his chest, punctuating her words. "I was damn good at my job. Or I would have been, if they'd given me a real chance. I didn't even make it through my probationary period." She rubbed at her eyes, her shoulders slumping. "God, I need a drink."

"That I *can* help you with. There's a nice bar in the hotel next door, where I'm staying."

He should know. He owned the hotel, too. As well as the parking garage in which they were standing. In fact, between his family's corporation, his own international hotel chain and his new, just-for-fun enterprise, he owned quite a bit of prime Arlington real estate. Not that he was going to reveal that to this woman. He far preferred that people not realize who he was when they first met him, wanting to be judged on his own merits and not on the size of his bank accounts.

She sighed heavily. "Oh, here we go."

"What?"

"See a helpless woman and move in for the kill, huh?"

He frowned. "First of all, you don't appear helpless."

"I'm not."

"Second, I'm not a killer."

"Maybe I worded that badly."

*I should think so.*

"Lady-killer is more like it."

His frown deepened. "I wasn't moving in for anything. I'm not trying to prey on your tearful state, ply you with drink and have my wicked way with you."

Well, not really. Mostly, he'd asked her to join him for a drink because she looked as if she'd been having a really crappy day. And, okay, he'd admit it, she was pretty damn stunning.

Damien hadn't been involved with anyone in a few months. He'd had his nose to the grindstone because of a major expansion in the family business, plus stealing what time he could to oversee his own personal endeavors.

But it wasn't just his work schedule that had kept him celibate. He'd also been trying to avoid the matrimonial traps single females sometimes laid out for him. Nobody was ever going to catch him in one of those—love and marriage just didn't seem to work for the men in his family.

Even purely physical relationships had been difficult to arrange lately. Hell, his own mother threw a never-ending stream of "appropriate" women in his direction. So he'd found it easier to just keep his head down and his libido in cold storage.

This blonde had made him begin to wonder if it was time to change that, though. It had been ages since he'd been so instantly attracted to someone. He'd gone from cold storage to overheated in fewer than ten minutes, and he wanted to know more about the woman who'd so easily thawed him out, even if that only involved a drink.

She shook her head and closed her eyes. "I'm sorry. I'm a bit of a man-hating psycho-bitch right now."

"Was there a recent breakup to go with the firing and the breakdown?"

"Let's start calling it 'car trouble.' 'Breakdown' sounds mental, and I haven't reached that point. At least not yet."

"Noted."

"And the break*up* was a few months ago. But more recently, a man made my work life hell, and another man fired me for it. I'm not fond of the male sex right at this moment."

"I don't blame you." Then he shrugged. "Their stupidity, my loss."

"I guess so." A frown tugging at her brow, she suddenly squared her shoulders and stared at him, hard. "Why not?"

"Why not what?"

"Why weren't you trying to pick me up?"

"Didn't you just accuse me of being a killer?"

"Lady-killer. But you weren't making moves on me. Why? Is there something wrong with me?"

Odd, now she seemed annoyed. He had thought by her reaction that she'd be glad he wasn't coming on to her. Even though, technically, he supposed he was. For altruistic reasons, of course…at least until later, when she'd recovered from her post-firing, car-breakdown slump.

Damien wasn't a hypocrite. He liked women; he especially liked beautiful women, as long as they didn't expect anything long-term. And this one was an interesting combination of beauty and brains.

He suspected she had problems because of that mixture, judging by the fact that she dressed severely to play down her appearance, and kept what he suspected was a glorious head of hair so tightly constrained.

"Nothing's wrong with you. Maybe I'm just a nice guy."

That amused him, since few in the corporate world thought of him as anything of the kind.

She snorted. "I'd like to meet one of those someday. Haven't come across any in a *long* time."

He sensed she was talking about her job again. He was suddenly curious about this position she'd lost. Given the way she spoke about the men she'd worked with, and the outfit, he suspected sexual harassment had been the underlying cause. Which totally pissed him off. He had younger sisters. If something like that had happened to them, he'd be out for blood. He also had a strict policy against sexual harassment in all his companies, even the hotels in countries where discrimination against women was rampant.

Nobody deserved to be judged or treated differently because of their sex or their looks. As ridiculous as it sounded, he'd learned that himself over the years. He'd been called a pretty boy when he'd inherited a huge mantle of responsibility at a young age and been underestimated more than once, though once was usually enough for most people. Of course, it hadn't been enough for those closest to him…his own mother, for instance. Which was one reason he spent most of his time in his hotels and rarely went back to his Miami home.

Shoving that situation out of his mind, he focused only on this stranger. "I suspect you could use a friend—and a mechanic—more than a date."

She glanced down at her suit and made a face. "It's these ugly clothes, isn't it? I guess that's one nice thing about losing my job, I don't have to dress like a seventy-year-old librarian anymore."

Noting she'd just confirmed his suspicions, he barked a laugh. God, did the woman really believe a baggy gray suit could disguise the fact that she had more curves than a circle?

"I doubt anyone would ever mistake you for an old lady."

"Still, you didn't try to pick me up, which means I've been playing good girl for so long, I have completely lost my touch."

Playing good girl? Hmm.

"There was a time when I would've had you offering to buy me a drink, dinner and breakfast, in that order, within five minutes of meeting me."

*Would you have accepted?*

"Under other circumstances, I probably would," he admitted. "But the truth is, I've got two kid sisters, and if one of them had had a day as bad as yours, I'd hope some nice guy would offer to help her without any selfish motives."

She eyed him steadily—God, those blue eyes—and finally a slow smile spread across her face. "You're really serious."

He couldn't help returning her smile with one of his own. It creaked across his face slowly. He wasn't used to smiling lately, given how hard he'd been working and the family nonsense he always had to deal with. "Yeah, I really am."

Nibbling her lip, she cast an uncertain eye toward her car.

"If you can't afford a tow," he said, "let me call somebody. I have a friend who's good with cars. He can be here in five minutes."

That would be his driver, Jed, who'd just dropped him off on the main floor of the garage, near the doors leading directly into the building. He'd gone up to park in the reserved corporate level one floor up.

"Five minutes?"

Damien didn't answer, instead pulling out his phone and dialing his driver. When Jed answered, he described the problem and then disconnected. "Less than five minutes," he told her with a shrug. "He said you can leave the car unlocked and the keys under the mat."

Her brow went up. "Seriously?" Quickly casting an eye over the dented vehicle, she added, "Then again, even if it could start—which it won't—who'd want to steal it?"

"Good point. Now, while he checks it out, you and I can go to the bar, get out of the heat and talk about your horrible, no-good, very bad day."

She glared. "You have kids!" Grabbing his left hand, she yanked it up. "You're married, aren't you? I should've figured."

He couldn't help chuckling at her indignant expression, and her assumption. "Not as much as a tan line on that finger, see? Not married. Never have been. No kids. But I have a three-year-old nephew who loves being read to."

Sheepish, she murmured, "Sorry, Uncle…?"

"Damien." He extended his hand to hers. "I'm Damien Black."

He waited for any sign of recognition, such as dollar signs rolling in her eyeballs—he'd certainly experienced that before. But he saw nothing in her eyes but that same wary interest, as if she was trying to decide whether she could trust anyone with a Y chromosome.

Or maybe she was wondering if she could trust herself?

If she'd been, as she said, "playing" good girl…who was she when she wasn't playing?

Hmm. He'd like to find out. He only hoped she decided to give him the chance.

Finally, after a long, breathless moment during which his heart started pounding with anticipation, she took his hand and said, "It's nice to meet you, Damien. I'm Viv Callahan. And if you can have a gin and tonic in my hand within thirty minutes, I might just revise my opinion of the male species."

# 2

VIV HAD BEEN a good girl for a long time.

She didn't just mean the nine weeks she'd been employed by the Virginia Vanguard. Even before that, she'd been steering clear of men, though she'd never come clean to her friends about why. They knew she'd been bothered by her breakup with her ex, Dale, last spring. They didn't know she'd actually been heartbroken, however.

It seemed as though the real Viv had been in hibernation ever since. But this guy, a complete stranger who in ten minutes had shown her more courtesy than any of her coworkers had in months, called to every wicked, suppressed instinct she owned.

As they walked together, side by side, out of the garage, she couldn't help casting surreptitious glances at him. Under the bright, late-afternoon sunshine, his black hair gleamed luxuriously, like a sleek cat's. His profile was incredibly masculine—the cheeks sharply cut, the jaw square, the nose strong without being overbearing, the brows thick over dark, chocolate-brown eyes.

Having been surrounded by beefy, brawny, self-important meatheads who'd been harassing her for weeks, she found his tall, lean-but-powerful body incredibly attractive. The tailored suit couldn't disguise his broad shoulders, strong arms, slim waist and hips and long legs. Absolutely delicious.

Vixen Viv, who'd been in hiding since being so badly burned, began to awaken within her.

Damien was gorgeous, sexy, unattached and interested. Judging by the clothes and where he was staying, he was probably a successful businessman visiting the DC area. Not being a local, he wouldn't be sticking around. That was just perfect, since she was in no mood to even think about anything serious. She hadn't been kidding when she'd told her friends she wanted some cock without complications. He could give her the one while letting her avoid the other. Win-win.

She had nothing to lose and no longer had a job to worry about holding on to. If she tried, she could seduce him into bed and not leave it until next week.

Besides, she was sick of allowing herself to live a life based on what one rotten man had done to her. If she'd told herself a year ago that a guy could hurt her so badly she'd give up men—and sex—for months, she'd have laughed.

Damien Black might end all that. He could help her shake off the unaccustomed insecurity she'd been experiencing since Dale had shattered her self-confidence.

She just had to make him want to.

Seeing a crack in the sidewalk, she edged closer to him, not wanting to trip. She also wanted to feel the brush of his sleeve against her arm, to catch a whiff of his spicy cologne.

"Watch your step." He put a hand against the small of her back as they reached the jagged crack in the cobblestone.

"Thanks," she murmured, not pulling away once they'd passed it. His hand stayed where it was, too, a fiery brand on her spine that she felt through her blouse and jacket. She didn't mind the possessiveness of it, because it was simple and noncontrolling. He made no effort to manhandle her, but the power of the touch reached her on a deep, visceral level.

It had been a long time since she'd given up control in a sexual relationship, and she sensed by the power this man exuded, as easily as he wore his designer suit, that he was used to being in control. Having a man *take* what he wanted—as that ignorant hockey player had done yesterday—infuriated her. But *letting* him take over, now, that was a totally different story.

The thought made her shiver with naughty anticipation.

They were heading toward the ritzy new Black Star Hotel, which was on the opposite side of the garage from the high-rise where she worked.

*Had worked, damn it.*

The hotel had opened fewer than six months ago. Viv had eaten lunch at the restaurant a few times, since the place was so close to her office—*former office*. But she'd never stayed there. It was definitely out of her price range, as it catered to wealthy international tourists, who came to explore the nation's capital, or Wall Street bigwigs on business trips.

Speaking of which… "I didn't ask, were you heading somewhere when you decided to play Sir Galahad wielding his mighty cell phone?"

"Yes, but it's nothing I can't reschedule."

"You're sure? I don't want to keep you from an important meeting or anything."

"No. I was planning to stop in and check out a business interest of mine, but I didn't have an appointment." He glanced over at her, his lips quirking up into a smile. "It can wait."

They reached the hotel, and the doorman immediately opened the door for him. "Good afternoon, Mr. Black."

Nice service they had here, at least for the registered guests. Keeping staff good enough to remember the names of the clientele had to be expensive, which could explain why the rooms started at five hundred dollars a night.

"Have you been staying here for a while?" she asked as they entered the opulent lobby, tiled in sleek, black marble.

Tasteful gold accents brought in some color without making it look ostentatious.

"I got into town last night. But I always stay here when I visit DC." He smiled and nodded at the concierge, who had immediately snapped to attention. "This is my favorite hotel chain."

"They're pretty new, aren't they?"

"Not really. They started in Miami around twenty years ago, and have about fifty locations around the world. The Paris one is my favorite."

Mmm, Paris. Visiting the city of lights was number one on her bucket list. She'd always loved the idea of it—the art, the music, the food, the romance.

Probably few people would believe it, but Viv was a romantic at heart. Most saw her as either a tough girl—as she'd had to be, being raised with all those brothers—or a sexual siren. So she seldom had a chance to reveal her softer side. And the one time she had…well, her ex hadn't exactly been the romantic type, and had been amused to find out she was.

She tried to shove Dale out of her mind. Not easy since his damn campaign signs were all over the place. Whenever she saw one, a chant of, "Lose, lose, lose," roared through her mind, but she had a sense that he was going to win his coveted-above-all-else Virginia delegate seat this fall. The bastard.

She supposed it wasn't a surprise that Dale was on her mind now, even though she was definitely over him. Well, she was over the tender emotions, not quite over the hurt or anger. Anyway, losing her job had brought all those feelings to the forefront again. Dale had commented when they'd broken up that a "woman like her, who worked around a lot of men" was bound to get into trouble. Damn, she hated that he might hear about this and decide he'd been proved right.

"Jackass," she mumbled.

Damien immediately stopped raised an eyebrow.

"Oh, sorry, I guess I was talking to myself." Feeling herself flush, she quickly added, "And I was *not* talking about you."

"Your boss?"

She shrugged, noncommittal.

"You talk to yourself a lot, don't you. I heard one of your scintillating conversations when I walked up behind you in the parking garage."

She winced. "Did I singe your ears?"

"Don't worry about it. Anybody who's had a day as bad as yours gets a pass on language and just about everything else."

"Everything else, huh?"

Possibilities flooded through her mind. She could think of a lot of things that would help her get her mind off her ex, her job, her car and all that ailed her. Getting back in the saddle, sexually speaking, was the perfect way to move past everything that had been going wrong for the past few months. She could get her rocks off, have an unforgettable night of passion and walk away tomorrow, clean slate, ready to start again. And doing it with the incredibly sexy man escorting her to a private table in a corner of the bar sounded heavenly.

*Remember—make him want to.*

She hadn't come on to a man in months, hadn't even really flirted, and definitely hadn't tried to get a guy into her bed. But it was kind of like riding a bike, wasn't it? A woman never really forgot how to make a man want her. At least, a woman as skilled at it as Viv Callahan had once been.

Instinct kicked in, her body making the decision one second ahead of her brain. As he pulled out her chair, she reached up and unbuttoned her suit jacket, slipping it off. There was nothing she could do about the shapeless skirt that reached her knees, but she was wearing a silky white blouse that could be considered sexy when it wasn't concealed by the jacket.

She made it even sexier by surreptitiously unfastening two more buttons while he took his seat opposite her. When he looked at her, his gaze traveled to her suddenly much-deeper neckline, lingered there for a moment and then moved up to her face.

His smile said he'd read her every move.

She didn't care.

Didn't blush.

Didn't retreat.

No.

Instead, she went one step further. Smiling innocently, she said, "Another good thing about unemployment. I no longer have to put my hair into hideous buns, either."

Reaching up, she pulled out the pins that constrained her thick, long hair, and shook it out, running her fingers through its length. It fell in a golden curtain around her shoulders.

He didn't take his eyes off her, as she'd known he wouldn't. There wasn't a man alive who didn't see an attractive woman's long, silky hair and imagine twining his fingers in it as she rode him into oblivion.

Damien watched her, his lips parted, his eyes hooded. And a surge of feminine power rose within her. For the first time in ages, she felt strong, sure of herself, certain of what she wanted and how she was going to get it.

The real Viv was back—in charge, in control and ready to get wicked.

STARING INTO THE face of a woman who'd gone from extremely attractive to drop-dead gorgeous, Damien felt like a baseball player standing on the field who'd just learned all the rules of the game had changed. Missed swings no longer counted as strikes, and three definitely didn't mean you were out. As for a grand slam, well, he had the sense that was suddenly well within his reach.

What, he wondered, had happened?

She'd been prickly when they met—with reason, given what she said she'd been going through. She'd warmed up and become a little flirtatious, but mostly just conversational. He'd noticed flashes of wit, but nothing that could have been described as provocative. And then, between the time he pulled out her chair and when he sat across from her, she'd armed herself with every potent, sexual tool in her arsenal. She'd gone from buttoned-up, sedate businesswoman to vamp with a few unbuttons and a swish of that glorious mane of blond hair.

Only a fool, or a male virgin, wouldn't get the message.

"What are you up to?" he asked, blunt, as always. He didn't play games, not when it came to anything important. And he sensed she could be important.

"Hmm? What do you mean?" she said with a shrug, playing innocent.

He nodded toward the hair, and cast another pointed glance at the extremely interesting cleavage. "I asked Miss Marple for a drink and ended up with Jessica Rabbit."

"Who's Miss Marple? And, uh, Jessica who?"

Not many people shared his enjoyment of old mystery novels, so he gave her a pass on that one. But a woman built like Roger Rabbit's wife ought to be familiar with the cartoon character.

"She…"

"Kidding." Batting her lashes and vamping her voice, she purred, "'I'm not bad, I'm just drawn that way.'"

Oh, yeah. She most definitely was.

"Why the costume change?"

She shifted her gaze away, but before she could reply, a server stopped by their table. The young woman deposited two glasses of ice water, garnished with lemon, and offered them each a perfunctory smile. That was good. He didn't want to be recognized and called by name by everyone in this place, not in front of Viv.

"Two gin and tonics, please," he said, remembering his companion's drink preference.

When the server was gone, Viv glanced around. "This is beautiful—the view of the river is lovely. It's even nicer than the one from the restaurant upstairs."

"Coward."

Her jaw fell. "What?"

"No subject change allowed."

"Did I do that?"

"You know you did. Now answer the question," he murmured, enjoying the sparkle in her eyes and the tiny smile lurking on those lush red lips. She was slightly annoyed that he was pressing her, but also, he suspected, excited that he was following her where she'd led him with those two unfastened buttons.

"I suppose you're right," she finally admitted. "Remember that librarian comment? Well, I have been wearing a costume. Not by choice. It was at the suggestion of my supervisor."

Back to the job with the shitty coworkers and asshole of a boss. He stiffened, instinctively growing angry on her behalf again. "Why was that?"

"I worked with a lot of poor, weak, helpless men. Isn't that sad?"

He rolled his eyes, knowing exactly where she was headed. "Men with no self-control?"

"You win the prize. You want to hear the really fun part, the kicker I found out today when I was being fired?"

He wasn't sure, but nodded anyway.

"I was a bet."

Damien's hands clenched into fists on the table.

"Excuse me?"

"Yeah, during his we've-decided-not-to-keep-you-through-the-rest-of-your-probationary-period speech, my boss's boss said the guys had bet on who could get me into bed first."

"Are you serious?" he asked through a clenched jaw.

Damien had the urge to hurt someone, and vowed that by the end of the day, he'd have found out the name of her ex-employer, invested in the company and fired her son-of-a-bitch supervisor. Hell, he could buy the damn company and fire every man who worked there.

"Entirely. Seems I was just too much of a distraction, so it was best for everyone—including me, for my personal safety—if I left."

"Jesus Christ," Damien muttered. Lifting his water glass, he half drained it, trying to cool himself off. He was stunned by the idiocy not only of her male colleagues, but also of a higher-up who would hear about that bet and react by firing the *victim*. If the man had been one of his employees, Damien would have hit the roof. Not only was it wrong on a moral level, but the guy had also just opened up his employer to serious lawsuits.

When he felt capable of being rational, he said, "Call your lawyer."

"I can't afford one."

"I'll call my lawyer."

"Thank you, but no." She offered him a small, humorless smile. That, and her slumped shoulders, told him how crushed she was by this entire situation. "I just want to forget it ever happened," she said. "I got severance, and I've been promised excellent references."

"All to keep you from suing or making trouble."

"Yes. Normally, I'm good at making trouble." She traced the tips of her fingers across the condensation on her own glass. "Maybe I'm losing my touch."

He watched her long, slender fingers, so delicate and feminine, but also strong. He sensed she wasn't so much giving up as she was choosing what she thought was a better option.

"I'm sorry. And I'm goddamn angry. Let me help you."

"I don't need any help."

Used to taking care of things, and bothered that he couldn't in this situation, Damien bit back a frustrated retort. She was independent, he respected that. But he couldn't stand the idea of anybody getting away with that kind of bullshit, especially when Viv was the injured party.

Their drinks arrived. Damien glanced at his watch. "Twenty-nine-and-a-half minutes," he pointed out before sipping, enjoying the icy bite of the alcohol.

Remembering her comment in the garage, she smiled. "Okay, I officially resign from Man Haters Anonymous. At least for the rest of the day."

Lucky him.

"Now, back to your situation…"

"I meant what I said. I know men like to solve things—boy, do I ever know that. But I have already made up my mind."

As if she sensed he was about to argue, Viv tossed her hair, lifted her chin and managed a real smile. He suspected she was trying to downplay her sadness and humiliation as she said, "I must say, though, I'm not happy my good behavior went to waste. I was so nice, so plain and sweet while trying to get those guys to lose interest."

Plain she could never be. He doubted sweet was used to describe her very often, either. No, she was spicy.

"The deck was stacked against you because of that bet. You could have come in to work literally wearing a nun's habit and it wouldn't have changed a thing."

"I understand that now. But I gave it my best shot, believe me. Though, I didn't think of the habit angle, and I should have, given my Catholic-school upbringing."

Something else they had in common. "Nuns are terrifying."

"No kidding. My second-grade teacher, Sister Margaret, wouldn't have recognized me over the past several weeks, I was so demure. If she had, she'd probably have fallen over dead of shock that her predictions of my future wickedness hadn't come true."

He sipped again, wondering just how wicked this woman could be. "Future wickedness, huh? Did she believe you were destined for damnation?"

"Or prison."

He chuckled.

"You think I'm kidding? Yeesh, let a nun catch you in a coat closet with two boys, playing my-underwear-are-better-than-yours, and she's pegged you as a bad girl for life."

"Were they?

She cocked her head. "Were who what?"

"Were yours better than theirs?"

Snorting and rolling her eyes, she said, "Well, duh. *Angry Beavers* beats *Darkwing Duck* or *Animaniacs* any day."

He had just taken another sip of his drink but her response made him swallow the wrong way, and he had to cough into his fist, half laughing, half groaning. When he could speak again, he asked, "Your parents let their seven-year-old daughter wear *Angry Beavers* panties?"

"Caught that, didja?" she replied with a snicker. "They worked a lot, raising six kids, five of them strapping, athletic, eating-them-out-of-house-and-home boys."

Ouch. Five brothers. He wondered where she fell in the Callahan family lineup.

She continued. "Because of my parents' work schedules, my oldest brother had to take me back-to-school shopping that year. He didn't want to be caught by any of his high school friends in the little girl's department at the mall, so I had free rein when it came to choosing panties. Heh. But hey, better than *Ren and Stimpy*, right?"

"I don't know, 'happy-happy, joy-joy' seems like a good underwear motto."

"Speaking from experience?"

"I don't think they make *Ren and Stimpy* drawers in my size."

"Bummer. That would be a wicked-good theme song to have in your pants at all times."

They laughed together, and Damien found himself relaxing more than he had in ages. Strange, considering the fact that he was sitting here, drinking gin and tonics, with a gorgeous woman he wanted to take to bed, and they were talking about childhood cartoons. He hadn't had a completely normal childhood, given his family's wealth, but he'd enjoyed the occasional after-school Nickelodeon binge, and remembered fighting with his sisters over who got to watch what.

Funny that this new stranger made him remember those days, so far in his past he'd nearly forgotten about them. He couldn't recall the last time he'd had a conversation like this. Lately, all he talked about was business when at work and shopping and finances when with his family. He avoided relationships, knowing he wasn't cut out for them, but, on occasion, he did talk sex with women who expected nothing more from him.

This one had him talking cartoons.

He suddenly realized he liked her. Quite a lot. Not

just because she was strong and independent after going through hell. Not just because she made him laugh. It was also because he suddenly realized she'd done what she'd set out to do. She'd distracted him from the issue of those two buttons and that tumbling sea of hair. Clever girl.

"So, Wicked Viv—"

"Vixen Viv," she interrupted.

"Even better. So, Vixen, was Sister Margaret right about your wickedness? Are you planning to seduce me?" he asked, not letting her evade the subject this time.

He kept his eyes focused directly on hers, so he saw the way they flared. She licked her lips, and a faint pink tinge rose in her cheeks. He knew she wasn't blushing; that wasn't embarrassment or modesty.

It was heat.

And he had his answer.

"Are you saying you would have to be seduced?" she finally asked.

"No, I'm not saying that at all."

Seduction implied having to be coerced or convinced to do something. That wouldn't be the case with Viv. He'd been attracted to her at first sight, and his interest had heightened with every passing minute.

It wouldn't take a seduction for him to ask her to come up to his suite on the top floor of this hotel. How had she put it—he could ask her to join him for a drink, and then dinner, and then breakfast. She most definitely wouldn't have to be the one doing the seducing. All she had to do was say yes.

"Viv, would you—"

She cut him off. "Yes."

He smiled. So did she.

And that was that.

# 3

VIV HADN'T BEEN sure how to answer his question about her seductive intentions. With Damien Black's unfinished invitation, however, she hadn't needed to. What was happening between them was on both their heads...and would soon, hopefully, be on their bodies.

No, this was not a seduction. This was all about instant connection, shared desire and pure heat. It also had something to do with timing. She was in the right frame of mind to have a wild, one-night fling, and he was the right man—oh, Lord, he was right in all the best ways—in the right place, to make it happen.

That was why she'd cut him off, not even needing to hear the rest of his question. The answer was yes to anything he cared to propose.

There was one thing, however. "One night," she said, wanting to make sure he knew where she stood.

"What?"

"I just want to make sure we're both on the same page. One night is all I'm interested in, and since you're here from out of town, hopefully that's all you want, too."

He stared at her, intent, assessing. Finally, he replied, "You're serious."

"Very."

"Why?"

"Why am I acting like a guy, wanting just a one-night stand?"

"Nobody could mistake you for a guy."

"Not in looks, maybe. But my attitude—about this, anyway—is probably more in line with a man's."

He didn't deny it.

She ran the tip of her finger around the rim of her glass. Would she turn him off by admitting she was a woman who wasn't afraid or ashamed to go after what she wanted?

"My life is too convoluted right now to consider any kind of relationship." Lifting her finger to her mouth, she licked off the condensation, eyeing him wickedly, making promises about what kind of night they could have. "But I want you. I want one hot night with somebody I won't have to deal with tomorrow when I start picking up the pieces of my life."

He appeared indignant. "*Deal* with? You don't want to have to *deal* with me?"

She shrugged, not repentant. Better to lay things on the table now. "Well, not you personally. I just don't want to care about any repercussions or expectations. I don't want to worry about whether you'll call, or have you worry whether I will."

He nodded slowly. "I can understand that. And yes, I'm here on business, and I won't be in town for too long."

"Perfect."

"And, for what it's worth, I don't do the love-and-relationship thing anyway. I don't have the right genes for it."

Fine by her. "So we're good?"

He held up a hand, palm out. "Just to make sure I've got this straight, you want me to fuck your brains out to-night, make you come in a dozen different ways, bring you breakfast in the morning and then go away?"

Wow. She swallowed hard, noting that he could give as good as he got. His words scooped out her insides and replaced them with boiling lava. Just the idea of the kind of night he promised made it hard for her to think.

So she didn't. She merely agreed. Finding her voice, she said, "Yeah. Pretty much."

A brief hesitation, and then he nodded. "All right."

Her heart leaped. Though she'd known he desired her, she was glad he hadn't been turned off by a woman who was so nongirlie about sex. Some men couldn't handle women who were blunt about what they wanted—and what they didn't want—and felt as if their masculinity was threatened, or something.

She suspected that had been partly why she and Dale hadn't worked out, though he'd used any number of other excuses when he'd dumped her. And she also imagined it also explained the ridiculous bet among her former co-workers.

Fortunately, Damien was an unusually confident man. He would never be threatened by a strong woman who was unafraid to admit what she was really thinking. He'd be challenged by her.

It was almost too bad they would only have one night. She suspected they were pretty spectacularly matched.

She quickly squelched the thought, because she'd set out the parameters and he'd agreed to them. They were both out for a one-night stand, and no possible future. She couldn't change her mind—or try to change his—ninety seconds later.

Licking her lips, she murmured, "So, a dozen different ways, huh?"

He gave her a confident smile.

Viv did a quick mental calculation, and could only come up with seven ways previous lovers had brought her to orgasm. Adding in what she could do with her own fingers, a sex toy or a handheld showerhead brought her to ten.

A dozen would be very interesting indeed.

Just picturing a few of them made all that lava boil over inside her, dripping down to her sex. She was swollen and sensitive, so wet she might leave a stain on her damn skirt.

Imagine…ninety minutes ago, she'd been at one of the lowest points of her adult life. Now, well, as the saying went, things certainly could turn on a dime. Or on a broken-down car.

"Maybe thirteen," he said, as if suddenly remembering something. Something wicked. But oh so good.

"I could live with that," she mumbled, halfway to her first climax without a single touch from the man.

Before she could say another word, however, his cell phone beeped, indicating a message. He glanced at the screen and said, "It's Jed. He's had a chance to check out the car."

If anything could cool off her rapidly burning self, it was that. She reached for her glass and sipped her drink. She could not afford any pricey car repairs. Part of her wished somebody had just stolen the thing before the mechanic had gotten there, but she knew it wasn't much of a temptation. Compared to most of the cars in this upscale Arlington neighborhood, hers was a top-of-the-line piece of crap. Nobody would want it.

"All fixed," he said, reading from the screen.

Her mouth fell open. "Seriously?"

"Dead battery, that was all."

"Finally something goes my way."

"You mean things weren't going your way?" His tone was silky; his eyes gleamed. "And here I thought your day had improved tremendously."

She licked her lips. "I'll clarify—things are *continuing* to go my way."

"As they should."

"Spoken like someone who's used to things always going his way."

"Not always," he admitted.

"Ninety percent of the time?" she asked, teasing him.

He shrugged, not smiling in response. "I didn't get where I am because of luck."

"Are you a workaholic?"

"Would I have blown off a business meeting to spend the afternoon with you if I were?"

"Thought you didn't have a meeting."

"I didn't, not officially. Sometimes I pop in on my staff by surprise."

"Your staff." She stiffened, recognizing the implications. "You run a business that has offices in this part of Arlington?"

Another shrug. "Just a start-up, and it's not entirely mine. There are other investors. I'm not even sure if it's going to last a year. It could all blow up in my face."

Just a start-up. In this zip code.

Viv found herself wondering if she'd gotten in over her head. Judging by his clothes and his self-confidence, she'd already pegged the guy as wealthy and successful. She hadn't, however, banked on him being a one-percenter. She'd had experience with a few *über*wealthy men. They were usually spoiled, and could be petulant when they didn't get what they wanted.

Of course, Damien *was* going to get what he wanted, as was she. And considering he wasn't an arrogant jerk, she suspected he was only moderately well-to-do, which suited her just fine.

He glanced at his gold watch. God, his hands were strong, yet elegant. Every inch of him was a mix of masculinity and grace. Again she found herself comparing him to the other men she'd interacted with recently, and found them all lacking.

She wanted him. Badly. And she didn't want to wait any longer to have him. Those dozen—or thirteen—orgasms were practically screaming for her to hurry things along.

"It's after five. Early dinner, or more drinks?" he said, his tone silky, as if he could read her mind.

"I don't want my senses dulled the least little bit to-night," she said, the words almost purred. "So let's skip the next round."

She noted with satisfaction that his hand shook the tini-est bit. He might be Mr. Calm, Smooth and Seductive, but he was definitely affected by her. God, it was good to feel the surge of feminine power that pushed up through her. It had been too long since she'd allowed herself to play this sexual game. She'd once played it very well, and was glad to know she hadn't completely lost her touch.

Dropping a few large bills on the table, Damien rose from his seat and walked around to pull her chair out. He didn't say a word. He didn't have to. They were both caught up in the excitement of what was about to happen.

Viv had had a few one-night stands over the years, but none had ever excited her like this. Knowing she would never see him again after tomorrow had forced away all her inhibitions—what few there were. There was a special kind of freedom in realizing she could do, have, take or give anything she wanted from the sexiest man she'd ever met. There would be no embarrassing run-ins in days to come, no wondering if he'd call, no stressing over whether he'd thought she was good. Nothing but wonderful memo-ries of a night she was already sure she would never forget.

It was the perfect treat she could give herself as conso-lation for her lousy day, week, month, summer and year.

Not that anybody would ever complain about having Damien Black for a consolation prize.

As they exited the bar, he put his hand low on her spine again and she shivered. Her jacket was slung over her arm now, and only her silky, thin blouse separated her skin from his. Her nerve endings sizzled and sparked at the faint brush of his fingertips on her body, and she almost arched her back, wanting to invite him to keep exploring downward. His big, strong hand would cup her rear end perfectly.

"The hotel restaurant is great, but the room service menu is pretty extensive, too," he murmured, his voice sounding a bit strained, as if he'd be disappointed if she said she wanted to eat in the restaurant.

She hadn't even considered that. "How's the room service breakfast menu?"

"Also extensive."

"Then we don't have to leave your room for a good fifteen hours, do we?" she said, certain it would be ages before they got around to eating anything resembling food.

His hand dipped the tiniest bit lower, and his laugh was low and sultry.

Crossing the foyer, Damien offered a short nod to a staff member who hailed him. Beelining for the elevators, he cast one hard glance over his shoulder, and the staff member backed off. When a ding signaled the car's arrival and the door slid open, she noted the interior was empty. Viv breathed a sigh of relief that no one was waiting to board it with them.

They entered together, in lockstep. The moment the door swished closed, he moved close...close enough that his breath fell upon her cheek. Holding her jaw, he tilted her face up and bent to brush his lips against hers.

Sparks erupted at that faint connection, and she quivered, melting against his body, drawn to him as metal was drawn to a magnet.

"Protection?" he asked, his voice low. He seemed the type who preferred to get business out of the way up front, and she appreciated that about him, too.

"I'm on the Pill," she replied. "And I have no communicable diseases. I had to get a physical for my job, and I haven't been with anyone in forever."

He stiffened and stepped away. "Forever?"

Laughter burst from her lips as she realized he'd momentarily thought she meant she was a virgin. Good lord, after the conversation they'd just shared?

"Five months is kind of forever for me. I haven't gone that long without sex since I lost my virginity to Ollie Winpigler in the computer lab in eleventh grade."

His tension eased. "Ollie?" His frown deepening, he added, "In the computer lab?"

"He was a nice guy—a total computer geek, not at all athletic, which was why I chose him. He flew under my brothers' radar. Any of the jocks who tried to get with me found themselves up against the Callahan defensive line and none of them could make an end run around it."

Huh. Maybe that was why she preferred smart, sexy guys to beefy jocks. And maybe that deep-down disinterest had communicated itself to her coworkers in recent weeks. She didn't think she'd done or said anything to throw down a gauntlet, to make them compete for her. Was it possible they were competing because they sensed her innate disinterest in their type? It bore considering.

Or maybe not. They were horny, spoiled jerks, and she was an attractive, available woman. End of story.

He cleared his throat. "Should I be worried about these brothers of yours? They're not going to burst into my room and try to sack me from the ten yard line tonight, are they?"

She appreciated that he'd continued her play with words. He was clever, as well as smart. "Well, we're all close, but they do live hundreds of miles away. I don't see them nearly often enough. I haven't been home since Christmas, though I am going next month to my parents' anniversary party."

"So nobody's nearby to defend your virtue?"

"Nope, you have me completely at your mercy." She stepped closer, putting her hands on that hard chest, toying with the buttons of his crisp, white shirt. "As to your original question…I'm protected and healthy. So if you're clean, too, bareback is fine with me."

Although a pleased smile widened those masculine lips, he also groaned, as if he'd suddenly imagined plunging into her, all heated strength to wet sheath. No barriers, nothing but hot, slick pleasure.

"Thank God I'm not a teenager and I don't go around with a rubber in my pocket. And, uh, I can say the same. I haven't been very active lately, either."

Curious, she watched him, wondering if he'd explain.

All he said was "It's complicated."

"As long as you're not cheating on somebody else with me, *complicated* is fine," she said, presenting him with her one unbreakable rule. She'd noticed he wore no ring, so she wasn't truly worried.

Some women might believe she had no boundaries, but she'd borne witness to what one of her brothers' affairs had done to his marriage and family. Seeing the devastation the big, dumb idiot and his trashy girlfriend had wrought on her sister-in-law, nieces and nephew, she'd erected a big No Trespassing sign in her head when it came to attached men. Viv abided by it, always. She might flirt indiscriminately, but when it came to men in relationships with other women, she was strictly hands-off.

"I'm definitely not a cheater. I just don't do relationships. I'm not cut out for them."

She slipped one button of his shirt free, licking her lips. "Then it's all good."

"It most certainly will be. God, I can't wait to get inside you," he said, grabbing her hips, his fingers digging in to her curves. Holding tight, he pulled her hard against him so she could feel the ridge contained behind his zipper.

A big ridge. An overstressed zipper.

A whimper escaped her mouth, but he took it from her lips, kissing her again—deeply, hungrily. He plunged his tongue against hers, exploring her, tasting her, ravishing her.

Twining her arms around his neck, she let him take her places with that kiss, loving the feel of him pressed against her. Every inch of him was hard, which so appealed to every inch of her softness that she moaned out of sheer helpless need.

His tongue continued to dance with hers, hard and then light, teasing a response out of her. She was responding as she never had to anyone, craving his kiss, his strength, his body. She loved everything about it, from the silkiness of his tongue, to the warmth of his breaths, to the taste of mint and lime and gin on his lips.

Pushing her into the rear corner of the elevator, he began to pull at her bunched skirt. Viv lifted a leg and twined it around his, arching against him, almost crying in anticipation of being filled by that powerful cock pressed against her sex. She was wet, steamy hot and separated from what she wanted by only a few layers of clothes. It was exquisite torture, for him as well as her.

Hearing his groan as he, too, bemoaned the barriers, she chuckled throatily.

"Witch," he grumbled. "Better be careful or I won't wait until we get to my suite."

"Who told you to wait?" she purred, her mood edgy, dangerous and wild. The elevator could stop at any floor before reaching the top one, where he said his suite was located. But she honestly didn't care. She'd never taken that kind of risk in public…but he made it sound worthwhile.

"Very well, then. I won't," he said, a dangerous smile widening his mouth and making those dark eyes gleam.

Called on her dare, Viv sucked in a surprised breath, wondering just how far he intended to go.

It turned out, he went too far for her liking—all the way to the front of the elevator car. Hmm.

Glancing over his shoulder at her, a self-satisfied expression on his face, he pushed the emergency-stop button on the control panel.

Viv gaped, hearing an alarm go off somewhere in the elevator tower. Damien wagged his brows, appearing utterly mischievous. There was nothing boyish about the man, he was all adult male, yet that expression said he'd probably been a holy terror as a kid.

God, she liked holy terrors.

A voice emerged from a speaker set below the panel. "This is security, what's happening?"

Damien pulled open a small box that contained a phone, obviously for emergencies only. He lifted it and spoke into the handset. "This is Damien Black, from the penthouse suite."

Penthouse? Nice! No wonder he'd suggested room service—if she was staying in the penthouse of a place as ritzy as this, she'd never leave.

*But you are leaving in the morning*, she reminded herself.

Right. This was a one-night stand so she could get back

in the saddle and get over being fired. She couldn't get emotionally involved with anyone until she got her life straightened out. And even then, it wouldn't be with a gorgeous rich guy who probably picked up women in cities all over the world. One who didn't "do" relationships.

She could take being his DC-area pickup…as long as she remained emotionally disengaged and never looked beyond tonight. It was when she expected or hoped for more that she got bitten in the ass. While she wouldn't mind this guy nibbling on her posterior, she didn't want to be left with any real, lingering scars.

"Yes, we're fine, thank you."

She couldn't hear the other end of the conversation, now taking place only through the emergency phone, and could only imagine the security guy was asking why they'd stopped the elevator. Part of her wished Damien hadn't bothered; they would have probably reached the top floor by now if he hadn't pushed that button. Another part loved that he'd pushed it because he hadn't wanted to wait one more minute to have her.

"There's no real problem, I just wanted to test the alarm and the emergency procedures."

The person on the other end of the call spoke more loudly, but Damien, staring at her, barely paid attention. Viv sensed a naughty opportunity to twist the screws even tighter. Reaching up, she slowly slid free the next button on her blouse to reveal the curves of her breasts, covered by a pretty, lacy bra. She had nice breasts, not huge, but high and firm. More than one man had gotten a little stupid over them.

His only reaction was a slight tightening of his grip on the phone handle.

"Give your supervisor my name and then put him on the

phone," he finally said with a heavy sigh, as if he'd grown tired of hearing the other man's arguments.

The fact that he was going over the security guy's head indicated he knew the hotel really wanted to keep his business. Of course, nobody wanted his *business* more than she did right at this minute, particularly judging by how big and hard that business had felt pressed against her.

After a brief pause, someone else apparently spoke on the other end of the phone call. She couldn't hear the conversation, but after a moment, Damien said, "Yes, I am. And it's quite all right. I'm sure you're doing a fine job in security. Please just give me five minutes and then I'll restart the car." He glanced up at the corner. "And turn off the in-car camera."

She stared up at the black dome, which concealed a camera. She'd been so heated up by her sexy companion that she hadn't even noticed it. Honestly, she wasn't entirely sure she'd have cared if she had noticed it. She wasn't an exhibitionist, but she wanted Damien Black *that* much.

To her shock, a small red indicator light blinked off. Amazement filled her as she wondered just how the guy could get a security camera shut off with a phone call.

"Who *are* you?" she asked.

"Somebody who spends a lot of money at these hotels."

"Are you a platinum member of their frequent guest program or something? Is that why they kiss up to you no matter what crazy request you make?"

He shrugged. "Something like that."

"You do realize they were watching us on the camera and know exactly what we're up to, even though it's now off?"

"Of course."

"And you don't care?"

"No."

"But…"

"Do you really want to waste what time we have talking about this?" he asked, stalking closer, each slow step an exercise in restraint, as if he wanted to make sure she hadn't changed her mind.

As if.

"No, I really don't," she replied.

"Good."

He burned her with a hot, possessive stare. The fire of it blazed down her neck, to her cleavage. Her breasts pushed up and out of her open blouse.

"Five minutes," he said as he reached her, sliding a hand into her hair to pull her face to his. "This is gonna be fast."

Fast, slow—she wanted both. She wanted it all. They had all night, and she wanted him every way she could have him. But fast would do for a start.

Then he was kissing her, returning her to the heights of insane want. Even as he devoured her, again eliciting all those crazy, hot sensations, raising the level of need into the stratosphere, he began undressing her. His hands were unfastening her buttons, pushing her blouse open, and he kissed his way down her throat to the swell of her cleavage.

"Gorgeous," he muttered as he licked along the edge of her bra. When he moved to the front and breathed on the dark nipples straining so hard against the lace, she squirmed, wanting a more intimate connection.

"An hour wouldn't be enough to suck you the way I want to," he muttered. "So that's going to have to wait."

She whimpered, both in disappointment and excitement of the promised hour to come.

"Are you hot for me, Viv?" he whispered as he kissed his way down her midriff, dropping to his knees to better reach her.

"Find out for yourself," she purred, lifting a leg and

draping it over one strong shoulder. She was wanton, arching toward him, inviting him to push her skirt up and explore her hottest, wettest secrets.

He did, gliding his hand along her thigh, pushing the skirt up inch by inch. When his fingers brushed the edge of her panties, she hissed. Her hiss became a moan of pleasure when he pulled the fabric out of the way to slide a finger into the crevice between her legs.

"So hot," he groaned.

Viv closed her eyes, wanting him so much. The circular motions of his thumb on her clit were driving her to madness, and the strokes of his tongue on her belly were timed to perfectly match it, filling her with a more primal need. But it was the slow thrust of his finger into her core that made her frantic to be filled by him. All of him.

"Three minutes left," he muttered against her skin.

"No," she groaned, not sure how she would survive if he stopped what he was doing for the painfully long ride up to the penthouse.

"What can I do for you?" he asked, teasing her clit again, and adding another long finger to the one slowly moving in and out of her channel.

"You can give me one of those orgasms you promised," she said, opening her eyes and looking down at him. She grabbed two handfuls of his hair and turned his head so he was gazing up at her. "Or proceed directly to fucking my brains out."

He immediately rose, unzipping his pants. "Maybe I can kill two birds with one…"

"Cock?"

He chuckled. "I love that sassy mouth of yours."

Viv reached out to help him, quivering at the satiny steel in her hand.

"Holy mother…" she mumbled, staring at the big, thick

erection. Though she hadn't ever been nervous about sex, not even that first time with Ollie in the computer lab, she hesitated. It had been five months. What if she'd...shrunk?

"What's wrong?"

"You're so big," she whispered, wondering if he could correctly interpret her tone as a combination of nervousness and pure, utter want.

"And you're so wet," he murmured, pressing a kiss on her mouth. "So soft and warm and ready for me."

"Okay then," she said, trusting him. He would certainly know.

"Hold on," he ordered, nodding toward the stainless-steel handrails on each wall of the elevator.

She quivered; she was in for a wild, fast ride.

Grabbing the handrails, she watched as he pulled her skirt back up, pushing her panties to the floor. He lifted her by the hips, arching her toward him. The panties fell off her ankles and she parted her legs wide in invitation.

Gripping her hips, he stepped between her thighs, that big, hard ridge nudging into the slick lips of her sex. She had a second to gasp at the amazing sensation before he plunged into her, filling her to her core.

Her gasps became cries as he claimed her. She couldn't believe how delicious it was to be so thoroughly taken. The emptiness that had been with her for so long—physically and emotionally—suddenly evaporated as she savored the ultimate connection with another human being.

God, how she'd missed this.

He gave her exactly what she'd asked for, thrusting hard, his hands almost punishing on her hips, his cock pounding so deep inside her she felt as though she was being split in half.

She loved it.

Meeting him thrust for thrust, she held on tight to his

shoulders, digging her nails into him. Their mouths met and locked in deep hungry kisses. Viv squeezed him deep inside, eliciting a guttural groan. The angle was perfect for penetration, but also gave her just the right amount of pressure on her clit, and she rode him as much as he took her, both of them drunk on the freedom of being able to throw away thought and inhibition and convention, and just have wild, crazy sex.

Waves of heat rolled through her, electricity dancing across every inch of her skin. The deliciously achy tension of need rolled through her body, wave after wave, and Viv knew she was going to come—had to come—or she'd lose her mind.

There would be time for a slow build later. Now she was desperate for an orgasm, and she rubbed against his pelvis, giving herself exactly the right amount of pressure to make sure she got it.

But just as she began to reach the highest wave of this churning surf of erotic sensation, a faint buzzing began to intrude. She didn't notice it at first, focused only on the wildness, their harsh breaths, the pounding of flesh on flesh. Soon, though, she realized the persistent sound wasn't coming from either of them, but rather from the emergency phone set in the front panel of the elevator.

He obviously heard it, too.

"Shit," he muttered. His hands still gripping her hips, his glorious erection still buried hilt-deep inside her, he stopped moving.

She groaned. "No."

Damien closed his eyes and banged his forehead against the wall. "Our time is up."

Viv squeezed him again, deep inside, and was rewarded with a slow thrust. His mind might imagine they could stop, but his body was nowhere ready to. "Five more minutes?" she cajoled, licking her lips, tightening her legs around his lean hips.

"It's going to take a lot longer than that," he told her, the words as much a promise as a declaration.

"Not for me." Not that she didn't want a lot more. But oh, she wanted an orgasm, and she wanted it now.

He pulled away so he could look down at her, and obviously noted the hot hunger she couldn't disguise. Her body was quaking, tingling, the pressure so enormous she felt sure she'd either have to climax or punch something, just to relieve the sensual stress. At no other time did pleasure and pain mix so exquisitely, with boundaries almost impossible to discern, than right before climax. When it came, there would be no better sensation in the world. When denied, nothing was worse.

"Two minutes," she begged. "I need... I have to..."

"No." He shook his head once, and let go of her hips, until she was standing on her own feet.

Viv was ready to cry, but when those lips curved up, she held off.

"Thirty seconds."

Her brows went up as she heard the confidence in his voice. But when he immediately dropped to his knees, lifting her leg over his shoulder, as he had before, she knew she wouldn't require the full thirty seconds. Not if he was going to... Oh, God.

He did.

A cry escaped her throat as he licked her sex, covering her clit with that warm tongue. She was panting, desperate for breath, hungry for release. Twining her fingers in his thick, black hair, she arched toward his hungry mouth, glorious sensation washing over her. He encircled the sensitive nub, licking at the base, sucking gently, and all brain function ceased. She closed her eyes and began to whimper as the heat centered and pooled right there…right… "There!"

Attaining the highest heights her body could reach, she let it rock her from head to toe. Warm waves of satisfaction rolled through her. She couldn't stop herself from gently thrusting her hips, loving that he continued to lap at her as the hot currents pulsed and scattered through her veins, bringing light and energy and pure deliciousness to every cell in her body.

She was so lost to it, she barely even noticed when he stood up, dropping her skirt into place. Missing his warmth, the intimate connection, she managed to open her eyes. Sucking in deep, hungry breaths, she watched him walk to the control panel and reengage the elevator. And then they were moving again, slowly rising, past one floor, heading to the next.

Finally, she found a functioning brain cell and muttered, "I might not be able to walk out of here."

"I'll carry you," he said, those dark eyes gleaming as he assessed her, from her tangled hair, to her gaping blouse and her crumpled skirt.

She gave him her most wicked, come-hither smile, but it faded from her lips when she realized the elevator was slowing. And they weren't yet to the top floor.

"We're stopping!" She ran a quick, assessing stare over him. For the most part, he looked perfect, gorgeous, the hair smooth, the face innocent—but for the gleam of hot woman on his lips—the jacket, shirt and tie just fine.

But, uh… "You might want to put that away," she said with a giggle, gesturing toward his unzipped pants. His penis was still free, all big, hard and delicious. If they weren't about to be boarded and invaded, she'd love to drop to her knees and repay the intimacy he'd just bestowed upon her.

He didn't immediately shove things into place again or try to zip and hide. No. Instead, he took a few steps toward her, to the back corner, and braced his hands on either side of her. Without even glancing over his shoulder or acknowledging that the door was sliding open behind them, he pressed his mouth to hers in a wet kiss, sucking on her tongue, letting her taste her own essence. Viv twined her arms around his neck, tilting her head, kissing him, not really giving a damn that someone else had boarded the elevator.

The kiss was long, slow and surprising. Damien cupped her face in both his hands, his thumbs scraping gently over her cheeks. His touch was tender, careful, his kiss a soft promise, not a demand. Viv was still dying for more, but she found her heartbeat slowing, and her breaths, too. She slid her fingers into his hair, stroking its silkiness, and gave herself over to the pleasure of a long, leisurely kiss.

Of course, this wasn't just a regular kiss, and in a tiny corner of her mind, she couldn't quite forget that. First, they had an audience, albeit a quiet, unobtrusive one. Second, she could still feel Damien's rock-solid erection pressed hard against her stomach. The people behind him couldn't possibly see, but oh, just knowing it was there— hot, throbbing, inviting—was enough to make her tingle all over.

Eventually, they came to another stop. Damien slowly ended the kiss. Smiling at how much she'd enjoyed it, Viv glanced over his shoulder, appraising their audience. It was a younger couple, both wearing workout clothes and carrying water bottles. They'd apparently gone downstairs to use the fitness center.

Both were watching them closely. Both were grinning. Viv wasn't the blushing sort, but still a bit of heat flashed up into her cheeks. If those people had any idea what had been going on in the elevator right before they'd stepped onto it, they wouldn't be grinning, they'd be wide-eyed with shock.

Then again...those grins said they were aware they'd stumbled onto more than a couple kissing in an elevator. Hmm.

When Viv inhaled a deep breath and caught the rich odors of earthy sex, she winced. There was no way those strangers didn't realize what they'd been doing. The very air betrayed them.

Resisting the urge to bury her face in Damien's shoulder, she groaned softly, praying she never ran into the other couple again. But just to make things a tiny bit worse, as they began to exit the elevator on their own floor, the young woman glanced at Viv over her shoulder. "Uh... don't forget those," she said with a wink, pointing to the floor.

Viv glanced down. And groaned. Her lacy white panties were tangled around Damien's black leather shoes.

# 4

"I BELIEVE WE'VE gone well past number twelve."

Making no effort to keep the satisfaction out of his voice for having beaten his stated goal, Damien rolled over onto his back. He breathed deeply, enjoying the rich, combined scents of sweat, sex and woman. His thudding heart gradually began to slow, and a lazy smile curled at his lips as he waited for Viv to respond, hopefully with admiration that he was a man who could make a plan and stick to his goals.

Wow. Talk about sticking to them. He'd found himself unable to let her go, not wanting her more than a few inches away from him for the past sixteen-or-so hours. He wasn't sure he was going to be able to walk today, considering the number of times and ways they'd had sex the night before. Not since he was a teenager had his sexual desire been so frantic, so unending. Throughout the night, no matter what they did, or where they did it, he'd found himself ready to plunge into Viv's tight, delicious body again minutes after leaving her.

It took a while for her to answer. He could hear her own heaving breaths begin to slow as she, too, sprawled out on the bed. Kicking the tangled sheets away from her calves she sighed as the air-conditioned breeze cooled her hot body.

*Oh, so hot.*

He couldn't stop himself from looking over at her. There wasn't an inch of her he hadn't tasted during the long, erotic hours of the night. He was tempted to roll over and press another kiss in the hollow of her throat, to taste his way down to a perfect nipple, so red and saucy from his avid attention. There wasn't a bit of her that wasn't delicious, not a thing they'd done that he would ever regret.

His only regret was the possibility that she'd meant what she said about this being a one-night stand. He might have agreed to it yesterday, out of habit, since he'd long ago realized he was much more the one-night-stand than the fall-in-love-and-settle-down type.

Frankly, he wasn't sure falling in love and staying that way forever was even programmed in his genetic code. His father had been the greatest dad on earth, but he'd borne no love for his wife, at least not that Damien had witnessed. Both sets of grandparents had divorced, as had his sister.

As for his mother—well, that chick in the *Frozen* movie had nothing on her. He'd started viewing her as the ice queen when he was just a kid, and the temperature had just grown colder as she'd aged.

So, no, Damien wasn't the love-and-romance type. Never had been.

He blinked, rubbing a hand over his eyes, pushing those images away. Now certainly wasn't the time to do a postmortem on his childhood or an evaluation of his ability to ever actually fall in love. He was lying in bed with a woman he craved, one he knew he couldn't let go of yet.

*She didn't mean it about just one night.*

Or, if she did, she would certainly change her mind after what they'd shared. Because he suspected encounters like that were earth-shattering, once-in-a-lifetime events that some people never even got to experience. And he was a greedy enough bastard to want to experience it again. He hoped she was, too.

Finally, she replied, but not with an appreciative purr.

"Let me guess, math wasn't your best subject in school," she said with a broad yawn.

"Excuse me?"

"Pretty sure it was eleven."

His eyes narrowed but then he noticed the hint of mischief lurking in her sleepy blue eyes. He played along, certain he'd given her far more than the eleven stated orgasms. Christ, she'd come twice in the five minutes after they'd left the elevator.

"Well, far be it for me to make a promise and not keep it. I figured you were worn out after getting such a small amount of sleep last night, but…."

She waggled her brows. "I'm never too tired for that."

"Guess I'd better get back to work then," he said, rolling toward her, an indulgent smile on his face.

"It's work?"

He nuzzled her neck, enjoying the brush of her silky hair against his cheek. "Only because it's a job worth doing well."

She rolled onto her side to face him, sliding one long, slender leg between his, draping an arm across his shoulders. "I don't want to be any trouble. I mean, heaven forbid you hurt yourself or something."

"Baby, if what we did on the desk didn't hurt me, I should be able to handle one more round of 'make a greedy woman come.'"

Swatting him, she said, "I'm not greedy. I just appreciate a person who keeps his promises."

"Okay," he said with a laugh, "but I fear you're the one who's math-challenged."

Licking her lips, she admitted, "The quantity was right."

He stiffened. "You complaining about my quality?"

"God, no," she said, vehemently shaking her head. "But I distinctly remember you saying twelve *different* ways."

Ahh, now he got it. "So I did."

"And while your tongue has a score of four all by itself, I don't remember twelve completely *unique* situations."

Hmm. That was an interesting challenge. He did a quick recap in his mind, remembering the elevator, the foyer, the bar, the desk, the shower and the bed. Oh, this bed. It—with her nestled beside him—was rapidly becoming his favorite place in the world. They'd rolled around on it in position after position, pausing to sleep, stopping for a snack sometime around midnight, then playing and sleeping some more. It had been a night he would never—ever—forget.

He intended to make this morning unforgettable, too.

*Twelve.*

"Well, I'll have to do something about that, won't I?" he said, already interested again in doing just that. His cock was still wet from their last joining, yet he was growing hard again. He felt like Superman, like a male virgin in a harem, like…like a thirty-year-old man who could still get it up eight times in a night. Christ, he might not be able to walk or take a piss for the next few days, but any sacrifices were entirely worth it.

"I'll understand if you're just not up to it," she said with a pitying smile.

"Anybody tell you you've got a smart mouth?"

"Only everybody who's ever met me."

He leaned over and busied that mouth with a slow, deep kiss. They'd kissed over and over during the night hours, but still, every time his lips met hers, he felt a jolt of excitement course through him all over again.

He wasn't sure what to call it, but there was no doubt he'd fallen hard and fast into a sexual addiction for the woman in his bed. Her beauty had stunned him at first sight, her wit had interested him, her intelligence intrigued him. Her sensuality, however, had captured him, holding him in its grip, until he wasn't sure if he was ever going to be the same again.

Sex, certainly, would never be the same—not with anyone else. Right now, he couldn't imagine of another woman on the planet who could tempt him away from the arms of his bewitching Vixen Viv. She had somehow made him forget all of his problems and daily stresses. With her, he became a creature of pure sensation. Damien couldn't remember another night in his life when he'd been as sexually satisfied, as well as simply happy.

"Roll over," he murmured, suddenly envisioning a unique way he could pleasure her.

She smiled lazily. "Well, as much as I like that, it's not exactly something we didn't do last night."

He managed to bite back a wolfish howl at those memories. "It's not that. Just roll over." He nibbled her jaw. "I'll make you glad you did."

She licked her lips, eyeing him through a strand of soft, blond hair. "If you mean, uh…that is, I've never…"

He laughed softly, immediately understanding what she was getting at. Embarrassed Viv was utterly charming. "No condoms, remember?" he reminded her. "No, I don't have to fuck your gorgeous ass to make you come again."

She hissed out a breath, that flush rising higher. Now, though, it wasn't embarrassment. She was interested, intrigued. Holy shit, the woman continued to amaze him. Admitting flat out what he wanted turned her on, and could say the same thing about himself. But he hadn't expected her to be so open to utterly any possibility. Even one he hadn't really been talking about.

"You really are wicked, aren't you?" he asked, admiration mixing with laughter in his tone.

"You'd better believe it."

"Good. Then roll over."

Sighing happily, she did, presenting him with a beautiful back, each delineated vertebrae demanding attention. The curves of that pert butt stopped his heart, and her shapely legs seemed long enough to wrap around him twice.

He moved over her, nudging her legs apart and lying between them. But while she lifted her hips invitingly, silently inviting him to slide right into all that juicy heat, he had something else in mind.

Not that he hadn't loved taking her like this last night. His front to her back, both of them on their knees, or once while they stood outside on the patio, overlooking the Potomac and the Capitol dome. She'd gripped the railing, he'd gripped her hips and they'd done all but bay at the moon.

Still…that lucky number twelve called.

He began to kiss his way down her spine, tasting the tiny indentations, nibbling each curve and line. When he reached the base, he paused, tormenting her. He knew she was wondering what he was up to, that she was waiting for him to move up, to glide into her soft heat from behind.

He didn't. Instead, he moved down, sliding his tongue along her coccyx, and farther.

She hissed. "What are you…?"

"Shh. I'm going for the even dozen here."

She glanced over her shoulder at him, and he offered her a wicked smile as he lifted her hips up. His steady gaze demanded she let him do what he wanted. She held his look, silent, her expression torn between shock and primal hunger. Her throat worked as she swallowed, hard, and she caught her lip between her teeth. Convention was telling her to close her legs, roll over, create some distance.

Excitement made her remain exactly where she was.

He smiled at her, nodding his approval that she was following him where he led.

"You taste delicious, every inch of you is sweet," he whispered, meaning it.

Then he got serious, exploring her with his lips, his tongue, his fingers. She was whimpering into the pillow. But he knew by the way she arched her spine, lifting herself for him, that she loved every naughty bit of what he was doing to her. She was shaking with it, her body a quivering bowstring of tension and heat. By the time he slid his lips against her warm, wet opening, she was moaning, and when he moved down to tongue her hard clit, she let out a tiny scream.

He doubted she even heard him whisper, "Twelve." But then, considering he immediately moved up to plunge into her, losing himself in the delights of her body, there was no need to brag.

This was lazy and slow, slippery limbs entwining as he pressed kisses to her neck and her shoulders. And after they climaxed again, she turned in his arms and curled in close, yawning and nuzzling against him like a sleepy cat that had drunk up all the cream and now just wanted a nap.

He stared at her for a while, watching her beautiful face relax in sleep, wondering how it was possible he hadn't even known she existed twenty-four hours ago. Because, right now, he feared his mind would crack if she walked out the door and he never saw her again.

For a man who'd long ago decided he wasn't cut out for relationships, the realization stunned him.

Eventually, he drifted off, falling into a heavy sleep, their bodies still glued together. When he next opened his eyes, he was shocked to glance at the bedside clock and see it was after ten. He hadn't slept this late in years.

"Oh, my," she said, following his gaze toward the clock. "I guess there won't be any sneaking out of here at dawn, avoiding that walk of shame through the lobby in my rumpled clothes."

He frowned, not liking the image for any number of reasons. "Don't say that. Shame has no part in this."

"Because I'm shameless?"

He chuckled, letting her get away with keeping things light and sexy. He suspected she'd heard the serious note in his voice and knew he'd been about to insist they give up on the idea of this being some kind of one-night stand.

"Maybe we both are. Maybe that's what makes us so well matched."

She licked her lips. "A perfect pair, huh?"

"Something like that."

"So what's the next step?"

"I don't want you to walk out of here."

"Are you planning to carry me? Because I'm not a lightweight."

He chuckled. She wasn't going to give up easily. "I've already carried you, remember?" A warm, sultry smile said she did. But it disappeared when he added, "I want you to stay."

"Indefinitely? The hotel might have other people who want this room at some point."

"I'll extend my reservation."

"What if somebody's already claimed it?"

"I've heard if you don't leave a hotel room, they can't kick you out as long as you keep paying."

She giggled. "I suspect your credit card would max out pretty quickly at these prices."

He would eventually explain his connection to Black Star, and the fact that he always had a penthouse reserved in any location, but still wasn't quite ready to bring his money into their relationship. "Maybe."

"And sooner or later you have to return to…where did you say you're from? Miami?"

"Yeah," he admitted with a sigh, not wanting to think about going home. Because the address imprinted on his driver's license wasn't home to him in any way, shape or form, and hadn't been for a long time. Not since his world had been upended by his dad's death twelve years ago.

Being only eighteen when he'd lost his father, Damien had immediately set out to get away from a home that had lost its heart and soul. If his mother had been cold before, she'd hardened into a piece of ice by that point. But she'd been particularly frigid to Damien. So he'd had to get away. He'd gone to the best schools—all out of state—and had then traveled from city to city, country to country.

He didn't require a shrink to tell him it had all been an effort to avoid returning to the place so strongly associated with the person he missed most in the world. A place that had been coopted by someone he simply couldn't get along with—his own mother—and her subsequent succession of husbands. Each relationship proved even more to him that his bloodline just wasn't capable of true love and lifelong devotion.

So, no. The Miami estate where he'd been raised wasn't home. It was merely an address. Frankly, living out of this hotel room for a year, with the woman lying beside him, sounded much more appealing than spending a single night in a house he was no longer comfortable in, even if his grandfather's will had given him full ownership of it. Something else his mother had never forgiven him for.

Maybe that was why he was so anxious for his new business to succeed. The resentment his own mother had exhibited toward him—even though he'd kept the family hotel dynasty in the black, and her in diamonds as icy cold as her personality—was hard to take. Though he'd loved them both, he'd felt trapped by his father and by his grandfather. Trapped into fulfilling their dreams, and not his own.

Was it so wrong to want to steal a few days out of his own life to do something he really wanted to do?

"Where did you go?" she asked softly, sensing his distraction.

"Just…memories."

"Not very happy ones?"

He shrugged. "It is what it is."

"That's such a cop-out phrase."

He rose onto an elbow and stared down at her, unable to prevent a grin at her eye roll and huffy breath. "Is that so?"

"That's so. Nothing *is what it is*, not if you're willing to work hard to change it."

"You believe there's nothing that can't be changed… fixed?"

"Nothing."

"I'll try to keep that in mind," he said, making a mental note. Then he shook off the family memories; there was no place for them now. His business in Arlington was only supposed to take a day or two. He'd have to return to Miami to deal with the company, and the Black family, sooner or later. But he'd make it as late as possible if it meant he could indulge himself with this beautiful woman for a while longer.

"To the point," he said. "I'm not in a huge hurry to fly home to Florida. You could stay with me while I'm here."

"Hmm. A wealthy businessman wants me to stay with him in his opulent hotel suite while he's in town." A wry grin tugged at that lush mouth. "That sounds awfully familiar. I think I saw it in a movie starring Julia Roberts and Richard Gere."

He immediately caught the reference and barked a laugh. "Well, you are a very pretty woman."

"Plus my name is Viv, just like hers, and I'm unemployed and broke. Unfortunately, though, I'm not a hooker."

"I'm glad. I'd never be able to afford you."

She smiled, hearing the compliment. "Lucky for you I'm an amateur, then."

"Doubly lucky. I'd die if I weren't allowed to kiss you on the mouth."

It took her a moment, then she realized what he meant. "You really know your chick flicks. I'd forgotten about that part of the movie."

"I have sisters, remember? And speaking of kisses…"

He leaned toward her and pressed his mouth to hers, kissing her good-morning, trying to distract her from where he suspected she was taking the conversation— toward their one-night-stand agreement and her determination to leave. Goodbye was the last thing he wanted her to say. Good morning, good afternoon, good night… hell, Merry Christmas and Happy New Year. It might take months to get her out of his system.

That didn't mean he was contemplating forever. Months was about the longest commitment he could possibly envision, even with a woman as intoxicating as this one.

She tasted warm, soft and sweet, and reminded him that he really—really—enjoyed kissing. When it finally ended and they drew apart, she let out a tiny sigh and returned to the unpleasant topic at hand.

"We had a deal. One night. Remember?"

"You know what they say about deals…"

"Never welsh on one?"

"Anything can be renegotiated."

"You sound like a businessman."

"I am a businessman."

He kissed her again, holding her close, tracing his palm

down her spine, caressing each soft curve and vulnerable hollow.

"You're trying to distract me," she eventually whispered.

"Is it working?"

"Depends on what you hope to accomplish."

"I'm hoping to get you to stay," he admitted.

"I do still have a home. I'm not desperate."

"Never thought you were. But maybe I am." He kissed her again, demanding, trying to get her to take a chance. "Don't go," he insisted. "Just stay and we'll see what happens."

She didn't immediately relent. Viv, as he'd already realized, was no pushover. "I can't think when you kiss me like that," she said, sounding disgruntled. "Go do something and let me pull my brain cells back into place."

He barked a laugh. "What should I do?"

"How about you call room service and get us some breakfast while I take a shower."

"That shower is enormous. Plenty big enough for two. Remember?"

She should. They'd taken a long, steamy shower last night.

She swatted his arm. "I'll take my own shower this time, thank you very much. I'm pretty sure I still have soap in my, uh...in some uncomfortable places from last night. You're good at lathering but not so hot at rinsing."

"There wasn't an inch of you I didn't take care of."

Licking those swollen, kiss-reddened lips, she breathed deeply. Remembering. Silently admitting he was right.

But she didn't relent, and instead scooted toward the opposite side of the bed.

He didn't argue or try to restrain her. Damien knew he had to give her what she was asking for. Space. Hopefully enough space so she wouldn't feel pressured and would decide to stay. "All right, you win."

This battle, anyway. Damien, however, intended to win the war. He usually got what he wanted, and right now, there was nothing more he wanted in the world than Viv Callahan—at least for the near future.

"Thank you," she said, her long lashes drifting half-closed over those startlingly blue eyes. Her tiny smile said she was glad he hadn't pressured her.

While she went into the bathroom to shower, he pulled on a robe and glanced over the room service menu. Calling down for breakfast, he ordered a bit of everything, since he wasn't sure what she would want. Adding Bloody Marys and champagne to the order, he hung up and went into the living room to wait. He doubted the delivery would take long. The staff was aware of his identity, and had been trying to impress him since the minute he'd arrived. Case in point—the elevator security guys.

He might just have to give them a bonus.

He turned on the TV, flipping to a sports station. Damien had been distracted since yesterday afternoon, but now that he had a moment, he realized it was time to check on the business that had brought him here to northern Virginia.

"And now for the latest on the Bruno Neeley scandal."

Damien stiffened, of course recognizing the name. Lowering himself to the edge of the soft leather sofa, he flicked the volume button, paying rapt attention to the two sportscasters.

"The bad boy of hockey is at it again," one of them said. "You all saw the shocking footage of Neeley getting smacked by an unidentified woman at the Virginia Vanguard press junket earlier this week."

"No, we all most certainly have not," Damien said with a groan. He'd been traveling—and having sex—for the past two days, and hadn't heard a thing about this. "Damn it," he muttered, wondering why professional athletes had to be so troublesome.

The other sportscaster smirked. "There was a lot of speculation about what he'd done to deserve it. Now, an attendee at that event has provided us with exclusive footage of the moments leading up to that already infamous slap."

Hating to watch and already starting to do mental damage control, Damien gritted his teeth as an amateur phone-video zoomed in on a crowded gathering. He recognized the general manager of the Vanguard, who stood behind a podium emblazoned with the new team's logo. But the person with the cell phone had been more interested in what was going on elsewhere in the room.

Despite the fuzzy, slightly out-of-focus picture, he easily recognized Neeley. The guy's swagger and bulk made him stand out in any crowd. Focused primarily on the player, Damien didn't notice right away that the attention of the camera operator had moved to a blond-haired woman seated on a chair in the back corner. But Neeley's actions most definitely drew his attention there. Because, to his shock, the spoiled player grabbed the woman's jaw and painfully twisted her face up for a kiss as he dropped a meaty hand high on her thigh.

"Jesus Christ," Damien snapped, livid on behalf of the woman, and humiliated on behalf of the whole organization.

He began calculating a response, already reaching for his cell phone so he could call the team's general manager. He probably had dozens of messages from the man and the other owners, frustrated that Damien had his phone off in the middle of a scandal. The general manager had called him as he'd arrived in DC, saying they had an HR issue, but he was dealing with it. Damien, already jet-lagged and juggling bigger issues, had dismissed it.

The sportscasters continued talking, slamming Neeley for his actions, even while chuckling snidely about the comeuppance he'd gotten from the woman. One of them mentioned that they'd managed to identify the blonde, and the screen segued to a more clear video of the press event. A pro cameraman had apparently swung his camera around in time to catch the slap, if not what had inspired it.

He couldn't wonder that the slap had made news before today, though he'd been oblivious to it. Bruno Neeley's head had jerked back under the strength of the woman's indignation. Now that he—and the whole world—had seen what the player had done to deserve the reaction, Damien could muster no surprise and silently applauded the woman.

And that was before he recognized her.

"Oh. My. God," he whispered, rising to step closer to the big screen. His eyes were telling him the truth—noting the familiar blond hair pulled back in a bun, those vivid blue eyes, the perfect mouth and soft face—even before his ears registered the name the sportscasters announced.

"Vivienne Callahan," one of them was saying. "Sources tell us she is with the Vanguard marketing team."

"Well, she's certainly getting a lot of press, and maybe that was her intention," the other guy said with an audible sneer, which just made Damien want to reach through the screen and throttle him.

As for Neeley—well, punching him wouldn't even begin to repay the disgusting way he'd treated Viv.

"We're waiting for the team to issue a statement regarding this shocking new twist in the situation that we now know involves a player and an employee. We will keep on top of this developing story."

A player and an employee of the Virginia Vanguard.

Wait. A *former* employee of the Virginia Vanguard…
because she'd been fired yesterday afternoon.

Damien thrust a hand through his hair, trying to make
sense of everything he'd just seen, and what he remembered of Viv's conversation yesterday. One thing was sure:
Viv had been assaulted, and had reacted with understandable anger. Yet the team's general manager had fired her?

What was it she'd said—she'd been accused of being a
"distraction." She was the subject of a bet among her male
coworkers. Jesus, and what a bunch of coworkers. They
were the tough, spoiled, testosterone-laden members of
a professional hockey team, who'd placed a bet on who
could get her into bed first.

"Son of a bitch," he snarled, punching the television's
off button and throwing the remote down onto the table.

He felt sick. And not just because of what she'd gone
through at the press junket, or at the hands of the team's
general manager, or at the mercy of a bunch of horny ass-
holes who'd made her life hell for weeks.

No. The real capper was that it was his fault. The buck
ended with Damien Black.

This team was the reason he'd come to town. It was
the one thing he'd wanted for himself—aside from Black
Star Hotels, the Black family, the foundation, the trust
and the corporation. The Vanguard was how he'd chosen
to indulge in his lifelong love of sports, his nostalgia for
his college hockey days and his need to have something
entirely his own.

Damien Black was the primary stockholder in the Virginia Vanguard.

And he'd just spent the wildest, most passionate night of
his life with one of his own former employees…who had
every justification in the world to sue his ass off.

# 5

ALTHOUGH VIV'S PLACE was nice, it was still just a basic one-bedroom, one-bath, with standard fixtures. Plus it was in Arlington, which had crazy-high square-footage prices. Which meant this hotel suite was about twice the size of her whole apartment and the bathroom here was bigger than her living room.

"I'm in heaven," she cooed as she used the soft washcloth to smooth divine-smelling gel all over her body. "I am never going to leave this shower."

Oh, the shower. It was one of those rainfall types, with multiple showerheads, spurting warm water on her from head to toe. It was like a summer rainfall, soft and sensuous. There was no curtain or door, just a glass-block half wall, the rest open to the remainder of the bathroom. To someone who'd grown up in a small, blue-collar Pennsylvania household with five brothers, this shower alone was like something out of a fantasy magazine or movie.

One thing was sure—Julia Roberts's bubble bath in *Pretty Woman* had absolutely nothing on this. The bathroom alone put the *sin* in *sinful opulence*. There was even a TV screen set *inside* the mirror, which was sort of freaky, but also very cool.

Well, it was cool until she saw her own face in it.

And it wasn't her reflection.

"No, please no!" she groaned, wishing curiosity hadn't

prompted her to flick the power on the remote as she dried off with a fluffy towel. The TV had been tuned in to a sports station, and she'd gotten a just *wonderful* view of herself being groped by, and then slugging, a hockey star.

It was one thing to mentally envision the slap ending up on the news. It was another thing entirely to see it— not only the slap, but also the humiliating kiss-and-grab that had inspired it.

She came across as an absolute idiot. Worse—like the type of woman men felt it was okay to grope. If Dale caught wind of this—confirming his own ideas about what kind of woman she was—she'd just die.

But she was kidding herself to hope he might not. *Everybody* would see this. All her friends back home, who'd been so excited for her as a woman breaking into a male-dominated industry. Her local friends, who'd cautioned her about what she might be getting herself into when she'd taken the job—wouldn't they be feeling justified right about now, at least the ones who were friends of the fair-weather variety? That certainly didn't include Lulu or Amelia, who already knew about the situation.

And then there was her family. Oh, God, her brothers. They were probably already piling into Dad's SUV and driving down here to protect her virtue by pounding the snot out of Bruno Neeley.

Not that he didn't deserve it. But considering she just wanted this whole thing to go away, she'd prefer that Neeley's snot stay right where it was—inside his fat, brainless head.

A quick rap gave her a moment's warning before Damien pushed the half-open door all the way open. She spun around to grab the remote. Unfortunately, her feet— and the glossy tile floor—were wet. Her heels flew out from under her, and she went caterwauling, destined for a face-plant on the marble counter. Her towel fell one way, her body another, and the remote skittered off the counter to land somewhere near—or possibly in—the toilet.

"Whoa, there," Damien said, diving to the rescue. He landed on one knee, probably crunching it painfully on the hard floor, but did manage to stop her fall. She collapsed into his strong arms with a whoosh, the breath knocked out of her.

"I've got you," he murmured.

He did. He'd taken a dive to catch her, playing the role of gentleman so easily it had to be an intrinsic part of his personality. Having such evidence of the goodness of a man, after confronting the visual evidence of pure ugliness, suddenly overwhelmed her.

Viv sniffed as moisture stabbed at her eyes. She hadn't cried since losing her job. Now, because of the sweet gesture of a man who could easily become an addiction, tears were welling up in her eyes and starting to drip down her cheeks.

"Baby, are you okay?" he asked, looking aghast when he noticed the tears. "Are you hurt? God, I didn't break you, did I?"

She sniffed again and managed a half laugh, half snort. "I'm not broken. You saved me from smashing my face on the counter. I might have cracked my head open."

"So what's wrong? Last night…"

"You didn't break me then, either. I guess I'm just in shock."

He nodded, reaching up to brush a long strand of wet hair off her face. She couldn't imagine how she looked— probably worse than a drowned rat—but he cupped her cheek tenderly and bent to brush his lips against hers.

She returned the kiss, both for the comfort—which she found herself desperately wanting—and in the hopes that the guys on the TV screen would segue into another story and Damien wouldn't see it.

She should have realized she'd used up her year's quota of good luck just in meeting the man.

"I saw the story," he said when they drew apart. Nodding toward the TV, he added, "I guess you did, too."

Viv hid a groan, and wiped the tears off her face with her hand. She struggled out of his arms, trying to stand, wanting to appear independent and competent. But her feet had other ideas. She slipped again and collapsed against him.

"Let me help you," he insisted, standing as well, a steadying hand on her shoulder, another at her waist.

"I'm fine. It's this stupid floor. Who was the genius who chose something this slick for the bathroom? This hotel is lucky you were here to save me or they'd be facing a big lawsuit."

He blanched, swallowing visibly. Feeling bad about worrying him, she admitted, "I'm fine. It's not a big deal, I wasn't hurt. And I really can stand on my own—once I dry my feet."

Obviously not believing her, he pulled her into his arms and hugged her close. Viv slipped her hands into his robe and pushed it open, wanting the connection of skin on skin. As far as comforting went, nothing beat warm, naked, sexy man.

Damien gently massaged her back, stroking her, soothing her, and she relaxed into him, taking what she could get. But she stiffened again when he asked, "Why didn't you tell me it was a famous hockey star who'd harassed you?"

"What difference does it make?" she mumbled. "He could have been a plumber and I still would have gotten fired."

"No, I don't believe you would have," Damien insisted, his voice low, throbbing with anger. He pulled away from her, though he kept his hands at her waist. Gazing down at her, heat in his eyes, he said, "They can't get away with this."

"I'm a distraction, remember?"

"Only for men who have no self-control or common decency."

He was skilled at this comforting thing. Viv's raging pulse began to slow, and the tension that had revved her into a live wire of energy eased. If she could just stay here, naked, close to him, with his warm hands on her hips, it might actually be possible to forget that she was the laughingstock of ESPN.

"How am I going to leave through the lobby now?" she muttered. "And I was worried about the walk of shame before. Does this place have a rear exit?"

"You have nothing to be ashamed of," he snapped. "That asshole player and bigger asshole general manager do."

"But somehow I'm the one the reporters are talking about."

Neeley's misconduct was sure to be laughed off as boys being boys. Those men on the news hadn't exactly talked about her as an assault victim. In fact, before she'd spun around to try to stop Damien from viewing what was on the screen, she was pretty sure she'd heard one of them speculate that the whole thing had been a PR stunt on her part.

As if she'd let that creep grope her and stick his nasty tongue down her throat in front of a room full of people for anything.

"God, I can't even imagine how my family and friends are going to react." She finally drew a deep, calming breath, and stepped away. Sweeping her hands through her wet hair, she nodded her thanks and added, "I should get out of here and start doing damage control."

"They announced your name. The press is going to be searching for you."

"Bastards. I'm not unlisted, either."

"So don't let them find you."

"Do you suggest I go into the witness protection program?"

"I suggest you stay right here until this blows over."

She'd been highly tempted before when he'd been trying to talk her in to staying. Now there was even more reason to. But Viv had never been the needy type, and she didn't like the idea now. "I can take care of myself."

"Have you ever been the fox chased by hunters and hounds? You can't even imagine how difficult the next few days will be."

She caught her lip between her teeth. "You really believe it will be that big a deal?"

He nodded, solemn, those dark eyes gleaming with support and regret. "I'm so sorry this has happened to you, Viv, but the truth is, your life is going to be hell until this gets straightened out."

"That's the problem," she snapped, swinging around and grabbing a fresh towel. She wrapped it around her body, tucking it in over her breasts. "This isn't going to get straightened out. It's done."

He was shaking his head before she'd finished speaking. "No, it's not. Not by a long shot."

Before she could ask what he meant, he walked toward the shower himself and turned it back on. "Our breakfast should be here any minute. Why don't you go out and wait for it. I remembered I have to go to a meeting in a while, but you can stay here and eat, and I'll come and join you later."

"You want me to hide out in your suite?"

"Yes."

"I don't have any clothes, not even a toothbrush."

He gestured toward his shaving kit. "There's a brand-new one in there. It's yours."

Viv lifted a brow. "You travel with a spare toothbrush?"

For whom? And how often did he give them out? Was he some kind of tooth fairy to sexy women all over the world?

She forced those worries away. Damien wasn't that kind of man. Even if he was, it was none of her business, anyway. She was his bar—or, parking garage—pickup. Nothing more. Even if he was being super nice this morning and trying to help her out of her mess, he'd made it clear that he didn't do love or relationships.

"The hotel always has a care packet waiting for these suites," he explained. "I've got loads of them."

Feeling small, she nodded and walked to the counter, getting the toothbrush in question. "Thanks." Then, her back to him, she smiled. "Does the hotel happen to provide thong panties in those care packages?"

She caught his eye in the mirror. Damien had been just about to step into the shower, and he laughed as he met her stare. Something about that laughter—the twinkle in his eyes, the flash of a dimple in his cheek—chipped away at her resistance. He'd let his guard down over the hours they'd spent together. She'd never have guessed him to be a dimple owner when they'd met, and was now certain she'd never meet a dimpled man again without picturing—dreaming of—this one.

"No, but there are some shops downstairs."

"None in my price range," she said with an eye roll, having seen those shops when they'd walked through the lobby yesterday. "I'm a Dollar General girl until I get a new job."

"Would you just shut up and agree that you staying here is the best option?"

Huh. So much for the charming, dimpled smile. Now he was practically glowering, reverting to the businessman who was used to getting his way.

Frankly, Viv liked that version of Damien, too.

"Stay, Viv. Just promise me you'll stay, at least until I get back later and we figure out what you're going to do next."

She gave it one more moment's thought, and then slowly spun around to face him. "All right. But just...just for a little while. Maybe just until you return."

"Or maybe for a week."

"Don't push your luck."

That boyish, sexy grin flashed again as he disappeared behind the glass-block wall and stepped into the steaming shower. But even through the mist and water, she heard him say, "I *always* push my luck. After all, if I don't, how am I ever going to get what I really want?"

What he really wanted. Meaning her?

She didn't want to read too much in to the flirtatious remark, but couldn't help but shiver in sheer pleasure that he still really wanted her. It was a powerful thing, being desired by a man who was so attractive, not to mention sensually addictive. He was an amazing lover, and she doubted anyone she was ever with for the rest of her life would measure up. Figuratively, or literally. It already broke her heart a little that she couldn't keep him for long...but maybe she'd keep him for just a little while.

Hearing a knock on the door to the suite, Viv rinsed her mouth, replaced the towel with a plush bathrobe and left the bathroom. Not one but two room service guys stood there. They pushed a table covered with a pristine linen tablecloth into the room. Domed dishes couldn't completely disguise a heavenly smell, and she realized she was famished. They'd never really gotten around to having a proper dinner last night.

"Do you need me to sign for this?" she asked the younger of the two servers—who kept sneaking peeks at her and blushing, ducking his head to hide his embarrassment. He looked about eighteen, and was apparently in training. He reminded her so much of her youngest brother—the only Callahan child younger than Viv—that she wanted to noogie his head. But she suspected that wouldn't go over well, especially under the stern gaze of his supervisor, who was as starched and stuffy as a British butler.

"That won't be necessary," the older man said, clasping his hands behind his back in quiet dignity. "Is there anything else we can do for you and for Mr. Black? Anything at all?"

"No, that's everything," she said.

"Yes, there is," a voice called, talking over her.

Damien emerged into the room, wearing nothing but a towel slung low around his hips. Viv stared at him. He'd dried off hurriedly and rivulets of water dripped from his dark hair onto those incredibly broad shoulders, riding ridges of muscle down into the light swirl of dark hair on his chest.

She parted her lips, breathing over them, unable to tear her eyes away. She'd touched, kissed, stroked and savored every inch of the man during the night, but now, seeing him standing there, steamy, wet, so unbelievably sexy, made her knees weak. She had to reach out and grab the back of the nearest chair to steady herself. There was such utter, nonchalant power in the man, from his body to his voice, and as he spoke, the starchy butler rammed his spine even straighter, and the young kid tried to disappear behind his boss.

"So you'll have her come up in an hour?"

Viv hadn't even been listening, she'd been focused only on Damien, and her unbelievable physical reaction to him.

"Certainly, Mr. Black."

"Great," he said, already moving away. "Thank you. That will be all."

The two men didn't turn around, they merely began to edge out of the room, bowing slightly. Like they were exiting an interview with a king.

"Wow. Impressive," she said.

"What?"

"Those guys were scared to death of you."

"Not too scared, I hope."

"No," she admitted, realizing she'd worded that poorly. "They were…in awe of you."

"Eat your breakfast," he said with a droll shrug. "I'll dress and be right out."

He headed toward the bathroom, which made her wonder what had drawn him out in the first place. "Who's *she*?" she called.

"Who?"

"The she who's supposed to be up here in an hour."

He glanced over his shoulder. "Mrs. Tate?"

"Uh, sure." She hadn't even heard the name. "Who is she? And why is she coming up here in an hour?"

"She manages one of the stores downstairs."

Viv wrinkled her brow in confusion.

Smiling, Damien returned to her, reaching up to brush a long strand of wet hair behind her ear. "And she's coming in an hour to get you fitted for some clothes."

Viv's jaw dropped open. No way was the man going to buy her clothes! She had only promised to stay for a few hours, and she could certainly wear her suit from yesterday. For that matter, she could just stay in this robe—or in one of his deliciously soft, obviously tailored dress shirts.

"No, that's not…"

Damien cut her off with a kiss. She tried to continue talking—to tell him he was being ridiculous—but he just deepened the kiss. When Damien Black kissed her, there was no thinking of anything else. Just him—strong, warm, sexy, gentle, demanding. Nothing and no one else existed.

By the time the kiss ended, she'd forgotten what she'd intended to say. And judging by the pleased expression on his face as he turned away, that suited him just fine.

"YOU KNOW YOU have to stay away from her, right?"

Sitting across the desk from Sam Donovan, the team's corporate attorney, Damien crossed his arms over his chest and glared at the man.

Stay away from Viv? The lawyer might well ask him to never again take a deep breath. It was not going to happen.

The meetings this morning had gone on for hours, and had been long, bitter and stressful. Frankly, only the thought of going back to the hotel to Viv had kept him from blowing his stack. She'd been the reason he'd kept his cool. The sooner he could finish with this legal shit, the sooner he could return to her and begin making her see that her career was not over.

"Forget it."

Sam wasn't giving up. "I mean it."

His glare deepened. Unlike most people, who would wither under such sharp attention, Sam glared back. He could get away with it. He was, after all, Damien's oldest friend—his college roommate, whom Damien had hired as the head of the legal department for the Vanguard.

"You *can't*, Damien."

"Don't be ridiculous."

"She's your employee." Sam glanced at his watch—a nice one, fitting the generous salary Damien had offered to lure him away from a big corporate firm in DC. Right now, Damien was regretting that move. "At least, she will be in a few minutes, once the acting general manager calls and tells her we want to rehire her."

Damien relaxed into his chair, trying to sound thoroughly reasonable, not wanting Sam to know he was desperate. "She'll have her job again. Stoker's out. Neeley's benched, pending a trade. All's well that ends well."

"Yeah, according to you. What about her?"

"Viv will understand."

Once he explained the truth—that he was the majority shareholder of the team, but he'd had no idea who she was, or what had happened to her—she'd let this go. They could get right back to where they'd left off this morning, before he'd switched on the TV and seen his world nearly blow up in his face.

"She could still sue."

"She won't."

"She could go to the press about the firing."

"She *won't*," he repeated. "Whatever you're worried about, forget it. She's a sharp, reasonable woman. She's not a shark, not at all cold and calculating."

Unlike some women with whom he'd been acquainted.

"I know that. I've met her, remember?"

Of course. He'd run in to Viv yesterday; the rest of the staff had been working with her for two months.

Sam went on. "And I respect her—she's smart, and she got a raw deal here. I'd give anything to make it not have happened, and I wish I'd been here yesterday to stop that Mensa candidate from firing her."

Sam hadn't been at the press event to witness the infamous incident, and he'd been at off-site meetings all day yesterday. He'd been as in the dark about the entire situation as Damien.

Until this morning. When the press had discovered Viv's name and where she worked.

"But it did happen," Sam said. "Now we have to handle it."

"Right, and we did. She just has to hear we're not standing behind Fred Stoker or Bruno Neeley, and she'll be fine."

"You can't be certain of that. She could make a stink about being let go." Sam pounded his palm on his desk. "I still can't believe that son of a bitch did it without even calling me."

"Ditto."

"Did you *hear* what he said?"

Damien had been trying to force the scene from his mind.

"He found her, what the hell was the word, *stimulating*? And since he is a happily married man, a devout man, but still felt that way, of course all these poor red-blooded American boys would, too. So she had to go. For the 'good of the players.'"

"And 'their souls,'" Damien snapped, the words gouged into his brain like a seared scar. God, one conversation with the small-minded asshole had given him just a tiny hint of what Viv had gone through. He didn't even want to imagine how demeaning it had been for her all those weeks working in this building.

"And as for Neeley…"

A growl escaped his mouth. Sam heard, and shut his own.

Damien had been the one to fire gernal manager Fred Stoker, with the corporate attorney there at his side. But he hadn't been in the room when Sam and the new acting general manager, a quickly promoted assistant, had informed Neeley he was being traded. Sam hadn't trusted Damien to be there, with good reason. Hell, Damien didn't trust himself around the guy. Damien had met Neeley, and knew the player had a hundred pounds on him. Still, Damien didn't think he'd have been able to resist trying to break Bruno's jaw. Damien would probably have snapped every bone in his hand, but it would have been worth it.

"How could anybody be so stupid? I mean, was the guy living in the Dark Ages or something? Who goes after the *victim* of sexual discrimination?" Sam asked, his mind back on Stoker.

"The Virginia Vanguard. At least, before today."

"Exactly." His friend leaned forward, crossing his arms on the desk. "Which is why you've got to steer clear of her."

Damien opened his mouth to argue, but Sam held up a hand, forestalling him. "Our team general manager and several players violated our sexual harassment policy— are you going to tell me you're ready to break your own rules against fraternization?"

"I don't work here," he snapped.

"Legally, it doesn't matter a damn," Sam explained. "You practically own the team, Damien. You can't get involved with an employee—especially not one who we want to keep happy and nonlitigious. I'm not just worried about the league wanting to stay squeaky clean before the launch. If she makes a stink, the rest of the shareholders might get antsy. You are aware they already believe you're too inexperienced with professional sports to be CEO."

Damien finally realized what Sam was really getting at. The lawyer wasn't as worried about Viv causing trouble immediately. He was afraid Damien would cause her to make trouble in the future, for more personal reasons.

"What, you're afraid I'll piss her off after you've gotten her calmed down, and she'll sue because of me?"

"It's happened before."

Damien slammed a hand down. "Don't fucking mention that."

Sam nodded slowly, not continuing the subject. He'd already put the thought in Damien's mind, which was bad enough. But even the silence was thick and heavy.

"This is nothing like Georgia," Damien finally said, anger making him tighten his grip on the arms of his chair. "That woman from the Atlanta hotel was running a scam. I didn't touch her. It was a bullshit lawsuit from start to finish."

"Yes, and it went away. You were vindicated." Sam slowly shook his head, getting that wise-old-soul expression on his face, the one he'd had from the day they'd met, when he'd been a skinny, nerdy, computer geek who hadn't been sure what to make of his rich and spoiled, but also sad and a little lost new roommate. "But this time, it wouldn't be bullshit, now would it? There *is* a personal connection. And eventually, when it ends, she could accuse you of just romancing her to keep her from making trouble."

"She wouldn't."

"You can't know that for sure."

Damien heard a note of unconcealed anger in the voice, and he eyed his friend closely. He suspected Sam was talking about his own recent relationship, one that had ended badly. Considering the person who had ended it was Damien's youngest sister, and that the breakup had almost destroyed his twelve-year friendship with the other man, he didn't want to go there.

"I would never hurt Viv," he finally insisted, not wanting to rehash something the two of them had already settled. Sam might still have issues with Damien's sister Johanna, but the two men had moved on.

"Not intentionally."

"What's that supposed to mean?"

"Your track record with women isn't exactly one of long, committed, happy relationships, Damien."

"Thanks for reminding me," he replied sourly. "That doesn't mean things can't change. What if she ends up being the love of my life?"

"Are you in love with her?"

He grunted. "Jesus, Sam, I met her a day ago."

"Plus, you're not capable of love, remember?" Sam said, treading out onto thin ice, walking a line between friend and employee. "You told me that in college. You said you were just like your dad, and you swore he never loved anyone except his kids."

"I don't have to be just like my father," Damien snapped before realizing his friend was making him argue something Damien had always held as an unchangeable fact.

Christ, was this woman really messing with his head so much after just twenty-four hours? Was he seriously questioning something he'd always believed about himself because he'd spent one night in her bed?

He threw his head back and glared at the ceiling. "This is crazy."

"I'm glad you're realized that. I'm also glad you've realized nobody is prewired to automatically fail at every relationship in his life. Now go fall in love…with any woman other than Viv Callahan."

"I don't want anyone else," he muttered.

"She can't be that important to you after one day, right?" his friend said, his voice soft, his tone annoyingly reasonable. "There are a lot of women in the world. So please,

Damien, for all our sakes, let this one go. Just forget about her."

Let her go? Forget about her? Impossible.

No, he might not be in love with her—he had never been in love, wasn't even sure he would recognize the emotion. But he wanted Viv, he craved her as an addict craved a drug.

There was more, though. Since he'd spied her in the parking garage yesterday, and heard about her no-good, very bad day, he'd felt protective of her. The image of that thug groping her hadn't left his mind, and the dark visions of what she'd experienced on a daily basis here were almost worse. He was responsible for all of that, for running a company where such things could happen. Where such things could happen to a woman he was rapidly becoming infatuated with!

No. He couldn't give her up. Not because his lawyer said he should. Not even if it meant putting his new company—the one thing he felt positive about in his business life—at risk. The other stockholders might try to use the bad press or sanctions from the league to force him to step down or sell out. But if they did, they'd have one hell of a fight on their hands.

He always fought for what he really wanted. Which was why he wasn't about to say goodbye to Viv.

"Please, at least consider it?"

A long pause. Finally, a low breath. "All right." He rose from his seat. "Thanks for your help today."

Sam rose, too, and extended his hand. "You'll be in town for a while, I guess? To make sure this thing blows over?"

He'd be staying for a lot more reasons than that. Well, only one more reason—but she was a major one. "Yes, I will."

"You're welcome to stay with me if you want out of the hotel. I have a huge place, and there are a lot of single women in my building."

He managed a small smile. The guy just never gave up. He had to wonder, not for the first time, what on earth his sister had done to make Sam give up on her.

"I think our partying bachelor days are behind us."

"Okay, just…"

"Don't."

Sam shrugged helplessly.

Few people had ever been able to make Damien do something he didn't want to—one of the big reasons he'd never gotten along with some members of his family. Sam had pushed as much as he could. Because Damien was in no way ready to give up Viv Callahan.

There was so much to explore between them, but they'd start with the truth. Who he really was, where he'd been for most of the day. He'd lay it all out and ask what she thought about them continuing to see each other. Maybe it would last a few nights, maybe months. Or, hell, he was thirty years old—maybe he'd finally found someone who could make him hear the word *family* and not immediately want to get to the nearest airport. Stranger things had happened, hadn't they?

But when he got to the hotel, walked into the penthouse and heard a thick silence that could only be caused by utter emptiness, he began to worry. "Viv? Where are you?"

His heart picking up its pace, he hurried through the huge suite, checking both bedrooms, the living area, dining room, media center and bathrooms. The patio was empty, as was every closet. Well, except for one, in which he found something strange. A pair of shoes—women's shoes. They were strappy heels, sexy and designer, and, he realized when he picked one up and checked the sole, brand-new.

"Where the hell are you?" he muttered, circling the room, holding the shoe in his hand like Cinderella's useless prince.

That was when he spotted the note on the pillow. He'd overlooked it because Viv had tucked it underneath the mints. Dropping the shoe, he grabbed the note and unfolded it, quickly reading the short message.

Damien—

I know the truth. I can't believe you lied to me about your "business." I've been such a fool. Please don't try to contact me, I honestly can't deal with yet another deceitful man right now.

Viv

PS: I did not want to keep the damn clothes, but they took mine to the laundry! I did leave the shoes in the closet—please give them to the snobby saleslady you sent up here to torture and humiliate me.

PSS: I'll return the clothes as soon as possible.

PSSS: Don't worry about me. I got my job back.

And that was all. Vixen Viv, Vivacious Viv, Vibrant Viv...was gone.

# 6

ALTHOUGH VIV HAD worried her return to the Vanguard would be stressful, her first full week had gone pretty well. She was beginning to believe she'd made the right decision in taking her job back, and they'd certainly made it worth her while to do so. She'd not only gotten a decent raise, but also an end to her probationary period and a bigger office.

The week had been full of meetings with the acting team's general manager, the director of Human Resources and somebody from the corporate attorney's office. They'd fallen over themselves to assure her that Fred Stoker had acted without authority, and that he was gone forever. She'd also been informed that the players had gotten a lesson about sexual harassment. There would be no more bets, no more grabs, gropes, kisses, or come-ons.

At least, so they said. And so far, they were right.

Viv was aware that the organization was trying to keep her happy so she wouldn't sue or spout off to the press— who finally appeared to have calmed down somewhat. Considering she'd had no intention of doing either, she felt bad about sucking up everything they were throwing at her. But not *too* bad. It would take a lot more than office perks to wipe away the memory of Neeley's hands and mouth on her, or the public ridicule.

Her family's reaction had been the worst. After spotting the TV coverage, her brothers had, as she'd feared, driven down from western Pennsylvania to make sure she was all right. All five of them. They'd growled and threatened, had tried to find out where Bruno Neeley lived. And they'd tried to drag her home.

Thank heaven she'd already been rehired by the time they showed up. Otherwise, considering how sad she'd been agonizing over the incident, and over Damien, she might have gone with them. But she'd be home again soon for her parents' anniversary.

"Damien," she mumbled, clenching one fist on her lap and tightening the other around a tortilla chip she'd just loaded up with salsa. The thing crumbled in her hand, sending bits of chip and tomato all over her fingers and the table.

"What?"

Grimacing, Viv grabbed a napkin and forced a strained smile at Lulu, who'd met her for Friday night happy hour to celebrate Viv's first week back at work. Amelia would be along shortly, with Lex. Lulu's new hubby, Chaz, would be joining them soon, too. As usual, Viv would be the fifth wheel, but considering how well things had turned out, Viv wasn't going to complain.

"Nothing. Just clumsy."

"You're thinking about him, aren't you? The guy?"

"Damien," she whispered again.

"No word, huh?"

"Of course not. I told him not to contact me. Even if I wanted to, he couldn't, because I never gave him my number."

"If he's as rich as you say, he could track you down."

"He wouldn't," she said, wishing her voice hadn't trembled. "I made it clear I didn't want to hear from him."

Lulu licked a bit of salt off the rim of her margarita

glass. "Explain to me again why you ran out on him? Why was it such a bad thing, him being a gazillionaire?"

"Because he lied about it."

"He said, 'Nope, no siree, I'm not a gazillionaire'?"

"Of course not. But for heaven's sake, we talked about the hotel chain—the Paris location being his favorite—and he didn't say one word about the fact that he owns the whole shebang."

"Maybe he's modest."

She snorted. "Not even close."

"Arrogant?"

"A little. But in a good way," she admitted.

Lulu eyed her speculatively. "So what's the problem again?"

"I don't want to be with a guy like that, who hides who he is, and can buy and sell people at the drop of a hat."

How could he have let her spend the night with him, and then remain in his suite, without mentioning that he owned the hotel? That elevator business alone was mortifying enough. Leaving the way he had, sending an army of officious salespeople up from the designer stores downstairs—what had he expected her to believe? They'd joked about Richard Gere and Julia Roberts, but from the moment she'd realized he really was a billionaire, and that he'd instructed his hotel staff to outfit her with an entirely new wardrobe, she had begun to feel cheap and purchased.

Well, okay, she'd loved the clothes. Damn it, any woman would. But she wouldn't have kept a stitch if not for the fact that her own had been whisked out of sight during the fittings, the manicure and the hairstyling.

"Was it really that bad?"

"Yes! I mean, who does he think he is, disappearing for the day, ordering me to stay put, sending people to fit me for clothes, but never telling me I'm a guest in *his* hotel?"

"Yeah, what a lousy jerk to want to protect you from the media, give you a place to regroup, drop a hundred grand on designer originals, while intending to come back and have hot, wild, monkey sex with you again all night. How dare that guy."

"I hate you."

"You love me. And you loved the monkey sex."

"Okay, yeah. And oh, hell yeah."

The sex had been amazing. Walking away from him—and that—had been painful. Still, she'd done it. She'd ordered everyone—and their clothes—out, had written a note and stormed from the hotel, intending to never see him again. He hadn't tracked her down. Hadn't called. And that was fine with her. *Right?*

"Maybe he didn't want to be desired only for his money."

"Bullshit. He knew I wanted *him*. The pheromones wafting off us could have been bottled and used in mating rituals."

"Eww."

"You're the one who mentioned monkey sex. No, he was just being sneaky, taking what he wanted, not trusting me with the truth. He should have come clean, should have let me decide whether I even wanted to be with somebody so…"

"Fabulous?"

"Out of my league. What would he see in me, anyway? Guy could have any woman in the world. No way would I measure up."

Lulu smacked a hand on the table. "Aha!"

"What?"

"That's it! You're worried you can't hold him. So rather than take a chance and risk being hurt again, you cut and ran."

Viv's mouth fell open. If there'd been food in it, she'd have spit it all over the table. "What are you talking about?"

"This is about last spring." Lulu was getting worked up. "That prick Dale said he was too good for you, didn't he? And deep down, you believed it. You fear you're hot and sexy, but that's about it, and no guy would want you for more."

Viv couldn't even muster a reply. She'd been so furious for the past week, she'd never considered such a thing. But could Lulu be right? Was she just using Damien's reticence about his wealth as an excuse? Somewhere between the Prada shoes and the Vera Wang dress, the saleswoman had asked what it was like to be staying with the owner, one of the richest men in the country, and she'd freaked out—and then bugged out. But she'd never stopped to wonder if it was because she was angry…or afraid.

"Hell," she muttered.

"I nailed it, didn't I?"

Viv didn't reply. She might, indeed, have thrown away a chance to be with someone amazing out of pure cowardice. Because she was afraid he might believe she was good enough to fuck but not good enough to actually care about.

But protecting her, urging her to stay so she could avoid the press, buying clothes so she wouldn't have to leave— those weren't the actions of someone who only wanted a piece of ass. He had cared, at least a bit. And she'd repaid him by running.

Stupid. She'd been so incredibly stupid.

She was saved from admitting as much to Lulu by Chaz's arrival. While Lulu kissed her husband, Viv headed for the restroom. Her friend's words kept repeating in her brain, so much so that, as she stood in the rear of the restaurant, she found herself wanting to explain her actions. Maybe even to apologize.

To Damien Black.

"You can't do this," she told herself, even as she pulled her phone out of her purse. "He's long gone, anyway."

But something made her look up the Arlington Black Star Hotel, and something made her dial the number, and something made her ask to be connected to Damien Black's room.

She waited, sure she'd be informed he had checked out. Instead, she was put through—there were a few clicks and a ring, and she almost hung up, an inner voice screaming at her to let it go.

He didn't answer. Instead, she got a recording. To her surprise, it wasn't a generic one. She heard his voice, firm and strong, demanding a message.

"Damien, it's me, Viv. I mean, Vivienne Callahan. We met last week." She swallowed hard. "Um, I've been thinking about how I left. It was pretty shitty to write that note and walk out. I reacted…well, maybe I overreacted."

*Ya think?*

"Anyway, I wanted to apologize. I know you were trying to help me. I should have stayed to tell you how everything worked out—about the job and all. And to thank you for trying to help."

What else was there to say? *I still want you. Do you still want me?* Jeez, she'd sound as juvenile as a fourth grader passing a note.

"Anyway, it's Friday night, I've had a couple of margaritas at my favorite Mexican place—Rosario's, a few blocks from where we met. And that made me think of you."

*Liar. You want him to know where you are…just in case.*

"So, um, I hope you're well. Thanks for everything.' Bye."

She disconnected, and then replayed each word, wondering if she'd sounded ridiculous, hoping nobody else had access to his phone. Then, wishing she'd just let things lie, Viv returned to the table. Amelia and Lex had arrived, and she took her chair, the five of them ignoring the empty sixth chair that hadn't been filled by anyone in Viv's life for months. Not since Dale.

Enough with Dale. And with Damien. And with men. She needed to forget all that, to focus only on the positives. She had her job again, and she had great friends and tonight was a celebration.

So she celebrated. The margaritas went down smoothly, and she ate lots of rich, spicy food, and she laughed, and eventually she even stopped watching the door.

Which was, perhaps, why she didn't notice him enter. Why she never even knew he was there. Not until Damien Black was standing right beside her.

"Hello, Vivienne."

She fell out of her chair.

She'd been sitting on the edge, leaning close to whisper something saucy to Amelia, who sat beside her.

Then he'd spoken her name, and the world had trembled. Her chair had teetered, and she'd slipped right off the end of it.

It could have been a catastrophe. But Damien reacted with that catlike quickness. He dropped on his knee to the floor, catching her in his arms, as he had in the bathroom last week.

"You're not very graceful, are you?" he asked, amused.

"What are you doing here?" she asked, her head spinning, a result of the slip, the tequila and oh, the incredibly sexy, spicy-smelling man holding her.

"Oh, my God. Viv, are you all right?" Lulu shrieked.

The others all got up and came around to check on her. If any of them thought it strange that A) a handsome stranger had startled her right out of her chair, and B) said handsome stranger had then taken a dive to catch her before she could hit the floor, they at least had the courtesy not to say anything.

"I'm fine," she insisted, not even trying to wriggle her way free. She told herself it was because she was still shaken about her near fall. Then again, she wasn't bad at lying to herself when the occasion warranted it. "Seriously, it's okay, go back to what you were doing."

The two couples, though wide-eyed with curiosity, retook their seats. Lulu leaned over to whisper to the others, and Viv knew she, at least, had figured out who the mysterious stranger was. Not surprising. How could Lulu not look at him and recognize the gorgeous, rich man Viv had described? Not because of any designer clothes—he wore simple jeans and a button-down shirt, the cuffs undone and sleeves rolled up his forearms.

Damn, she loved those arms.

But no, the outfit didn't reveal who and what he was. The way he carried himself did. His confidence bespoke wealth and success. Plus, of course, Lulu might have ID'd him because he was on his knee on the dingy floor, holding Viv around the waist as if loathe to let her go.

That was nice.

If Viv had been completely sober, she would have gotten back into her chair, coolly invited Damien to join them and introduced him. Instead, she stayed right where she was, eye-to-eye with the most glorious man she'd ever met. She smiled at him, studying the face, the eyes, the mouth, all of which had become so familiar to her in one long, sensuous night. All of which she'd missed in the eight days since she'd seen him.

"You came," she murmured, still in shock.

His presence meant something, right? He didn't have to be here, he certainly hadn't needed to track her down.

There was no reason for him to seek her out...unless he really *wanted* to.

"I came."

"I hoped you would." She hiccupped, cursed the tequila and went on with her confession. Her voice low, she admitted, "I just didn't want you to *know* that I hoped you would."

"Of course I knew you hoped I would."

She blinked. "Wait, did I say that right? I'm confused."

"Not as confused as me."

"As I."

"What?"

"Not as confused as I."

"Thank you, Grammar Granny."

She pinched his shoulder, for three reasons. For the Granny remark, for the teasing and to make sure he was really here.

One dark eyebrow went up, but she'd swear his lips quirked with humor. "What was that for?"

"Why'd it take hours for you to show up? Couldn't you read between the lines? I was ready to order dessert, and God knows my hips don't need any cheesecake."

"Your hips are perfect," he insisted, cupping one in his hand. "Why didn't you just come right out and invite me?"

She tried to rise off his knee, struggling to appear graceful, but failing miserably. Sighing and giving up, she admitted, "I didn't want to seem desperate."

"You could never seem desperate." He leaned closer and kissed the tip of her nose. "Just clumsy."

"I'm not clumsy," she insisted, succeeding in sliding into her chair. It didn't wobble, thank heaven. But her stomach was doing enough wobbling of its own with all those butterflies flitting around in there. That nose kiss had been too flirty and adorable. Definitely not an I-just-want-to-fuck-you gesture. But a cute, we're-sort-of-dating one.

He was here. He was *really* here. Moreover, he wanted to be. How crazy was that?

He sat in the chair next to her. "As for why it took so long, I was out and just heard your message a little while ago."

"I'm surprised I caught you still in town."

"I've been waiting."

Her whole body tensed. "Waiting for what?"

"To see if you'd call."

Viv couldn't breathe—she swore even her heart stopped beating in her chest for one long moment. She stared into his eyes, searching for deceit, seeing none.

He meant it. He'd waited for her. She'd run out on him, leaving him a cowardly note, and he'd waited for her to get in touch, not pushing, not demanding. It surprised her, honestly, given how strong and impatient she knew he could be—deliciously so. But his admission also made something warm and sweet open up within her. A flower of optimism, which she'd ruthlessly crushed last spring, began to bloom in her heart.

He'd waited. For *her*.

"I thought you had to get home to Miami," she finally replied.

"I was planning to leave tomorrow if you still hadn't reached out." He covered her hand on the table, lacing his fingers with hers. "I'm glad you did."

Viv licked her lips, suddenly nervous. The effects of the margaritas wore off quickly, like a veil she'd dropped to the floor. Reality crashed in. She'd invited him back into her life. She'd opened herself up to this gorgeous, rich, perfect man, and he'd accepted her invitation. So what now?

"Are you going to introduce me to your friends?"

Okay, that was a start. Nodding, she cleared her throat. Of course, the other two couples had been pretending to mind their own business and keep up with their conversations, but the moment she made the noise, four pairs of eyes turned toward her.

"Everyone, this is my friend Damien." She nodded toward the couple on Damien's right. "Damien, meet Lulu and Chaz Browning."

They smiled and said their hellos, and then Viv gestured to the couple on her left. "And here are Amelia and Lex, aka Bridezilla and her hapless groom-to-be."

Amelia wrinkled her nose at Viv before offering Damien a smile. "Ignore her. She's just mad because I'm making her wear an orange bridesmaid dress."

"God, don't remind me," Viv said, reaching for her drink. "The wedding's on Halloween weekend," she explained. "So can't I just wear black? Let Lulu wear the orange?"

Lulu glared. "If you're wearing black, I'm wearing black."

"Orange!" Amelia pronounced, not a bit moved. *Ugh*, Viv thought.

"You look familiar," Lex said to Damien, his eyes narrowed as if he was trying to place the other man. "Have we met?"

"I don't believe so," Damien replied. "But I've seen you on TV. I enjoyed your interview with Pete Whitecastle."

"He's a nice guy."

Viv groaned, recognizing the name of the NHL star, who'd come out in support of gay players earlier in the year. "No. No hockey talk tonight. I get enough of it Monday through Friday."

Lex smiled. "So…baseball? Who are you rooting for in the series?"

Damien went along, his smirk saying he knew well that she was seething in her chair. "LA's looking good."

"Their star player is, anyway," said Lulu. "Hubba hubba. I hate sports, and even I know who Rand McConnell is. Yum."

When Damien coughed lightly into his fist, Viv raised a questioning brow. "What?"

"Oh, it's nothing. Just…I know the guy. Had a run-in with him in Chicago a couple of years ago."

Everyone at the table eyed him, all intrigued. Including Viv. "A run-in? Like, a fight?"

He shook his head. "No. There was, uh, a sort of mix-up with the rooms at our hotel. I accidentally ended up in bed with his girlfriend."

Viv's jaw fell open, and Lulu's husband, Chaz, chortled. "Do you mean his now wife? I've seen pictures of her. To quote my wife—hubba hubba, indeed."

Lulu elbowed him in the ribs. He leaned over and grabbed her around the waist, pulling her close, and they shared a kiss. Despite their comments, the two were crazy about each other, having shared a love-hate relationship since childhood.

"I don't suppose you ever accidentally end up in bed with an unattractive girl, huh?" Viv said, not hiding her snark.

"Not if he's lucky," said Lex. The three men at the table exchanged knowing glances. All three burst into laughter, Damien melting into the group so easily, she could almost forget he was a freaking billionaire who could buy and sell any of them a thousand times over.

"When did you realize you were in the wrong bed?" Amelia asked.

"I wasn't. She was." He lifted a glass of water the server had just deposited on the table and took a sip. As he lowered it, a twinkle appeared in his eyes. "And we didn't figure out the mix-up until two of the three of us were practically naked."

"Holy crap, was it you and Rand McConnell? Because I woulda paid money to witness that," said Lulu.

Viv snickered as Damien's eyes rounded. They went even rounder when Amelia murmured, "Me, too."

"Alas, no," he finally said, his face perhaps the tiniest bit flushed. "Sorry I can't add to anyone's baseball-player slash shipping."

Lulu smiled at Viv. "I like this one. A guy who's confident enough not to mind chicks slash shipping him with a baseball stud is a-okay by me."

"Thanks," he said. "Just don't go shipping me with any hockey players." He squeezed Viv's hand. "Not after last week."

Viv nodded. "Hear, hear! Now, can we stop the sports talk? I've had enough of it."

"Can we at least toast to your getting your job back, and that asshole Bruno Neeley being traded?" Lex asked, lifting his glass. "I hate what he did to you, and I couldn't be happier that the city's getting rid of him. He's scum."

Damien was nodding, and his hand tightened even more. They hadn't even had a chance to discuss what had happened with her job, other than what she'd said in her note. But that was fine. Frankly, she'd talked about it enough. As far as she was concerned, it was over. Her professional life was settled; now Viv was ready to move forward and focus on her personal one. And considering the man of any girl's dreams was sitting beside her, having come to find her for no other reason than that he wanted to be with her, she seemed to be making a pretty good start.

ALTHOUGH DAMIEN LIKED Viv's friends, he couldn't wait to get her to himself. He'd been waiting for more than a week, hoping for some sign that she'd calmed down about him not telling her he owned the Vanguard. He'd refrained from chasing her—hadn't gone to the office, or lurked around the parking garage after work hoping to accidentally bump into her. Realizing he owed it to Sam, and his company—as well as, of course, to Viv—to let her figure out how to proceed, he'd steered clear.

Still, he'd been honest about having stuck around for her. He'd dodged calls from his family. Inventing reasons to stay in the area, he'd actually gotten some work done, including negotiating a trade for Neeley to a Canadian team. The bastard wouldn't be happy about moving to the great white north, but contractually, he couldn't do anything about it. Hopefully the guy wouldn't harass anybody except the polar bears.

Damien had also been pleased that the acting general manager, Zane Koch, a former player, had leaped feet-first into the job and was exceeding all expectations. The promotion might end up actually being a permanent one. According to the reports, Koch had handled the transition smoothly, and had done everything he could to ensure Viv, and every other woman working for the team, was treated equally and with respect.

So yes, everything had come together. Except Viv. He'd begun to worry she'd never get over it. So when he'd heard her voice mail tonight as he was leaving the practice arena, he hadn't even gone to the hotel to change clothes. Instead, he'd had his driver take him straight to the restaurant she'd mentioned, hoping it wasn't too late and he hadn't missed her.

Seeing her sitting there—her golden hair gleaming under the soft restaurant lights, her lips curved into a smile, her eyes bright—had made his blood roar in his veins. He'd missed her. More, his hunger for her had not diminished one bit in the days they'd been apart. Judging by the way she'd eaten him up with her stare, the feeling was entirely mutual.

Which was why, the moment they slid into the backseat of the limo, separated from the outside world and from his driver, by tinted windows, he pulled her onto his lap. She immediately slid her arms around his neck and tilted her head, her lips parted in invitation. Their tongues swept together, tangling and thrusting. She tasted of tequila, lime and hot, spicy woman. He reached up and cupped her face in both hands, stroking her cheeks, his thumbs tracing the line of her throat. He memorized the feel of her, glad to realize he hadn't been wrong—she really had the softest skin he'd ever touched.

"I've missed you," he growled against her mouth when they paused to draw breath.

"Then why didn't you come sooner?" Her voice held a pout.

"You didn't leave me your number, remember?"

"You could have found me." She scooted even closer, until her soft, curvy butt was pressed right into his groin. His cock throbbed with heat, and she cooed, wriggling as she felt his raging hunger for her.

"Yes, but I thought you wanted space," he admitted.

"If you'd read my Facebook statuses all week, you'd have realized I was lonely and hoping you'd get in touch."

"I don't do social media."

She snickered. "You barely do social."

"You saying I wasn't social with your friends?"

"Yes, you were. But it was quite obvious you weren't interested in being there."

"Only because you weren't, either."

"I love my friends."

"I'm sure they're wonderful people. But you know you wanted to be alone with me."

"Sure of yourself, aren't you?"

"Sure of what I heard in your voice in that message."

She licked her lips, not trying to deny it. "Could we pretend I didn't sound totally pathetic?"

He lifted one of her hands to his mouth and brushed his lips across her knuckles. "That was not the word I'd use."

"Whiny?"

"Shut up, Viv, and kiss me again."

She shut up and kissed him. Damien slid his fingers into her hair, twining that silkiness around his skin. They tasted and sipped from each other's mouths, and all the questions, the embarrassment, the worries of the past week… just drifted away.

When they again drew apart, he murmured, "There hasn't been a minute since you left that I haven't thought about you."

"Not one?"

"Not one," he said, dropping a hand to her long, slim thigh. She was wearing a business suit, but it fit better than the last outfit, highlighting that incredible body rather than concealing it. Considering she no longer had to worry about being harassed at work, her wardrobe had definitely improved since the day they met.

Speaking of which… "You should have taken the clothes."

"I didn't need them. Just one outfit to make my getaway, which I returned to the hotel the next day. Did you get it?"

"I got it."

It was hanging in the closet in the suite. Along with her original suit, plus every other thing she'd tried on but refused to accept that day. He hadn't been ready to admit she wasn't coming back.

"Anyway, thanks for finding me."

"Thanks for calling."

"You're welcome." She sighed happily, dropping her head onto his shoulder, nuzzling into his neck.

Although he was dying with want for her, he also found himself enjoying this softer, sweeter Viv. This wasn't frantic, as things had been last week. Instead, she seemed happy to stay curled on his lap, wrapped in his arms. And while he wanted her with a desperation that bordered on insanity, he found himself savoring the moment, just as it was. This slightly tipsy Viv seemed younger, more vulnerable. He liked that she'd lowered her defenses, and he'd make damn sure she didn't live to regret it.

There was one thing to clear up, though. "I apologize for not admitting who I was before I left you that morning. I guess my brain was scrambled because of that frigging TV story."

"You were worried about me?"

"More than you can imagine."

"You're forgiven."

"Maybe. Still, I can't express how sorry I am about everything that happened to you. It was wrong on every level."

"It all worked out. Let's not talk about it," she said before yawning audibly near his ear. His warm, soft kitten had her claws sheathed, and appeared ready to soak up his heat and take a cozy nap. This wasn't exactly what he'd intended when he'd dragged her into his arms. And yet, he was enjoying it anyway.

Laughing softly, he squeezed her and dropped a soft kiss on the top of her head. She mumbled something, but was already drifting off to sleep, and he couldn't make sense of it.

A buzzer sounded from the console phone. Damien carefully disengaged an arm to answer.

"We're almost to the hotel, sir."

It had, of course, been a quick ride. Too quick. He wasn't ready to give up this quiet interlude, the two of them cocooned in his car, her cuddled in his arms.

"Just drive around the city for a while, Jed, will you?"

"Certainly, sir."

Damien hung up the phone, watching as the car left the downtown area of Arlington and headed toward the parkway. The Friday-night traffic wasn't too heavy, the car gliding on the road as smoothly as soft butter on a knife. And as crazy as it seemed, considering he'd been a raging hormone for the past week, all because of the woman lying so vulnerable and soft in his arms, he found himself drifting off, too.

He was lulled by the sounds of her low, even breaths. Damien hadn't slept well in a week, tossing and turning in the big bed, made bigger by her absence. Now, though, everything seemed right, and he was able to relax for the first time in days.

He awoke minutes later when he realized a soft, warm mouth was kissing his bare chest. It took him a second before he realized a wide-awake Viv had begun to open the buttons of his shirt and was exploring his body, her sweet tongue gliding along his pecs, swirling around his nipple. He hissed, tightening his hand on her thigh.

"Stay asleep, you're having a nice dream," she murmured as she shifted on his lap to face him, straddling his thighs. Her shirt scooted high on her legs and he helped it along, pushing up the fabric, caressing her silky skin. When he reached the edge of her panties, he slid his fingers under it, gently toying with the soft curls concealing her sex. She let out a sigh, but quickly wriggled away, evading his touch, as if determined to focus only on him for right now.

He wasn't about to argue. Not when her mouth was so… damn…amazing.

"What am I going to find when I wake up from this dream?" he asked.

She laughed wickedly. "What do you want to find?"

"You. Just you."

Sliding farther away, she pushed herself off his lap and nudged his legs apart. He said nothing as he watched her drop to her knees on the floor of the limo, between his thighs. His breaths were coming unevenly out of his lungs, the anticipation of her touch making him throb all over.

Viv leaned close again, continuing to unbutton his shirt, nibbling and licking her way down his body. Her soft tongue swirled around his navel, and then she tasted her way to the waistband of his jeans.

"I mean it, go to sleep," she said.

"Fat chance."

"Afraid you'll wake up and realize some vixen has taken advantage of you?"

He was more afraid she wouldn't.

He twisted his hands in her hair. "I enoy the way you take advantage of me," he said, remembering how she'd used her mouth on him last week. The memory of that soft tongue lapping against his sensitive skin had haunted his fantasies. Viv had explored him with utter sensuality, tasting every inch of him, as he had her. He didn't remember being with a woman who seemed to love giving pleasure as much as she enjoyed receiving it.

She must have read his mind. Viv worked his belt open, and then unbuttoned and unzipped his jeans.

"Oh, God," he groaned as a small, soft hand slipped beneath his jeans to brush against his throbbing dick.

"My, oh my, Mr. Black!" A saucy smirk. "I fear you forgot your drawers."

"Maybe you should give me another pair of yours."

"I doubt they'd fit," she purred.

"No, but they'd be nice to keep in my pocket, so I can imagine you all day long when we're apart."

"Wait, another pair?" She stopped what she was doing and stared up at him, her mouth agape. "I never got my underwear back from the hotel laundry."

He smiled wickedly.

"Damien Black, did you steal my panties?"

"Guilty."

"What have you done with them?"

"All sorts of wicked things."

Looking pleased, she stroked his cock, from base to tip, her nails scratching ever-so-lightly. Then she encircled him in her hand. "Did you wrap them around yourself like this?"

*Heaven.* "Mmm. Oh, God. Yes, Viv."

A light squeeze, but she released him. "What else?"

Groaning, he asked, "Do you want me to admit that I used your panties to beat off?"

"Did you?"

"Of course."

She gasped softly. "Tell me about it."

He stared down at her, the golden moonlight coming through the sunroof giving her a soft glow. She moved her lips ever closer to the wet tip of his cock, and he growled, "Taste me."

"*Tell* me."

Gritting his teeth, he clenched his fists on the seat as he watched her sway so close, he could feel the warmth of her exhalations touch the drop of cum seeping from the tip of his cock. "All right. Your panties did not go to the laundry, because I had them in my pocket when I left the hotel."

"Oh?"

"Uh-huh. And when I was sitting in this car on the way to and from my meetings, I pulled them out."

Her turn to hiss.

"They smelled like you—like hot, sultry Vivienne, and just the scent was enough to make my dick so hard I could've used it to pound nails." Frowning, he growled, "So you can imagine how disappointed I was to get to the hotel and find you gone."

"I'm sorry about that," she whispered.

"Me, too."

She forced a smile. "But you had my undergarments to keep you company."

"Indeed I did." Closing his eyes, he gave her more of what she'd wanted—details. "I loved the way you sucked me off that night. Your silk undies weren't quite as soft as your mouth, or as warm and wet as your pussy, but they did the job."

"Oh, my," she whispered.

"You asked for it."

"I'll take it."

More? Okay. *More.* "I cupped my balls first, remembering how you licked me there."

If it had been light enough in the car, he might see a blush on her cheeks. But hell, he doubted it. His vixen wasn't the blushing short—one of the things he adored about her.

"I wrapped the fabric around my cock and stroked myself, my eyes closed, imagining it was you I was sinking into."

"Soft or hard?" she whispered.

"Both. Soft, at first. Then harder. Faster."

She was panting, he could hear her breaths. "And?"

"And I couldn't help myself. I came all over your panties, wishing with every bone in my body that it was you instead."

Viv didn't wait to tell him he'd pleased her by admitting the down-and-dirty truth. She showed him. Without any further warning, she bent over him, nudging his pants farther open, and slid her tongue all the way up the long ridge of his cock.

Damien groaned, threw his head back and gave himself over to her. Her tongue was the second closest thing to heaven, and as she kissed and sucked him, he was unable to stop himself from slowly thrusting up toward her greedy mouth.

She took what he gave her, making love to him with lips, tongue, hands. The interior of the car got hot and steamy.

More than anything, he wanted to pluck her off the floor, yank her onto his lap and impale her. But she wouldn't let him. When he tried to pull her up, she shook off his hand, determined to bring him all the way home.

It didn't take long. When the waves of pulsing pleasure began to roar through him, signaling his release, he tried to push her mouth away. She wouldn't, however, let go and sucked deeper, taking everything he had to give and swallowing it down. Damien could only sit there, sliding his fingers through her hair, trying to regain his breath, watching as she finally withdrew and looked up at him, a smile on her beautiful face.

"That was…"

"That was number one," she told him, the words nearly purred. "And I believe the goal is twelve?"

Twelve. Damn. Easier for her to say than for a guy.

But he was game to try. As long as Viv wanted to play, he'd do his damndest to keep up with her.

# 7

ALTHOUGH THE UPSCALE restaurant in the lobby of the Arlington Black Star Hotel was famous for its Sunday brunch, Viv was quite content to savor another room service meal in the penthouse.

Unlike last week, there was no rush. Damien didn't have to hurry out for a day of meetings and Viv wasn't wallowing in the misery of public humiliation. In fact, the two of them had completely forgotten about anyone and anything else the minute they'd gotten in his car outside the restaurant Friday night. Well, except for Jed. The driver had been remarkably discreet and friendly, accepting her thanks for working on her car, but refusing the compensation she'd offered.

Other than him, though, they hadn't exchanged more than a dozen words with anyone, which was fine with Viv. Because the past thirty-six hours had been remarkable. And not just because of the intense, utterly unbelievable sex. The truth was, she'd just enjoyed being with him.

Washington, DC, was a great city to explore if you had the time and a willing victim...er, tourist. Damien had said he'd come to the area for business on multiple occasions, but he'd never been to a single one of the museums. He'd never walked up the steps of the Lincoln Memorial, or read the names on the beautiful onyx wall that memorialized those who'd fallen in Vietnam.

Having a car and driver made things so much simpler, and they'd managed to shove a week's worth of sightseeing into one day. They'd hit everything from the monuments, to the National Zoo, to the Smithsonian, finishing up at Viv's favorite, the National Museum of Natural History, for a peek at the Hope Diamond.

"I've seen nicer," he'd mused, staring at the stone through a thick wall of security glass.

"Maybe. But not bigger, I'll bet."

He'd never taken his eyes off the rock. "I thought women didn't care about size."

Viv had snickered. Of all the things Damien the billionaire might have to worry about, size was *not* one of them. "Of course we don't…except when it comes to diamonds. Oh, and penises."

He'd reached around and pinched her butt to punish her, and she'd emitted a squeal that had echoed through the gallery. They hadn't stayed long at the museum after that, taking a walk along the reflecting pool before Jed picked them up and took them across the river into Virginia.

It was there they'd had the only unpleasant moment of the day. They'd been walking down a cobbled sidewalk, coming from an adorable French restaurant where they'd enjoyed dinner, and she'd spied a campaign sign with a familiar name on it. Damien had apparently felt her tense up, and asked what was wrong.

"Just a goose walking over my grave."

He frowned. "Huh?"

"Sorry, aren't you from the South? Don't they use that expression in Florida?"

"We say it all the time when we travel back to the 1940s."

Giggling, aware he was trying to lighten her suddenly

dark mood, she'd admitted, "I used to go out with that guy. The one running for delegate."

His turn to tense. "And?"

"And nothing. It's not fun seeing his name everywhere."

Even worse was seeing his face on the damn signs. Dale was nothing if not proud of his looks, and his dumb, smiling mug was used as a selling point in all his promotional materials.

She couldn't help comparing him to Damien, and her ex paled in every way. Damien was far hotter, smarter, more charming, more successful. But he was not at all in-your-face about it. He never had to make himself seem bigger or more important at anyone else's—*her*—expense. And, funny, since the moment she'd met him, Viv had never worried she wasn't good enough, like she had to be on her best behavior for fear of doing or saying the wrong thing. With Damien, she was free to be herself, and was never pressured to be any other way.

What a wonderful, amazing thing. It was a gift Damien had given her that he didn't even realize, was one she already cherished.

"More champagne?" he asked, lifting an icy bottle from a bucket, bringing her thoughts forward from last night into the bright light of Sunday morning.

Viv looked up from her plate, which she'd just cleaned of not only a delicious serving of eggs Benedict but also half a Belgian waffle, and nodded happily. She watched as Damien splashed the sparkling liquid into her glass of orange juice, then she accepted the glass and stretched in her chair. "I could get used to this," she murmured, staring out over the river through the bank of floor-to-ceiling windows that spanned the penthouse dining room. From up here, she had an unobstructed view of the Capitol dome, the Washington Monument, all the beautiful structures people around the world only ever saw in books.

The breakfast, the view, the champagne, the softness of the robe, the closetful of clothes he'd insisted he couldn't return…all of it suddenly became a bit much for Viv. Because she *could* get used to this, all too easily. And that was not a good thing. At the end of the day—or the week, the month, whatever—Damien would be heading for Miami. To his real life. She'd be staying here and going on with hers.

High-rises, penthouses, limo rides, designer clothes and two-hundred-dollar bottles of champagne had no place in her life. While she, with her sassy mouth, her bad reputation, her snarky attitude, her blue-collar family and her entry-level job, had no real place in his. Despite how wonderful he made her feel about just being herself, she knew that was true. He might like her as she was, might make her feel comfortable enough to be totally herself around him, but to the rest of the world, she would never be good enough.

A feeling of melancholy suddenly washed over her. She'd managed to keep all those worries at bay for the past day and a half. Now, knowing he'd meant to leave yesterday, and could probably only postpone his trip home for a few more days, she began to realize her tactical error. In taking all the wicked, spoiled, exotic moments she could with him, had she simply opened a window in her mind to miss him all the more when she returned to the real world? *Her* world?

"Finished?"

Nodding, she rose from the table and walked over to the couch. She sat down, continuing to stare outside, suddenly unsure of what to say, how to behave. She was aware she was being was ridiculous, considering the amazing intimacies they'd shared throughout the weekend. It might have taken her longer than just Friday night, but Damien had definitely hit twelve and kept right on going. As for Viv? Well, she'd stopped keeping count.

So why was this suddenly so awkward?

"What's on your mind?"

"Nothing."

He walked over to stand behind her, dropping his hands onto her shoulders, gently kneading them. Viv sighed with pleasure, tilting her head to the side to give him better access. If there was a man on the planet who was more skilled with his hands, she'd like to meet him. Or, no, she wouldn't. She was quite happy with this one…at least, for as long as she had him.

"Tell me what you're thinking."

"Nothing, really."

"Is it that guy?"

"What guy?"

"The one with the big chin—on the campaign sign."

She barked a harsh laugh. "No, Dale was definitely not on my mind. I can't imagine why he'd be on yours."

"Because of the way you tensed up last night. The hint of hurt in your voice when you talked about him."

"I'm not hurt anymore. Maybe just my pride."

Damien sat down, pulling her close and draping an arm over her shoulders. "How long ago did you break up?"

"I said he wasn't on my mind."

He shrugged. "But I admitted he's on mine. So humor me."

"It's no big deal. We dated for four months last spring."

"That doesn't sound like 'no big deal.'"

She kept her tone light, not wanting him to realize how badly she'd been hurt by the affair.

"What can I say? Lulu and Chaz had just gotten engaged, Amelia was head over heels for Lex. I guess I saw my two best friends with great guys, and suddenly wanted that for myself. So I made myself believe I felt something I didn't really feel."

"So you weren't in love with him."

"No," she said, meaning it. Even if she hadn't realized it at the time. Looking back, though, she understood she hadn't been.

"But you were in love with the idea of being in love?"

"I suppose. I made myself believe it, anyway."

"And him? Did he love the idea of being in love with you?"

She couldn't contain a snort. "Definitely not. He loved the idea of me using my marketing skills to help his campaign."

"God, please tell me you weren't responsible for putting that chin on those signs."

That brought a giggle from her lips. He was already making her feel better. Laughing about what had happened with Dale had been something she envisioned in the *distant* future. As in years from now. She'd been too raw and humiliated to laugh before now. Before Damien.

"No, but I did organize a lot of the early stuff. Enough to get him the nomination."

Damien had taken a strand of her hair between his fingers and was toying with it. The brush of his skin on her neck was a gentle connection, one that silently urged her to continue.

"Once he had the nomination, though, he decided having someone *like me* on his arm wouldn't win him votes in the general election. The Virginia state government isn't the extent of his ambitions—he intends to cross the river and sit inside that national dome someday."

She wouldn't have even known Damien had reacted to

her words if not for the tiniest pull on her hair. She turned to see his hand had clenched. "What do you mean, some-one *like you*?"

She didn't want to rehash the ugly conversation, so she simply replied, "I'm not politician's-wife material."

"Are you kidding? Men would vote for him just to shake your hand."

"He needed more than just the male vote," she said, her tone dry. "Although you might not have noticed, since we were with my two best friends the other night, a lot of women don't approve of me."

"They're jealous."

"Maybe, but Dale feared the older, more proper voters wouldn't, either."

"There's nothing wrong with you. Being sexy isn't a crime."

"Being in-your-face about it is, according to Dale. Ap-parently, I'm the kind of woman men want to fuck, but definitely not the one they take home to Mama."

He muttered a curse, and then drew her close, holding her tightly in his arms. "I officially hate that son of a bitch."

"He's a politician. I was aware of what I was getting into. But I didn't know how to not be the blunt, slightly outrageous person I've always been." Frowning, she added, "I sure gave it my best shot at work, though. I played the good-girl role as if I'd invented it."

"To prove him wrong after the breakup?"

"You already have me figured out, don't you?"

"Getting there." He traced the tips of his fingers across her jaw. "Can I admit, I've never been a fan of good girls?"

"Lucky for me."

"No," he whispered, "lucky for *me*. I like you just the way you are. Good and bad. Sweet and oh, so spicy."

He leaned over and kissed her, his lips soft, warm. Sitting here in the sunshine, in his arms, sharing a kiss, she could almost forget there'd ever been any darkness in her life.

When they drew apart, he said, "I'm going to need an hour at my desk this afternoon. Do I have to tie you up to make sure you don't leave?"

Her eyes glittered. "If you tie me up, you'd better stay with me to make it worth my while."

He swallowed hard. Viv had never tried bondage, being far too strong to submit to anyone. But with him, well, she suspected Damien could make her love it. She was already putty in his hands—being forced to stay still and take whatever pleasure he chose to give her sounded like a perfect way to spend the day.

"Is that an invitation?"

"I thought you had work to do."

"It won't take long," he said. "I just have to quickly set up a Super PAC and donate a shit-ton of money to you-know-who's opponent."

A merry peal of laughter escaped her mouth.

"You think I'm kidding?"

"Of course."

"Baby, I'd buy an election to screw over the guy who hurt you in a heartbeat."

"That's one of the sweetest things anyone's ever said to me," she said, still amused. "But it's not necessary. I've become a believer in karma—sometimes things work out the way they're supposed to, and people get what they deserve."

She, herself, was a prime example. She'd reacted pretty maturely to last week's work fiasco, and everything had worked out all right. She had to believe that somewhere down the road, Dale would get what was coming to him, too.

"If you really want to stop me, you're going to have

to focus my mind on something else," he said, nuzzling her neck.

"Such as?"

"Maybe how gorgeous you'd look wearing nothing but the sunshine spilling in that window?"

She pointed. "That sunshine?"

"Uh-huh."

Rising, she walked across the plush carpet and tapped a nail on the glass. "This window?"

"Yep."

"I could do that."

Moving slowly, she turned her back to him, focusing on the blue sky right outside. She breathed deeply as she untied the sash at her waist. Dipping her shoulder, she let the thick, plush robe glide down one arm, and then the other. She didn't need to see or hear Damien to know he was watching her every move.

She felt powerful, a completely sexual being. Bringing up all that old darkness of her last relationship had actually made her realize something. She'd been playing good for so long—trying to please her ex, and then her employer. But there was something freeing in being bad, in giving in to her deepest, darkest urges. Damien aroused feelings in her she'd never experienced before, and while she had him in her life, she wanted to act on every single one of them. Even if they were wicked. Even if they made her the bad girl, the temptress, the vixen.

He liked the vixen. And screw it, so did she.

The robe fell with a whoosh to puddle at her feet, and she lifted both hands, pressing them flat against the glass window. Closing her eyes, she tilted her head back, letting the warmth of the morning bathe her skin. In the space of two breaths, she felt the heat of his body behind her.

"Are you distracted?"

"From what? I can't remember a thing except how much I want you," he mumbled, lifting her hair so he could place his mouth on the nape of her neck.

He moved closer, pressing against her. He'd dropped his robe, too, and all that hot, naked strength around her made her go weak in the knees. He seemed to realize it, because he reached around to hold her, his hand low on her belly. Gripping her even more roughly against him, he let her feel his body's reaction.

"God, are you ever not hard?" she groaned.

"Are you ever not wet for me?" he countered.

"Hasn't happened so far."

"Ditto." Another brush of his mouth on her neck. "Stay still, Vivienne. Keep your hands on the glass."

She heard the command in his voice, but verified it anyway. "Is that an order?"

He didn't even hesitate. "Yes."

Ooh. He'd caught her mood, the craziness, the frenzy.

"Will you punish me if I disobey?"

No hesitation this time, either. "Yes." He licked her earlobe, breathing into her ear. "But I promise I'll hurt you in ways you enjoy."

The strength seeped from her legs. She was glad for the support of the window, and for his arm around her waist.

"Trust me," he urged.

She licked her lips. Nodded. "I do."

It was true. Damien had taken control many times since they'd met, and he'd never hurt her, never done a thing she hadn't desperately wanted him to do. Now, well, she wasn't entirely sure what she desperately wanted him to do.

Other than…everything.

Maybe that was why, when they'd stopped at a store yesterday, she'd grabbed condoms and lube, which right now rested inside the pocket of the robe on the floor.

*Everything.*

No more words passed between them. Damien began to focus solely on exploring her body. She wasn't embarrassed to stand completely naked directly in front of a floor-to-ceiling window. The penthouse faced the river; anybody on the other side of it would have to have binoculars to see her.

Even if they didn't have complete privacy, though, she wouldn't care. Not when his mouth was so warm and wet, when his hands were so strong yet subtle—his fingertips brushing against her collarbone, his other hand gliding down her spine. She didn't know where he would touch her next, or what he would do, and could only stand there, staring at all that clear blue sky, as storms—thunder, lightning, a volcanic eruption—built within her.

He reached around to cup her breast, his thumb teasing the tip into a hot point of sensation. She arched into his hand, wanting intensity, not tenderness. More pressure, more ache, more need, more satisfaction. All of it. They'd made love in almost every conceivable way, but still his touch excited her as nothing in her life ever had, and now, with that sexily worded threat/promise, she wanted to experience everything it was possible to experience as a lover. Even pain.

"More?" he asked, reading her body's response.

"More," she whimpered as his fingers encircled her nipple in a gentle but firm grasp. His gentle stroke became the tiniest pinch, and she gasped at the swift combination of a hint of discomfort and a gush of pleasure.

"You are the most beautiful woman I've ever seen," he murmured as he kissed his way down her body. "I want to memorize you."

"I think you already have."

"No. It's going to take more effort to really know you the way I want to. A whole lot more."

He seemed ready to put in that effort. Viv let out a gasp when he slowly dropped to his knees, his tongue gliding down the small of her back. He continued to move his mouth—low, hot, wicked—over her most secret places.

She didn't protest. In fact, when he gently nudged his tongue between her cheeks, she leaned forward, understanding what he wanted. And then his tongue was there, rimming her, testing her resolve, seeing just how far she really wanted to go.

"Yes," she hissed, sensation surging through her.

It was bold, wicked, dangerous. But oh, how she loved it.

Damien groaned when she urged him on, reaching up to grip her ass in both hands. He squeezed, kneaded, and she suddenly wondered what it would be like to feel the sting of a slap there. They were treading onto new, bold paths, going places she'd never been—had never wanted to go with anyone else. She suddenly understood why pleasure and pain could so easily coexist: it wasn't just the physical sensations, but the mental ones. The wild imaginings in her brain were turning her on almost as much as his seductive hands and tongue. She wanted the new, the shocking, the forbidden. Wanted it all. With him.

When he moved his mouth farther down, so he could dip his tongue into the wetness of her vagina, she cried out. She craved him, needed him so much. She wasn't sure she could stand much more pleasure until he showed her she could.

When he gently slid a wet finger against her puckered rear, she didn't resist at all, inviting him to explore, to invade.

He did, dipping into her, charting new, previously unclaimed territory.

"Oh, Damien," she moaned, arching into his hand, telling him yes, *yes*.

Saying nothing, Damien turned around to sit underneath her, moving between her parted legs. The angle gave him access to her clit, which he covered with his warm tongue while his finger played wicked magic in her bottom.

Her climax didn't rise slowly or come on in waves. It crashed into her hard, violently, shattering her so she had to clench one fist and shove it in her mouth to stop herself from screaming. Her muscles didn't so much tremble as tremor, an earthquake pounding every inch of her, inside and out.

Damien didn't stop. He kept loving her with his mouth and his hands, and she realized the orgasm hadn't taken the pressure off entirely. No. It quickly began to build again, making her greedy, mindless.

"More," she cried, suddenly wanting to scratch and claw and claim. "Take me now, Damien, please."

"My pleasure."

He began to move up, but she stopped him, making a quick, heart-stopping decision. "Wait. My robe. In the pocket."

He didn't ask questions, merely did what she suggested, checking the robe. With two items in his hand, he rose in front of her, between her and the glass. He kissed his way up her body, sucking one nipple, pinching the other, biting her throat, his mood as edgy and dangerous as hers. Then he was kissing her, his tongue plunging deep in her mouth, as it had into her core.

"You're so wet and hot. This won't be required," he mumbled against her lips, lifting the lube. Then he waved the condom. "And we've done okay without these."

"You're wrong. We do need them," she said, gripping

two fistfuls of his hair. She ground against him, telling him this wasn't normal desire, this was raging lust. She wanted more wickedness, more naughty pleasure than anyone had ever given her. And she wanted it from him. Now.

"Wait." He looked down into her face, his eyes questioning.

Staring unflinchingly into his eyes, Viv smiled in challenge, silently explaining to him exactly what she wanted him to do to her.

"You want…"

"Yes."

"Are you sure?"

She yanked him close and pressed a hot, openmouthed kiss on him, plunging her tongue into his mouth as he had hers. Then she whispered, "Yes, I'm sure. Take me. Do it. I want it now, right here."

He didn't protest further, his jaw tightening, the cords of muscle on his shoulders and neck flexing. After one more wet kiss, he moved behind her. He gently pushed her so she was half-bent at the waist, and then gripped her hips.

He was big, so big. A tremor of nervousness attacked her.

He noticed immediately. "Are you all right?"

"Just…slowly."

She heard a crunch of foil, then felt his fingers, slick with lube, readying her. All those wild sensations she'd experienced a few minutes ago rushed back, and she knew she was, indeed, ready. Ready to be wild, wicked, bad to the bone. But only because she trusted him completely and because she was sure he would never judge her for that wickedness.

Because he was just as wicked as her.

"God, Viv," he groaned as he gently eased his way between her cheeks, his hands tight on her hips, his cock nudging into her the tiniest bit.

She breathed slowly, deeply, trying to relax, torn between embarrassment, nervousness and utter mindless want.

The want won. The tension was driving her mad, his patience just making her *im*patient. She pushed toward him, inviting him to take more. And so he did, moving into her ever so slowly, creating all kinds of sensations, not one of which made her inclined to change her mind.

"Tell me when to stop," he demanded, the words coming out between harsh, choppy breaths.

"Don't stop," she demanded, battered by emotions and physical sensations. He was being so careful, so tender, but he felt so good inside her.

This moment was one she would never forget. She'd finally broken out of the shell into which she'd confined herself, taken her identity back, become the fully realized, sexual being she'd always been meant to be.

And he'd brought her here. With his kiss and his touch, his charm and his patience, his mouth, his hands, his cock, his lips, his amazing laugh, his dark, dreamy eyes.

Everything about him had seduced her to this point of utter freedom. She'd given up all her reservations, every inhibition…and she didn't regret one damn moment of it.

ALTHOUGH DAMIEN WANTED her to stay with him, to sleep in his arms every night while he was in town, Viv had insisted on going home Sunday evening. And while she'd met him for dinner—and more amazing sex—just about every day after work, she never spent the night. She seemed determined to keep their personal relationship separate from their work one. In fact, she wouldn't even let him mention the team, beyond informing him at dinner every night that she'd had a fine day at the office. She would then change the subject.

Although they never discussed it, he was aware there was another reason she wouldn't let him see her at the office. They were walking a fine line, that whole fraternization thing looming large in his mind. He could handle Sam if the attorney made an issue of it. But as a subordinate, Viv couldn't. Nor did he want her to have to explain that she was dating the team's owner to anyone else.

"Dating," he muttered, laughing under his breath at the word. He hadn't dated in forever. And yet that's what it felt like they were doing. He would pick her up at her place, they'd go out for dinner or, even one night, a sappy movie that he hated and she adored. There would sometimes be a long drive in the limo afterward, where they made slow, seductive love. Other nights it was right back to his suite, or her place, for hotter, louder sex.

They'd done things he'd only ever fantasized about. He'd made good on his threat to tie her up…and then had let her repay the favor.

Christ, what a night that had been.

What a week, really. The best one of his life. Worth every long phone call or video conference he'd had to make to keep up with work, and every snarky email he'd ignored from his family about why he was staying away for so long.

"What did you say?" she asked, eyeing him from the other side of the elevator. He was riding with her up to her apartment, but, as if not trusting him not to seduce her during the trip—as he usually did when they were in the elevators at the Black Star—she'd edged to the far corner and put up a hand to stop him when he'd tried to join her there.

"Just thinking."

"About?"

"About the fact that we're dating."

She sucked in a tiny gasp, her eyes widening, as if she hadn't really considered that, either. "Are we?"

"I think so. I'm picking up you at your door, and escorting you back to it."

She snickered. "Uh, well, until today, you haven't been stopping at the door, buddy. In fact, you haven't been stopping until you're through my bedroom door and naked in my bed."

"Are you complaining?"

"If I ever do, you'd better stick a thermometer in me and run a CAT scan, because I'm obviously sick in the head."

He slid an arm around her waist. "It's all right with you? I mean, I know you didn't want to have to *deal* with me after that first night."

She gazed up at him, her blue eyes bright, her lips soft and moist, and slowly smiled. "It's fine with me, Damien," she whispered. "In fact, I've come to enjoy having you around."

He brushed a kiss across her lips, murmuring, "Ditto."

They reached her floor and stepped off the elevator. Viv lived in a newer Arlington high-rise that catered to young city professionals. Impersonal enough that he'd never seen the same neighbor, but still warmer and cozier than the rather cold hotel room he'd been living in for weeks.

That wasn't really a huge change for him. He was used to living in hotel rooms, since he tried to stay on the road as much as possible. Running a hotel chain did have its perks. But those perks did not include homey touches like family photos on the wall—there were tons of Viv's family on her walls, especially all those big, athletic brothers. There was a worn rocking chair that she said her parents had given her, one used to rock her and her siblings as babies. On it was draped a tenderly crafted afghan, made for

Viv by her late grandmother, and which he suspected was one of her favorite possessions.

Her furniture was inexpensive, but comfortable, the TV an old console with a grainy picture, the dishes colorful but mismatched. Everything about the place screamed home and, truthfully, he'd come to prefer being here with her, rather than at the penthouse. And it was definitely better than the ice castle that had replaced his father's once warm home on a hot, sunny, Florida beach.

Inside, just to prove her wrong about what she'd said in the elevator, he purposely did not head for the bedroom. Instead, he watched as Viv went into the kitchen and put the foam container full of her leftover dinner in the fridge. She always got to-go boxes from the restaurants they frequented, taking the leftovers for lunch the next day. He'd laughed when she'd admitted it was because she didn't trust him enough to leave the building to go out and get food, for fear he'd be lying in wait to seduce her to the hotel.

"I'm going to go change," she said, when she returned, heading past him toward her room.

"Okay." He noted that she didn't invite him to come along, and wondered at her mood. She'd been quiet throughout dinner, not her usual vivacious self. He hoped nothing had happened at work today, but considering they weren't allowed to talk about it, he hadn't asked.

Tossing his jacket aside, he went into the bathroom to splash cold water on his face—something to cool himself down, since he'd gotten the unvoiced message that she didn't want to be jumped on right this minute. When he came out of the bathroom, he heard a popping sound and smelled an unmistakable scent wafting from the kitchen, and his impressions were confirmed.

Viv made it even more obvious when she walked into

the room, carrying the large, steaming bowl of popcorn. She'd changed out of her work clothes and was now wearing a baggy pair of sweatpants and a long T-shirt. She had pulled her hair from its secure bun, leaving it to hang in a long ponytail down her back. While any other woman might merely have looked cute, Viv couldn't help but be as sexy as hell no matter what she wore. The sweatpants clung to that pert butt, and the long hair bounced with each move.

*Down, boy*, he reminded himself. He only hoped she would be in the mood later, because, just eyeing her had him ready to cover her with that popcorn and eat it off her.

"Do you like popcorn?"

"I could be persuaded to sample some," he murmured.

"Cool," she said, popping a handful into her mouth. As she munched, she said, "I thought we'd have a movie night."

He lifted a brow. "Movie, huh? Please say it's going to be a winner like the one we watched on Tuesday. I just can't get enough of cancer-stricken women married to scumbags."

Viv threw a piece of popcorn at his chest, and then sat down beside him on the couch. "I have a lot of DVDs. You pick."

"Then I'll pick something we can watch in bed," he said, leaning over to nibble her ear. Having witnessed what the woman could do for a pair of sweatpants, he couldn't *not* try. Hell, the very fact that he was a man made it impossible. "Have anything X-rated in that collection of yours?"

She quirked a half smile. "Maybe. But not tonight."

"Okay. We don't have to watch a movie, I'm happy to just lie in your bed and eat...popcorn."

Sighing heavily, she shook her head. "No can do."

"You have a rule against eating in bed? You haven't mentioned that one before."

"It's a new rule. Starting now," she admitted, not sounding happy about it.

"Why?"

"I'm not feeling so well."

He reached up and put a hand on her forehead. "No temperature. Should I go get the CAT scan machine?"

"It's not that kind of unwell."

Beginning to worry, he asked, "You're serious?"

"Yeah."

"What's wrong? Was it something you ate at dinner?"

She shot him a glare. "No. I'm just…not doing great. It's no big deal."

"Viv, if you're sick, we should get you to the doctor."

Sinking into the far corner of the couch, she tossed a pillow at his head. "God, you're clueless. My brothers would have recognized where this was going the minute I came out here with the popcorn."

He still didn't understand what she was driving at.

"I thought you had sisters," she said.

"I do."

"Did none of them ever occasionally get cranky, wear baggy clothes and eat junk food? At certain times of the month?"

It sank in at last. Regretting his own stupidity, he mumbled, "Oh."

"Yeah. Oh." She wrapped her arms around herself, her spine stiffening. "So, as you can imagine, the playground is closed for a few nights. Sorry about that."

"It's okay." Moving closer on the couch, he put an arm around her and tugged her close. "Need a foot rub or anything?"

She gaped at him. "Seriously?"

Her astonishment amused him. Had she expected him to whine, to throw a fit because biology said he couldn't have what he wanted for a change? Not that he wouldn't mind telling biology to go screw itself, but Viv didn't seem comfortable with the idea, at least not on day one. "Seriously."

"I—I waas afraid…"

"That I'd be an asshole about it?"

"Well, no, not that. Just figured maybe you'd be asking for some alternate compensation."

"Tit for tat? Jeez, you think I can't go a night without sex? That I'd demand a blow job or something?"

"Well, we've established that we're both pretty adept at the *or something.*"

"Huh?"

"I mean, you know, some guys might ask for the buttsecks."

He inhaled a piece of popcorn and promptly choked on it. Leaning forward to cough into his fist, he nodded his thanks as she pounded on his back. When he'd gotten himself under control, he looked up to see the mischief in those beautiful blue eyes.

"You are a bad, bad girl, Viv Callahan."

"So glad you noticed."

"For the record? I believe you were the one who initiated the, er, buttsecks."

Her pink cheeks said he'd gotten even with her.

"How in the name of God can you be blushing?"

"That's ridiculous," she insisted, chin going up. "I'm absolutely not blushing."

"Yes, you are. Your face is as red as an apple."

"It's a hot flash. I'm on my period."

"Bullshit. The vixen is embarrassed. And it's adorable."

She fisted a hand and punched him in the upper arm. "I kinda hate you right now."

"Nah, you don't," he said, more sure of that than he was of anything. In fact, he suspected she kinda loved him.

The idea flashed across his mind, and then quickly disappeared. Because, really, what did he know about love? Hell, it wasn't as if he'd ever really witnessed it. His parents hadn't loved each other, one of his sisters was a divorced mom, the other one bitter after whatever had happened with Sam. All of his friends were single or paying alimony.

Love? What the hell did that have to do with anything?

He forced all the uncomfortable memories away, focusing on the here and now. The here was sweet, sexy Viv, inviting him to stay for a movie night.

He leaned back and pulled her against him, until her head was tucked under his chin. "Now, about this film. Got anything with lots of blood and gore?"

She grimaced.

"Okay, no blood and gore. How about serial killers?"

"Not a chance."

He sighed. "Rabid dogs?"

"I've got *Old Yeller*!"

He'd been thinking more along the lines of *Cujo*. "That is the most depressing movie ever. I'd rather watch *American Psycho*."

Whatever color had been in her cheeks fell out of it. His Viv might have balls, but she was not the horror-movie type.

Suddenly snapping her fingers, she got up, opened her movie cabinet and searched for something. In a moment, she held up a recognizable case.

*"Star Wars?"*

She bit her lip and nodded. "Is that okay?"

"Perfect!" he said. Then, glad that she was finally starting to smile, he added, "Some Darth-Vader Jedi action for me, and Luke and Leia romance for you."

"Eww." Her nose wrinkled in distaste. "They're siblings. No incesty movies for me, thank you."

"Guess that means you hate that coffee commercial that comes around every Christmas then."

Her eyes widening, she nodded quickly. "Oh, God, yes, with the brother and sister? Ick!"

"I *know*, right?"

She caught his inflection, realized he was trying to make her laugh by mimicking every teenage girl on the planet, and giggled happily. Putting the DVD in, she rejoined him on the couch. She curled next to him, and they settled in to watch the movie. But as the famous opening credits started to roll up the screen, talking about a galaxy far, far away, he noted that Viv still felt stiff. Despite their laughter, the tiniest hint of tension remained in her body.

She confirmed it when she whispered, "You really don't mind?"

"Why would I mind?"

"It's so normal," she said, twisting her hands in her lap. "And it isn't leading to anything."

There was trepidation in her voice. His strong, sexy woman, who was an utter wildcat in bed, who wasn't afraid to take what she wanted, was feeling vulnerable. Viv was unsure of herself, and of him. All because she feared he'd be angry that they couldn't have sex tonight.

In all the moments he'd shared with Viv, even the ones when she'd been so devastated about what had happened to her at work the day they'd met, he'd never heard her sounding so forlorn. It was as if she didn't really believe he'd want to spend a simple, easygoing night just eating popcorn and watching TV with her, with no expectations of anything else.

That, more than anything, made him want to track down that asshole whose massive chin was littering the streets of Arlington. If he could find him, Damien would shove one of his campaign signs down Dale what's-his-name's stupid throat for ever making Viv believe she was good only for one thing.

Doing that wouldn't help now, though. It would do nothing to ease Viv's concerns. So instead, he tightened his arms, kissed her temple and replied, "Honestly? I can't think of anything else in the world I'd rather be doing, or anyone else I'd rather be doing it with."

Her tension eased, her muscles relaxing. Viv nodded slightly and then turned her attention to the screen. Confident, at last, that he was here with her, doing this, for no other reason than that he cared about her.

As that realization crossed his mind, he forced himself not to tense up as she had. Because the realization was such a new, shocking one. But as he evaluated it, Damien realized he had to admit it was true. He cared about Viv Callahan as he'd never cared about another woman in his entire life.

He hadn't expected it, hadn't ever really supposed it would happen, but his emotions were getting involved here. What that might mean for the future, he couldn't say. They lived a thousand miles apart, their jobs supposedly excluded them from being together, his family was pretty psycho, neither of them had a great romantic track record. So what chance did they have for something real?

Probably none.

But maybe…maybe more than he'd ever dreamed of.

# 8

OVER THE NEXT few days, Viv kept waiting for Damien to tell her he had to return to Miami, to his real life. But the days slipped by, each better than the last. They were inseparable when she wasn't working, and he swore he kept busy during the day, too. She noticed he'd set up an office in the spare room of the penthouse, and she supposed it was possible an international hotel magnate could run his empire from one of his own hotels.

Their relationship had begun with sex. Wild, fabulous, amazing, never-to-be-forgotten-as-long-as-she-lived sex. And she'd told herself that was all she wanted, because, even though she knew nothing could come of it and that there was no future for them, he was worth it. What they had together was worth it.

Now, though, she had begun to suspect it wasn't just about sex. Something had changed. Since Friday night in her apartment, when he'd held her close and they'd watched a movie, eating popcorn, kissing and cuddling, she'd begun to accept the possibility that he wasn't just sticking around because they were so good together in bed.

Damien required nothing from her, had no reason to be with her other than sex. And yet when they couldn't have sex, he'd stayed. He'd held her, teased her, done normal things and seemed perfectly happy about it.

This was becoming more than a sexual affair.

That should have scared her to death. The truth was, however, that when she thought about how he made her feel, not physically, but emotionally, she was incredibly happy instead. Seriously, down-to-her-toes, never-more-elated-than-this happy.

Because she was falling in love with the man.

She wouldn't tell him, of course. No matter how he acted, being confronted with a woman's emotions was enough to scare off any guy.

Part of her worried it wouldn't matter, that his rich, jet-setting life, into which she *so* didn't fit, would pull him away sooner or later. She'd be left alone with nothing but memories.

But even that fear didn't make her want to close up her heart, to build her defenses against that possible day. Instead, she wanted to grab what she could get, certain any future moments of sadness or loneliness would never outweigh the sheer joy she got from being with him now.

"What's on your mind?" he asked her early one morning. "You have a big smile on your face."

She stretched and curled up next to him, having relented and spent last night in the penthouse. It had been their first night in bed together since the movie night, and she hadn't been able to drag herself away after their incredibly erotic, but still somehow tender, lovemaking. "Just, uh..."

"I know, I know. You're thinking about me," he said, sounding self-satisfied.

"Not at all." He was right, but no woman wanted a man to be *too* sure of her.

She scrambled to come up with something to hide the fact that she had been lying here, soaking in the sunshine and his body heat, building castles in her mind constructed of his smiles and his laughter and his touch.

"Um, I was just thinking about my parents."

A groan. "Not what a guy wants to hear when he's in bed with a beautiful naked woman."

He sounded so disgruntled, she had to laugh. "Their thirty-fifth anniversary is next month. My brothers and I are planning a party." Rolling her eyes, she added, "Since it's two weeks from Halloween, my younger brother, Aidan, wants to make it a costume party and have everyone come dressed as their favorite *Grease* character. That was the movie my parents went to see on their first date."

"Oh, God."

"You saying I couldn't totally rock black leather and a chick fro?"

"I have no doubt you could," he said with a leer.

"We're having the party at the Blue Mountain Lodge. Too bad there's no Black Star location in Gerryville, Pennsylvania."

"We don't build in cities of less than a million people."

"Bummer. So close. Gerryville misses that mark by only about nine hundred and ninety thousand."

"You're the proverbial small-town girl, huh?"

"Yep. With five brothers. Why else do you think I now live in the city?"

He toyed with her hair, twining a long strand around his fingers. "Where do you fall in that hierarchy, anyway?"

"I'm number five out of six."

He grimaced. "Four big brothers?"

"Yep. *Big* being the operative word."

"No hockey players among them?"

She made a face. "No, thankfully, though all of them played football in high school."

"Do they all still live in your hometown?"

"Yep. Joe, the oldest—he's divorced with two boys—works with my dad in his plumbing business. Neil's second. He went into the military and then went back to Gerryville

to open a gun shop. Third, Evan, is a firefighter. Andy—
he's eleven months older than me—just got married and
is taking over his wife's family's dairy farm. And Aidan,
who is pretty smart, his party suggestions notwithstand-
ing, is at Penn State, studying sports medicine."

"No wonder you had to sneak into the computer lab to
lose your virginity to Ollie the nerd."

Blinking in surprise, she said, "You have a good memory."

"Only when it comes to the important stuff."

"Like when and where I lost my virginity?"

"Your sex life is of critical importance to me," he said
with a wolfish growl. "So your family is close?"

"Very. My brothers can be idiots, but there's nothing
any of us wouldn't do for each other." Her voice softened,
as did her heart, as she continued. "And my parents are
the best. Still crazy in love with each other, even though
my mom gripes about Dad's snoring and he groans about
the credit card bills."

Although he smiled, a shadow seemed to cross his face,
and he glanced away. Damien didn't talk much about his
own family. She remembered his father was dead, and
that he had two sisters—both younger. She also knew he
didn't get along with his mother. Other than that, though,
he was pretty quiet about his background. Which made
her feel more gabby than ever for having mentioned all the
branches on the Callahan family tree.

When he didn't reciprocate with any kind of stories
about his own home life, she bit the bullet and asked out-
right.

"What about you? You said you have sisters. No brothers?"

"No, there's just me, Johanna and Holly. Oh, but I do
have a nephew—Holly's little boy."

She remembered. "The one who enjoys being read to."

"Right."

Licking her lips, emboldened by his willingness to talk about it, she said, "And your father died many years ago?"

His body stiffened a bit. But he drew in a slow breath and replied, "Yeah, when he was forty-one."

"So young!"

"It was the day before I graduated from high school."

"Oh, no," she said, her heart aching for him. What an awful time to lose a parent. She wished she hadn't asked, not sure she wanted him to relive it.

But Damien was lost in the memory, already telling it. "He was in New Orleans overseeing a new hotel construction, but a storm system came in, shutting down commercial flights. He had his pilot's license and wasn't about to miss my graduation." His whole body was taut, as tight as a wire. "He went down in the Gulf of Mexico. Some wreckage washed up in the panhandle a few weeks later."

"Oh, God, Damien, I'm so sorry." Tears welled in her eyes. She couldn't imagine losing one of her parents. And to lose them in such a way, without even having a body to bury. *Agonizing.*

"It was…not a good period in my life."

"I can imagine. What did you do?"

"What he'd have wanted me to—I graduated, went ahead with my plans." He traced his hand down her arm, absently drawing circles on her skin. "His father came out of retirement to manage the business while I got through college. Then my grandfather had a massive heart attack and died right before I got my MBA."

"Oh, no."

"Yeah." He managed a hard laugh. "I decided then and there I'd never go for a doctorate. Who knows who'd fall over dead?"

She heard through the humor to the heartache under-neath. Damien was a strong man, but this part of his past was incredibly painful for him to remember, and to talk about.

Viv was gratified that he trusted her enough to share the memories with her. And that her own younger years, while the epitome of the hard-working, blue-collar life-style, at least hadn't included such tragedies.

"You've run the company ever since?"

He nodded. "Dad was an only child—no aunts or uncles to step in. My sisters weren't interested. My mother just wanted the money to keep coming in so she could con-tinue to support her latest husband in the style to which he'd become accustomed."

An unkind word crossed her mind about Damien's mother, but Viv didn't voice it.

Damien wasn't finished. "In my house."

*"What?"*

"She got a lot of money from my dad, but the estate where I grew up technically belonged to my grandfather. He left big cash settlements to my sisters, but left the is-land just to me. My mother was living there at the time… and still is."

Viv managed to not goggle at the word *island*, and fo-cused instead on what he was saying. He'd lost his beloved father, and his grandfather. Meanwhile his mother—with whom he had a strained relationship—had remarried, maybe more than once, and was supporting a succession of husbands in Damien's house.

Ouch. Talk about the lifestyles of the rich and shame-less.

But at least everything began to make sense to her now, why he lived out of hotels, why he was in no hurry to get "home." She understood why he lived a vagabond's life, so quick to set up an office in a hotel room. Of course he didn't mind eating out every meal, or that there wasn't a picture on the wall or a pillow he could call his own when he laid his head down at night. Damien Black, one of the richest men in the country, was, for all intents and purposes, homeless.

"Why don't you get a new place?"

"Because it's my dad's childhood home. *My* childhood home." He breathed deeply, the subject obviously a sore one. "I mean, I have a condo on the beach, on the top floor of the flagship hotel. That's where I usually stay. But even that is just too close. I prefer to steer clear of south Florida altogether."

"I get it," she whispered. And she did. He didn't want to live there—couldn't possibly live there now—but he couldn't just let go of the home he so closely associated with his own childhood, with his father, with his grandfather. Even though she sensed his relationship with his mother was strained, he probably also held on to it for her sake, not wanting to take away the home she'd lived in for decades.

He wouldn't appreciate her saying it out loud, but he was a fine man. "I'm sorry about everything that happened to you, Damien," she murmured, pressing a kiss onto his shoulder. She dropped her hand across his waist and gently squeezed him closer. "Life can be so unfair."

"Don't cry for the poor little rich boy," he said, his tone droll. "My fifty-foot yacht and private jet are pretty decent consolation prizes."

Viv couldn't help gasping at that, though, of course, she knew Damien was filthy rich—*private island, remember*?

He'd never flaunted his wealth, but there'd been no denying it, either. At first, whenever they walked by a high-end store, he'd wanted to buy her something. She'd refused diamonds and clothes, even ignoring the ones he'd already bought, leaving them to hang in the penthouse closet. All because she hadn't wanted him to put her in that category—as the kind of woman who'd take what she could get while she could get it. Not when what she most wanted to take, while she could get it, was *him*.

That was why she hadn't worn the clothes, and hadn't let him buy her another thing. Well, there had been *one* thing. Last weekend when they'd walked through a farmers market, he'd bought her a fresh, delicious peach. As the juice had dribbled down her cheeks, she'd assured him it was the best present anybody had ever given her. He'd looked at her as if she was crazy, and then kissed the nectar off her lips, afterward agreeing that it had been a damn fine peach.

That had been a turning point, when he'd finally stopped offering, accepting the fact that she didn't want any goodies.

He wasn't finished. "And I do have penthouse apartments in every major city in the world, whenever I want them."

"They're nice," she replied with a shrug.

"Nice?" He drew her closer, and she slid a bare thigh between his legs, curling into him as though they were two strands of the same vine.

"Not very homey."

"In my opinion, home is defined by the people who remain behind the front door when it closes at night."

She heard something in his voice—something intense. As if he was admitting that here, with her, over the past couple of weeks, had been as much a home to him as anyplace.

"I'm glad," she murmured, not asking him to confirm her theory.

Hugging her, he insisted, "I'm fine, Viv."

"I'm sure you are. Still, you were pretty young to take on the world. So much responsibility at, what, twenty-four?"

"Three."

Twenty-three years old. She hadn't even finished college at that age, being a five-year slacker. But Damien was already running a multimillion-dollar international corporation. And, judging by where he was today, doing it well.

"It doesn't sound like you've had many opportunities to do anything just for yourself."

His stare grew more intense. "So you can probably get what I'm doing here, then."

"Here, in this bed?"

"Here in Arlington, taking a break from the hotel business and indulging in my real interest—sports. And you."

She was so glad to be included on that short list that she didn't dwell on the sports part of the equation. She'd had no idea he loved sports, and wasn't sure how he was indulging that love. But now that she knew about it, she realized there was one thing she could give him that he couldn't easily get for himself. After all, he ran hotels... but *she* worked for a professional hockey team.

"I see."

She leaned over to press a kiss on his slightly grizzled cheek. Damn the man was sexy in the morning. But it *was* morning—and it was growing later by the second. She glanced at the clock and sighed. She had to get up or she'd be late to work. Luckily, her office was right up the street.

"I have to get moving, but first, there was something I wanted to ask you. About work."

"I thought we didn't talk about that."

"We don't. Well, we haven't. But, I'm ready to at least discuss the topic again. My job's great, I'm no longer having any issues. In fact, there's a special celebration tomorrow night, and I want you to come as my guest."

"You mean the season-ticket-holders event?" he asked, appearing surprised.

"You've heard about it?"

He merely laughed in response. "Ha ha. Very funny."

Okay, as a sports fan, of course he would.

"Yes, well, why don't you come? It's being held right downstairs, in one of your own ballrooms. There shouldn't be much press—thank God—but lots of local celebs will be there, plus dozens of other people. The entire Vanguard staff has been invited to bring dates. It's a chance to get all fancied up and go out in public together."

He rolled toward her, scraping the tip of his finger along her jawline. "I'd already accepted my invitation, of course."

Huh. Okay. Well, she supposed it did make sense that a sports-fan millionaire would buy season tickets to the team his girlfriend—or whatever she was—worked for. She felt a little deflated at not being able to give him a superspecial treat, but was still glad he would be there.

"You don't mind people knowing we're together?" he added.

"Because of what happened with Neeley?"

"Don't mention that bastard's name. I just don't want there to be any awkwardness for you."

"Why would there be? I'm an adult, I have a right to a personal life."

"What about the lawyers and HR people? I mean, I don't give a damn myself, but are you sure you don't mind if they nose around and ask questions about who you're with and why?"

She snorted. "They believe I'm not going to file a lawsuit, and that's all they care about. My private life shouldn't factor into it."

"I suppose not."

Surprisingly, Damien was the one who suddenly seemed uncertain about them being seen together. But Viv was nothing if not persistent when she wanted something. Now, having come up with the idea, she couldn't imagine anything she wanted more than to go to that banquet, which was as much a celebration for the staff as it was for the players and the public, on the arm of this remarkable man.

Fortunately, as she got up to go into the shower, Damien cleared his throat and gave her what she wanted.

"Okay, if you're sure, I'd be delighted to be the man on your arm tomorrow night."

"Excellent," she said. Feeling sassy, she said, "You don't have to do a thing but look pretty and keep your mouth shut. You'll be the perfect arm candy."

Being Damien, he took no offense, instead bursting into laughter. "I think I can do that."

"I'm sure you can," she said before sashaying away, sure his stare was glued to her bare butt.

She smiled as she started the shower, imagining how great it would be to have Damien Black as her arm candy. There only remained one thing to do. She just had to ease her righteous stance…and sneak a gorgeous dress, and some to-die-for shoes, out of that front closet.

DAMIEN WANTED TO walk through the door of the banquet hall with Viv on his arm, to make it clear to Sam, and anybody else, that they were together. It was what she wanted, what she'd asked of him, and he had long passed the point of being able to refuse her anything. The invitation—her willingness to open their relationship to potential comment from her coworkers—had been a sign of her trust in him, and he would never do anything to betray that trust.

Unfortunately, though, walking in with her on his arm

wasn't possible. Viv had a role to play in the event, which her department had organized. She'd hurried back to her own place after work, and then returned to the hotel ballroom, promising to meet him there.

Just after seven, dressed in a fitted tux he never traveled without, Damien headed downstairs. He was anticipating the sight of Viv in the deep blue dress he'd noticed her grabbing from the closet yesterday, when she'd thought he was in the shower. Viv was incredibly stubborn, and wouldn't take a thing he offered her, but she'd been unable to resist "borrowing" the designer gown. He had no doubt it would be cleaned, pressed and returned to the closet by the end of the week.

But for now, since she'd taken the garment, he'd decided to get her something to go with it. He remembered the dress well—the cut, the color, which was the exact shade of her eyes—and had stopped by the downstairs jewelry shop that afternoon. He looked forward to seeing his gift against that fabric…and her smooth, silky skin.

The event didn't officially get under way until seven thirty, but he wanted a few minutes with Viv to give her the present. He didn't intend to drag her out of the ballroom—if he got her alone, she'd probably just refuse the gift. But if they were within sight of anyone else, she'd accept gracefully. And then she'd try to give him the jewelry back when the night was over, like a star borrowing a piece for an award show. Only his Viv wasn't going to get away with being just a renter. Not this time.

He didn't spot her right away. The banquet hall wasn't crowded, but some key people were already here. A few of the players and their wives chatted near the bar. Some office staff had claimed a table up front. The general manager, newly promoted to the position permanently, spotted him, blanched and made as if to come over. Damien shook his head once. He was here as Viv's date tonight, not as the owner. He would prefer to fly under the radar, which was one reason he'd created an LLC to purchase the team, and had enlisted other investors. His name wasn't on the letterhead and he preferred it that way.

Then he spotted Sam. His friend saw him, waved and came over to join him.

"Spiffy suit," he said. "Custom-fitted, I presume?"

Damien nodded and glanced at his friend's tux. "Rented, I presume?"

Sam feigned offense, and they both laughed. Glad the ice was broken, and his oldest friend seemed in a good mood—with at least one Scotch under his belt, judging by the nearly empty glass he carried—Damien was direct.

"I'm looking for Viv."

"Who?"

"You know damn well who," he said. "Vivienne Callahan. I'm her date."

Sam immediately lowered his glass onto the nearest table. "You're joking."

"Do I ever joke?"

His friend frowned. "I thought we'd straightened that out."

"*You* might have believed so. I never agreed there was anything to be straightened."

Sam began to grumble. Damien cut him off.

"Viv found out who I was right away, and had no problem with it." Seeing his friend was unconvinced, he said, "I know her, Sam. We've been dating for weeks. I promise you, the whole thing with Neeley and Stoker is over and done with. Our 'fraternizing' is not going to cause any trouble."

"Women always cause trouble, bro."

He hated to believe that his own sister had made the

normally sunny-natured attorney a whole lot more pessimistic about women. But he suspected it was true.

"Not Viv."

"She could stab you in the back…"

"I'm not going to discuss this with you anymore," he said, cutting the man off. "I'm involved with Viv. If anybody has a problem with that, they're welcome to go fuck themselves."

Sam obviously recognized that Damien was in a mood where it was best for everyone else to back off, and he did just that. Holding both hands up, palms out, he said, "Okay I get it. I can't talk you in to doing anything you don't want to do. Never could."

"Never will."

They eyed each other, and then Sam smiled, his good humor never gone for long. "She is beautiful."

"No kidding."

Sam glanced over Damien's shoulder, and his eyes became saucers. His mouth fell open. Somehow, Damien was sure of what his friend was going to say even before he said it.

"Holy shit, maybe I'll fight you for her. Did I say beautiful? Jesus, she's gorgeous."

Damien slowly turned, watching as Viv emerged from another side of the ballroom, near an area set up as a dance floor. The overhead lights were revolving in a kaleidoscope of different colors, and she stepped into a pool of gold that made her long, flowing hair luminescent. Like a molten river falling down her back in thick, shiny waves. His breath caught in his throat, and his heart skipped a beat just at the sight of her. Smiling, young, beautiful. *Mine.*

Yes. His. He was shocked at the surge of possessiveness that swelled through him, having never felt so lost under the spell of any woman. But Viv had him by the gut—or the heart or the cock, he honestly wasn't sure which. Nor did he really care.

He wanted her. Just her. For as long as he could have her.

Right now, if he was asked, he'd have to say that forever couldn't possibly be long enough.

She said a word to the leader of a string quartet strumming softly in the corner, and then glanced across the room, catching his eye. The light above her segued into a soft blue that caught the gleaming, glittery strands of material sewn into her royal blue gown. The dress was long and form-fitting, strapless, with a heart-shaped neckline, and a full bottom that flared out below the knee. He didn't know the name of the style, but recognized the Jessica Rabbit look immediately, and smiled at how perfectly the hourglass design suited her figure.

He was not the only man in the room under her spell. Every other guy there, alone or in a group, had his eyes glued to the beautiful blonde.

Possessiveness put Damien's feet into motion. He strode across the room toward her, watching the way her eyes sparkled and her lips curved up in a welcoming smile.

Before he'd even gotten to her, he'd reached into his pocket to withdraw his special present. And when he stood in front of her, he immediately said, "Close your eyes."

"What?" She glanced around and laughed nervously. "Uh, why?"

"Just do it," he whispered.

She licked her lips, a flush rising into her cheeks, and then nodded. Her eyes drifted closed, those thick, dark lashes resting on her high cheekbones. Without a word, Damien lifted the necklace and draped it around her neck, fastening it and letting the long strand of diamonds and sapphires fall into a *V* right above that perfect cleavage.

She gasped at the touch of cold metal on her skin, and immediately opened her eyes, trying to peer past his hands to what he'd put on her.

"Damien, I can't…"

"Shut up."

To his surprise, she did. Maybe because she'd spun around to the mirrored wall behind them and had glimpsed how perfectly the necklace complemented the dress.

"It's beautiful. I'm not sure what to say."

"Say, 'I'm not going to try to give this back later tonight, Damien.'"

She nibbled her lip, and he knew she'd already thought of doing exactly that. Considering for a moment, she finally murmured, "Thank you. I love it."

"I'm glad."

Twining her fingers in his, he led her away from the dance floor, toward the bar. He recognized a few faces and nodded greetings, but hoped his impersonal, generic smile kept anyone from getting too close.

The ballroom began to fill. The Vanguard was a new team. To his gratification, however, the season ticket drive had been successful. There was a lot of energy and enthusiasm in the gathering, and he found himself caught up in it, even if he was trying to be incognito tonight.

"Damien, isn't it?" a voice asked.

Turning, he spied Viv's friend's fiancé, whom he'd met a few weeks ago at the Mexican place. "Yes. Lex, right?"

The other man put out his hand. "Yep."

"Is Amelia with you?"

The other man pointed toward Viv and Amelia, who were hugging hello.

"Are you here in an official capacity?" Damien asked, only slightly concerned. He had no worries about Lex doing anything to hurt Viv, or put another embarrassing spotlight on her. But if the press was going to be a presence here, he'd have to make a point of sticking close to her.

"Nah. I'm a hockey fan. I bought season tickets as soon as they went on sale."

"Glad to hear it."

Lex glanced toward Amelia and Viv. "It'll be okay," the man murmured. "What happened is yesterday's news."

"I hope so," Damien replied.

As speech-making time approached, Damien and Lex joined Amelia and Viv at a table near the front. He'd already informed the GM that he didn't want to speak, or be acknowledged in any way. Tonight wasn't about him; it was about the staff, the players and the fans. So he was comfortable just sitting with Viv and her friends, as well as several others at the table, enjoying the evening.

The dinner was, he was pleased to note, first-rate. Every Black Star Hotel had a top-notch catering team, and tonight's did him proud.

"You have to track down whoever made the pastries and give him a big fat raise," Viv said, cooing as she took another tiny bite of a chocolate-and-raspberry confection.

He leaned close to whisper in her ear. "I'll have a tray sent up to the penthouse for later. I only want to eat it if I can lick it off your body."

She shushed him, but also dropped a hand on his thigh, squeezing it. Excitement and energy snapped between them, the sexual tension as high as it had ever been. Perhaps it was because they were in public, unable to touch or kiss, or maybe it was that she looked so incredibly stunning and had drawn the attention of every man in the room. Whatever the reason, he suddenly wanted her with an intensity that made him shake.

"Wait, did I hear that right?" asked the woman seated next to him. "Are you the manager of this hotel?"

The woman and her husband, a doctor whose face had grown redder with each martini he'd consumed, had monopolized the conversation all evening. She kept leaning close to whisper to Damien, making him uncomfortable. He recognized a wealthy trophy wife on the prowl when he met one. There wasn't a more recognizable species, nor one he hated more.

"Not exactly," he said, not wanting to get into it.

Lex, sitting beside him, suddenly exclaimed, "Holy shit, I just realized who you are!"

Damien cast him a quelling glance.

"You're Damien *Black*. As in Black Star Hotels and Black Ice LLC." Lex frowned at Viv. "Jeez, why don't you tell a guy? If I'd known who he was, I woulda arranged an interview."

Before Viv could say anything, the doctor's wife, her nails as red as her lips and her dress, dropped a hand on his arm.

"Oh, my, you *own* Black Star? We love your hotels."

"Thank you."

"I've never slept in more comfortable beds," the woman said with a feline grin. "They're like big playgrounds."

Damien was about to pull his arm away when Viv, his vixen, leaped in, defending her turf.

"Oh, that's wonderful," Viv said, her smile bright and disarming. "I've heard so many other *older* guests such as yourself say the same thing. Those orthopedic beds are perfect for aches, pains and rheumatism." She glanced at Damien. "Right, babe?"

Damien held in a laugh. The woman in red appeared ready to spit nails, but Viv merely lifted her champagne glass and refocused her attention on Amelia.

Viv might have been protecting her territory in a woman's game, but he found himself amused by it. Probably not what she'd been going for, but he enjoyed the feeling, any-way. Her hands-off-bitch-he's-mine attitude only aroused him more, and he was dying to get out of here.

First, though, there was one more thing he wanted to do. He'd held Viv in his arms many times now, but never while there was music playing. "Dance with me?"

She glanced at the nearly empty dance floor, obviously wondering if she should make a spectacle of herself. But he knew she wouldn't let him down. Finally, she nodded and let him take her hand to help her out of the chair. He led her out onto the dance floor and swept her into his arms.

Damien had been stuck in dance classes as a kid. He hadn't remembered them in years, but when he drew Viv close, one arm around her waist, his other hand raised and entwined with hers, he found them coming back. It was schmaltzy and a little silly, but the steps of the waltz sud-denly seemed exactly right. She looked like Cinderella, so why shouldn't she be swept into a formal glide around the ballroom?

"You dance very well," she said.

"So do you."

"Where did you learn?"

"Madame Fleming's Dance Academy for Young Ladies and Gentleman in Miami Beach."

She snickered. "Old lady Sneed's after-school dance-a-palooza, Gerryville YMCA."

They spun and twirled, and out of the corner of his eye, Damien noticed the few other couples on the floor leaving it. Soon he and Viv were entirely alone, turning in broad circles, oblivious to everyone else but the music and the twinkling lights and each other.

They were halfway through a three-quarter turn, be-tween a potted palm and the raised stage where the musi-cians sat, when he realized he was falling in love with her.

Staring into those blue eyes, hearing that delighted laughter, smelling her soft, evocative scent, even noticing the way her brow creased as she concentrated on her counting absolutely delighted him. He found himself wanting to do nothing but stare at her, talk to her, be with her. She was his first thought every morning, and if her face wasn't literally the last thing he saw every night, it was most certainly the last image in his mind.

He had never experienced it before, always doubted he would…but he truly believed he had fallen in love. It went against all odds and expectations—hell, practically against his own genetics—and probably against common sense, considering the obstacles. Proximity being one of them, the fact that his family was pretty fucked up being another. But it suddenly didn't matter.

For the first time in his life, he actually began to believe he understood what the whole love thing was all about. Because of her.

"I'm glad we came," he said, not yet ready to actually say anything to her about his strange emotional self-revelation.

"So am I."

He kissed her temple. "But now I'm ready to get out of here. I want to take you upstairs and strip that dress off you so I can make love to you for hours."

Her mouth trembling, she nodded. They abruptly halted their dance, heading without a word toward their table. Before they reached it, though, she said, "I left my wrap in the prep room we were using before the party. Actually, I left my overnight bag there, too."

"Oh, were you planning on having a sleepover?"

She smirked and lowered her voice. "You've done a great job tonight, baby, being pretty and keeping your mouth shut and all. I guess I'll give you somethin' to make it worth your while."

He had no doubt of that. Anything she cared to *give* him would undoubtedly go on his list of favorite things ever. "I'll go get your wrap and your bag."

"That's not necessary," she insisted. "Give excuses to Lex and Amelia for me, and meet me out in the corridor. I can slip out of the prep room, cut through the service wing and avoid the farewells." She reached down and lightly pinched his ass. "I'll meet you at the elevators. The sooner we're in one, the sooner I can shimmy out of my panties."

Whistling as he imagined how much fun it would be to test the elevator's safety systems again, he strode to the table. Lex and Amelia were going as well, and they ended up leaving the ballroom together, along with a handful of other guests.

As they walked out the doors, Damien glanced down a side corridor and spotted a flash of blue that could only be Viv's dress. He smiled, wondering if her panties were the same color. Or if she'd already slipped them off and intended to hand them to him the minute they were alone. With Viv, anything was possible.

The idea of her being pantieless and alone suddenly worried him. Rather than heading to the elevator, he decided to go to her, not wanting her to walk through the rear service hallways of the hotel alone. He turned to give a final wave to Viv's friends, but froze when he heard the sound of a woman's shriek.

His blood went cold. Some might have confused the noise for a shrill laugh, but Damien knew it hadn't been. His instincts—already heightened even before he'd heard the sound—were now pinging, tension flooding him. He couldn't see who'd made the distressed sound.

But he didn't have to.

He knew Viv. By now, he knew every inch of her, from the dimple on her pert butt to the freckles on her collarbone, to the sound she made when she was excited. Or happy.

Or frightened.

Damien spun around, his body reacting before his mind had a chance to. He didn't spare a glance for Lex or Amelia, or anyone else, including the startled-looking staff members. There was no time. Viv needed him.

He pounded down the hall at a dead run, toward where he'd last spotted her.

Frantic for her, he rounded the corner and his heart fell from his chest. Because there stood Viv, one hand gripping her torn dress, the other touching her swollen lip. Her blue eyes swam with tears of pain, which filled Damien with a level of rage he'd never experienced before in his life.

There was no evaluating the situation, no wondering who, what, why. He simply saw Viv—his Viv—struggling with a massive guy wearing jeans and a hoody, and launched.

# 9

WITH HER WRAP in her hand and anticipation filling her mind and heart, Viv hadn't experienced the slightest hint of worry as she'd entered a secluded hallway of the hotel. She'd been practically skipping, still cocooned in the bliss she'd experienced when Damien had whisked her across the floor. Viv had always been more of a shake-it-don't-break-it kind of girl when it came to dancing. But when Damien Black had waltzed her around the room, she wasn't sure she'd touched the ground.

She'd felt, for one heart-stopping moment, cherished, as if she was living out her most romantic girlhood fairy-tale dream.

And then she'd walked by herself into the small hallway near an access door used for loading and unloading into the catering kitchens, and entered her worst nightmare.

"You fucking bitch."

The words had hit her a split second before the body did.

Big. Hard. Smelling of sweat and liquor.

She hadn't recognized him at first, too shocked to do anything but throw her hands up as he came at her. But she might has well have been trying to stop a tsunami with two open palms. Her strength was no match for his, her defenses completely ineffectual against the hundreds of pounds of angry, muscled man.

He grabbed her hair, pulled it painfully, while, with the

other hand, he yanked a fistful of her dress and twisted. She heard seams tear, cried out at the agony of skin being sliced and abraded, then found herself thrust off her feet and shoved into the wall so hard her head thunked against it.

Her breath whooshing out of her, the world spun. Confusion warred with pain, but both immediately lost ground to fear. "What do you want?" she said, her voice shaking.

"Whatya owe me, y-you teasing whore."

Her vision was blurry, tears, terror and pain confusing her, but at last she recognized the face and the voice.

"Bruno?"

"Should remember my name since you ruined my life."

Genuine terror had her in its grip and now it squeezed tight. Bruno Neeley had always been a giant asshole, but he'd at least tried to hide his jerkish tendencies behind an aw-shucks-I-didn't-mean-any-harm act.

Now there was no charm. His mask was off, the real man—big, angry, drunk—was fully revealed.

"I didn't ruin your…"

"My wife took my kids, you cunt."

Anger swelled, momentarily shoving the fear aside. Along with every other female in the world, she *hated* that word. "Smart woman," she muttered.

He shoved her again, but this time he didn't let go of her dress, and it ripped further. She crossed her arms over her breasts, struggling to keep herself covered. Though it went against her nature, Viv said nothing, instinctively aware she had to avoid provoking him further while she waited for an opportunity to escape him.

Viv tried to remember where the door to the next banquet room was, wondering if Damien had emerged through it yet. Nobody inside would hear her scream, but those leaving might.

"She's divorcing me and is gonna get more in alimony than that stupid Canadian team can pay me."

"Bruno, please, let me go. It wasn't my fault."

"Yes it was!" He leaned close, spittle landing on her skin as he shouted, "You acted like you wanted me, and when I took you up on it, you slapped me and humiliated me in front of the press. You cost me my job, and my family."

"No, no I didn't." She swallowed, trying reason, though he was probably too far gone for that to work. "I never meant to lead you on. And I had no idea you would be traded."

"Bullshit!" He rubbed his hand on his mouth, something she'd seen alcoholics do. Considering the man's reputation for bad behavior, she had to wonder if he'd had an alcohol problem long before he'd gotten drunk to drown his woes tonight.

"You've got to let me go. I'm sure we can work this out."

"Yeah, you gonna get your boyfriend to cancel the trade and give me my job back?"

She shook her head. "What?"

"You got me fired, you can fix it. Spread your legs, make him happy and get me on the team again."

Now he was just rambling. "I have no idea what you're talking about."

"Stop lying, I saw you with him! You're fucking the team owner."

"No, I'm certainly not. That's crazy."

"Well, you will be soon, 'cause that's the only reason anybody would be with you. You stupid bitch, he just wants a piece of ass." He let out an ugly laugh. "Oh, and to keep you from suing or something. When his pussy lawyer threw me out, he said the owner was sooo worried about you suing them all."

"Bruno, I'm sorry for your problems, but you're very confused right now."

"You're the one who's confused if you really believe some billionaire gives a shit about a trashy slut like you."

She swallowed hard, determined not to let his words get to her. She couldn't let her anger lead her to make a mistake that would goad him into more violence.

But he wasn't finished. "You ain't livin' no fairy tale, sweetheart. I don't care how much you dance around the room with him."

He meant Damien. Apparently Bruno had heard about tonight's event, come here drunk and spied on what was going on. The fact that he'd caught her alone had been icing on his revenge cake.

"He uses people like me...and like you. He'll trade you when he's done with you, too."

His words confused her, but she tried to keep her tone calm, treating him as she would a wild bear she'd encountered in the woods. "Bruno, why don't you go next door— some of the guys are there. I'm sure one of them would take you home."

"Are you deaf? I don't have a home no more!"

He shook her violently, so hard that she lost her grip on her dress. The silky blue fabric fell down, exposing her breast, and he immediately focused his attention there, an ugly smile pulling up his mouth, revealing his broken teeth.

"Or maybe we can make a deal." He licked his lips. "You give me what you're giving your boss, Mr. Black. Let's find out if your pussy is worth the cost of that necklace he put on you tonight."

"You're disgusting. You're also confused, and you're drunk," she said, trying to sound calm and strong, though she was trembling and her heart was galloping in her chest.

"Drunk. Not confused."

He crowded closer, bending to try to kiss her. Viv jerked her head away, but he grabbed her jaw to hold her still, gripping painfully with his strong fingers. She would have bruises tomorrow.

*Dear Lord, please let it be only bruises.*

She wasn't about to give up without a fight. When he moved his mouth to hers, she bit him, satisfied by his yelp of pain.

Her satisfaction was short-lived. Growling, Bruno slapped her hard across the face, making her whole head jerk to the side. Her ears rang, her face ached, but even through the shock, Viv saw his fury when he realized she'd drawn blood. It spilled off his lip, and he angrily rubbed it away with his arm. An almost visible blanket of rage dropped over him, and every ounce of it was directed at her.

She was in trouble now. Serious trouble. Viv had no doubt he intended to hurt her. She could smell his intentions in his fetid, whiskey-soaked breaths blasting her in the face.

His big hand fisted.

She reacted instinctively, diving away from him, hearing a crash as he landed a punch on the wall behind where she'd just been standing. Stumbling, she spun around the corner into a broader corridor that led out toward the lobby. She managed to get a few feet ahead of him, aiming for the far end of the hallway that led out of this service-room maze. At the end of it, she beheld a tall, dark-haired man in a tux, and her heart leaped.

Opening her mouth to scream for help, she found herself yanked out of sight of the man she prayed was Damien, and a beefy hand slammed on her lips. Viv twisted and struggled, not caring that the dress was falling off her. She bit at his hand, scratched at his face and finally was able to draw breath enough to scream.

Only once, but she gave it everything she had.

*God, please let Damien have heard.*

Bruno picked her up and began dragging her toward a storeroom. She was well aware if he got her inside, she would not escape rape. Or worse. He was out of his mind, blaming her for all that had gone wrong in his life, determined to mete out punishment. Tied up in that anger and drunkenness was lust, violence and a seething desire for revenge.

They neared the door.

She remembered something she'd read once about how to evade an attacker. Letting her body go limp, she forced him to support her entire dead weight.

If he'd been a normal-sized guy, it might have helped. Neeley, however, wasn't slowed down a bit. Instead, as if to punish her for trying, he began to squeeze her around the middle. His crushing grip made her bones audibly crack. The air was being forced out of her lungs, and she was unable to fill them again, breathing in desperate pants.

Hot tears filled her eyes. Viv became light-headed, and wanted to sob at the pain in her ribs, when suddenly, to her shock, Bruno dropped her onto the ground as he stumbled to his knees.

Gasping for breath, she scooted out of the way as Damien landed on the other man. The two of them rolled across the floor, crashing into the opposite wall. Damien was pummeling the hockey player, cursing him, threatening him. His face was a twisted mask of rage; she'd never seen him like this, oblivious to everything except the thug who was staggering to his feet, ready to fight against someone closer to his own size.

But not that close.

Bruno Neeley had to weigh almost three hundred pounds. He was acknowledged as a brute on the ice, a right wing who gave out concussions by the boatload to opposing players. Yes, he was drunk, unsteady, and Damien had caught him off guard. But he was quickly rebounding, throwing his weight behind a counterattack.

The two men went flying by her in the other direction, each struggling for an advantage. Bruno was all brawn, but Damien was quick, strong and driven by an almost insane bloodlust. Fists thudded against bodies. Harsh breaths became snarls. Viv looked frantically around, wanting to find something to help Damien, and spied only her bag, which held nothing but clothes. There had to be other people nearby. She ran to the hallway for help, beyond happy to see Lex and Amelia hurrying toward them, apparently having followed Damien.

"Help him!" she screamed.

Lex barked something to Amelia and came toward her at a run. He rounded the corner, realized what was happening and dived in to assist Damien. Amelia, meanwhile, darted toward the lobby, calling for security.

Helpless to do anything, Viv stood there biting her nails, watching as two strong men she cared about worked in unison to contain an enraged animal. Fortunately, between them, Damien and Lex got Bruno under control. By the time the two security guards joined them in the alcove, the hockey player was sitting on the floor, his head between his knees, moaning.

Viv began to breathe again as they took control, radioing for the security office to call the police. Once she was sure that Bruno wasn't going to get up again, she ran into Damien's arms, sobbing in a delayed reaction made half of fear and half of relief.

He grabbed her, pulled her close, running his hands up

and down her sides as if to make sure she wasn't broken. "Are you all right?"

"I'm fine," she insisted, almost choking on the words. Her breaths were coming on hoarse gasps and she was caught between tears and screams.

"He hurt you."

"No, no, it's nothing."

He grabbed her shoulders and gently pushed her away so he could examine her face, which was probably reddened from the slap. Worse, she actually tasted a bit of blood in her mouth. Then he noticed her torn dress, and an almost inarticulate rage washed over Damien's face all over again.

She grabbed him tight and collapsed against his chest. "Just hold me," she insisted, more to keep him from returning to pummel Bruno again than anything else. She was calming down, realizing that yes, she'd had a close call, but no, she wasn't actually hurt.

"I'm gonna kill him."

"Don't. Please, let the police handle it."

"I'm sorry. Jesus, I'm so sorry, Viv. I should never have left you alone."

"How could you expect some lunatic would attack me?"

"I *should* have expected it. He was furious when I had him traded, and more than one person informed me he'd been making threats against me. I should have realized you'd be a target, too, and that he hadn't given up."

Viv had been slowly recovering from the trauma as she let herself soak up Damien's warmth and comfort, but his words confused her. "Wait…what do you mean?"

He kept touching her, caressing her hip, stroking her hair, kissing her cheek. "I mean, I should have had a bodyguard protecting you the minute I found out what happened. Or I should have had him escorted to a plane to take him to his new city, or convinced you to press assault charges. But I promise you, Viv, he won't get near you again."

Viv scrunched her eyes closed, trying to get past the anxiety, trying to calm down and make sense of everything that had just happened. Bruno's words about Damien had sounded crazy, a mixed-up amalgamation of resentments in the muddled mind of an alcoholic. But now, with what Damien was saying, she was beginning to visualize another possibility.

"Damien, Bruno seemed to believe you had something to do with him being traded."

"Well, of course I did."

"How?"

He stared down at her, puzzled. "The new GM and I made a lot of calls until somebody took him off our hands."

"*You* did that."

"Yes."

"But why?"

"Because he hurt you."

"No, I mean, why would you be involved. Damien, was Bruno telling the truth when he said you own the team?"

It was his turn to appear confused. "Well, yes, of course."

Such an easy thing to say. *Yes, of course.* But the words hit her like boulders thrown from a cliff. Her head was reeling, and it had nothing to do with the slap.

*Yes, of course* he owned the Vanguard.

*Yes, of course* he had arranged for Bruno's trade.

*Yes, of course* he would have been the one who'd gotten Viv her job back.

*Yes, of course* he was the one who got rid of Stoker.

*Yes, of course* he would want to make sure she didn't sue the organization or cause them any more bad publicity.

*Yes, of course* he had swept her off her feet until she would have done anything—absolutely *anything*—for him.

But had he done it intentionally? Had all of it been some sort of plan to keep her from making trouble, to prevent a lawsuit, as Bruno had said?

Could Bruno Neeley, in all his demented anger, have been right?

"Viv, are you okay?"

She shook her head slowly, trying to process it. "No, actually, I'm not."

The room began to spin, the floor rising and falling beneath her feet, as if she stood on the deck of a ship trying to stay afloat on a stormy sea. Her dress was torn, her skin bruised, her face sore, her body shaking and her heart…oh, her heart was playing all kinds of crazy games with her head.

*Yes, of course.*

It was all just too much. Everything overwhelmed her, and nothing made sense.

And suddenly, without warning, all the strength drained from Viv's body, and she fainted right into Damien's arms.

DAMIEN SAT BY her hospital bed all night.

He held her hand, consoled her when she cried out in her sleep, barked at each doctor or nurse who came into the private room to make sure they kept her safe and well.

She wasn't badly hurt, thank God. Not physically, anyway.

But she'd been stalked, terrified and assaulted. Her emotional reaction to Bruno Neeley's attack had left her confused and frightened.

After she'd fainted, he'd insisted that paramedics take her to the hospital, and had further insisted on riding with her in the ambulance. Lex and Amelia had followed, and they'd waited with him while doctors examined Viv. None of them were family, but Damien had lied and called himself her fiancé, finding the word a lot easier to utter than he'd ever have imagined.

With no one else to talk to about her condition, the doctor had confirmed for him that Viv had no life-threatening injuries. Her ribs were bruised, and she had some other abrasions and cuts. Worse, she was probably suffering from shock. She'd been admitted and Damien hadn't left her side since.

Throughout the night, she'd ranged from dozing to crying. Eventually, somewhere around 3:00 a.m., she'd shared the details of the whole story in soft whispers while he'd lain in the narrow hospital bed, holding her.

The recounting seemed to help, and she'd finally fallen into a real sleep. While she'd slumbered, Damien had sat in the chair beside her, keeping watch. Still wearing his tux, he'd tossed the jacket and tie aside, and unbuttoned his shirt. Nothing would induce him to leave, and he'd glared at anyone who suggested that he do so. He'd stayed there, for hours, sending up prayers of thanks that she was all right, fully aware of how close she'd come to calamity.

If he hadn't heard that scream, Viv might have been in need of a rape kit, or worse. Bruno Neeley had been enraged, drunk and, apparently, high. There would have been no stopping him, and she would have been helpless to fight him off.

"Thank you, God," he mumbled again as he brought her pale hand to his lips and kissed it.

"Damien?"

He immediately rose from his chair and leaned over her. "I'm sorry, I didn't mean to wake you."

She blinked and glanced around the room. Early morning sunshine had brightened the room. "I guess I really slept."

"The doctor said that was the best thing you could do."

He would have urged her to get even more rest, but the police officers who'd taken Neeley into custody last night had said they'd be by first thing this morning to get Viv's statement.

"So it wasn't a dream," she whispered.

"Nightmare, maybe"

"Yeah." She took a deep, calming breath. "You stayed all night?"

"Of course.

"Thank you."

"Lex and Amelia left at around midnight. Amelia said she'd come again this morning."

"She doesn't have to do that," she said, struggling to sit up.

He helped her, tucking the sheet and blanket around her, then pushing the button to raise the bed to an inclining position. "Are you hungry? Thirsty?"

"Water?"

Glad to have something to do, he crossed the room and poured her a glass from the plastic pitcher a nurse had left. Bringing the glass to the bed, he held it to her lips, supporting her head while she sipped.

She winced as the cup scraped against her swollen, bloodstained lip, and Damien flinched. His hand tightened on the cup, but he managed to hold it steady and not spill it, not wanting to reveal his fury. It had been hard enough not to bellow with rage when he watched the rising sun send shards of light over her face, highlighting the faint bruises on her jaw.

"Thanks." Then, apparently remembering some of their jumbled conversation during the night, she added, "You didn't call my family, right?"

He frowned down at her. "I should have, but no."

She'd argued with him about it last night, begging him

not to worry her parents or brothers since she wasn't seriously hurt. Damien had almost done it anyway, but understood Viv wanted to prepare herself for the conversations she faced. Hearing their daughter—their only girl—had been attacked and almost raped would not be easy for her parents. Christ, he could hardly stand the thought of it himself.

"When can I get out of here?"

"The doctor should be here soon." He brushed a long strand of hair away from her face, touching her gently, not wanting to hurt her further. "The police, too."

"Oh, God," she groaned.

"It'll be fine," he said, bending to brush a kiss on her forehead. "I'll be right here with you."

She stiffened the tiniest bit, and shifted her eyes to gaze past him. "To look out for the team's interests?"

The muttered comment shocked him so much, he jerked up and took a step away from the bed. "What?"

Shaking her head and closing her eyes, she mumbled, "I'm sorry. I didn't… I shouldn't have said that."

"You don't really believe it."

"No. Of course not." She didn't sound terribly convinced.

"What, exactly, did Neeley say to you?" he asked, still confused over some of what Viv had relayed to him during those late-night hours.

She didn't answer the question, instead countering with one of her own. "Why didn't you let me know you owned the team?"

"What are you talking about?"

"It's a simple question. Why didn't you say anything about it?"

He had to wonder if Viv was suffering from more than

shock. Maybe she had a concussion. "I really don't understand."

"It's a simple question."

"Viv, you *knew* I was one of the owners."

She gaped, her brow furrowed, her mouth open. "No. I didn't."

"That's not possible. The day—that first day at the hotel, you left me a note saying you'd found out who I was. That's why you took off on me!" Realizing he'd never actually voiced it, he assured her, "I swear to you, I had no idea who you were or who had fired you until I saw that story on the news."

Viv rubbed at her temples, as if to soothe an ache. "That note, I left it because I'd learned you owned the hotel."

He stiffened. "And?"

"And nothing. That was it. The salesclerk mentioned you were a billionaire, that you owned the building I was standing in. I was…well, I was pretty mad at men at that point, and felt lied to."

The truth began to sink in. "Are you saying you ran out because I was rich? It had nothing to do with me being CEO of Black Ice, the company that owns the Vanguard?"

"That's exactly what I'm saying." She slapped her hand down on the bed. "I had no clue you were the team's primary owner until last night, when that disgusting pig said he'd been traded because of my relationship with you."

Damien's thoughts reeled. It made no sense, how could she not have realized? All these weeks… Well, of course, he'd never done any work with the team while she was present. He'd steered clear of the office for her sake. But still…

"You never wanted to talk about work," he mumbled. "I assumed it was because you were trying to keep your professional life separate from your personal one. Trying to keep the owner-employee thing totally away from us."

"No, it was because I live sports nine-to-five, five days a week, and I just didn't want to talk about it anymore. Especially after what happened." She licked her lips. "I didn't want you worrying about me and my problems. I wanted it to just be about you and me."

He stepped to her bedside again, stroking her unbruised cheek. "It *was* just about you and me."

He stared at her, willing her to believe him. He hated the idea that she'd believe he'd only been involved with her as some way to avoid a lawsuit or trouble for the team. The concept was ludicrous, and he could beat Bruno Neeley all over again for putting it into his head.

Of course, Sam and the other attorneys had certainly floated the possibility, too. So Viv might have gotten this impression anyway. But, damn it, that still didn't make it true.

"Viv, listen to me," he insisted, sitting on the edge of the bed. "I hate what happened to you, all of it, from that TV fiasco to last night. I'd do anything to make it not have happened."

"I know," she said with a weary sigh.

"No, you don't," he persisted. "If you want to sue me, you go right ahead. I won't fight it. I'll give you whatever you want."

"That's ridiculous."

"I mean it." He leaned closer to her, searching those blue eyes for some sign she believed him, wanting her to understand, wanting most of all for her to stay.

"I'll do anything you want," he whispered. "Just, please...don't leave me."

Her eyes grew misty, luminous, and he saw she was trying not to cry. "Leave you?"

"I don't want to lose you."

It wasn't a declaration of love. Damien still wasn't entirely sure he was capable of that emotion, much less say it out loud. But the idea of something happening to her—the way Bruno had hurt her, or the possibility of her cutting off their relationship because she no longer trusted him—threatened to crush the heart of him.

He would do whatever it took to keep that from happening. If it cost him the team, or every penny he had. Whatever it took.

"Damien?" she finally asked.

"Yes?"

She reached up and brushed her fingers through his hair, cupping his cheek. "Would you please take me home?"

"As soon as I can, Viv. And I promise, nobody will ever hurt you again.

# *10*

---

AFTER VIV WAS finally released from the hospital, following another checkup and a police interview, Damien made good on his promise to take her home. She'd been wheeled to the exit, and he lifted her out of the wheelchair and into the backseat of the limo, holding her on his lap.

Damien asked Jed to head for her apartment, but as they drove through Arlington, Viv realized she wasn't ready to go to her own place yet. She wasn't frightened, precisely; Bruno was in custody. He hadn't even had a bail hearing yet.

But her nerves were still rattled. She didn't know if she would be able to fall asleep without fearing she might be awakened by a coarse hand covering her mouth and a powerful arm crushing the breath from her body.

Damien would stay with her if she asked him to—he'd spent one or two nights with her in the past. But she would feel more secure, more capable of keeping herself safe, if they were in the penthouse, behind security, elevators and locked doors.

"Would you mind if we went to your place?" she asked, having come to consider the penthouse Damien's home, since she'd never seen him living in any other.

He frowned. "Are you sure? I mean, after what happened there?"

That was another reason to return to the Black Star.

She'd grown to love the place, and didn't want her feelings about it ruined by the attack. Viv had given Bruno Neeley control over enough of her life in recent weeks.

"I'm sure."

Damien called Jed and changed their destination. He kept his arm around her waist as they walked through the lobby, positioning himself so she wouldn't even have a view down the side hallway that led to the scene of her nightmare, his protectiveness intuitive.

Once they were inside the penthouse, Damien insisted on taking care of her. She'd barely removed her jacket before he was sitting her down on the couch and heading into the bathroom to draw her a steamy, relaxing bath.

"I'm fine, I can walk," she called after him.

"Let me do this," he insisted, returning to carry her. She was beginning to feel like one of those petite, fragile women whom men could easily sweep into their arms, and couldn't deny she kind of enjoyed it.

Once in the bathroom, Damien stripped off her clothes— a sweater and pair of jeans Amelia had brought to the hospital for her this morning—and lowered her into the bubbles. Even then, he wasn't finished. He kneeled beside the tub, washing every strand of her hair, gently bathing each sore and scrape. She felt boneless and relaxed even before he began to massage her shoulders and aching muscles.

"This is heavenly," she murmured.

"I'm going to spoil you."

"I'm really fine, Damien," she insisted, reaching a soapy hand up to brush against his cheek. "I appreciate all of this, but I promise you, I'm not in pain."

"Not physically, maybe," he muttered.

She couldn't argue that, because he was right. Emotionally, she was still in a great deal of pain, unable to forget the violation of Bruno Neeley's hands on her. Which, she realized, was probably why Damien had so lovingly washed every inch of her. As if he could remove those memories by his tender touch alone.

And perhaps he could.

As the water grew cool, Damien lifted her out, dried her off, carried her into the bedroom and tucked her into bed. She lay there as he ordered room service, surprised when he asked for chicken soup, ginger ale, chocolate pudding and ice cream. All the comfort food anyone could want. When it arrived, he wouldn't allow anyone to enter the bedroom, bringing it in himself. He'd fed her, coaxed her into eating all her soup before she could have the junk.

Afterward, he did the most important thing of all.

He held her hand when she called her parents to tell them what had happened. The story of Neeley's arrest would make national news, there was no way they wouldn't find out about her involvement.

It hadn't been easy to talk to them. But Damien hadn't left her side.

After the call, after she'd promised them she was fine and had elicited their promise not to come, saying she'd see them in a few days for the anniversary party, she collapsed into Damien's arms.

"I've never heard my father cry like that," she sobbed.

"I know, baby, I'm sorry."

"They're crushed."

"They're terrified…imagining the could-haves rather than being thankful for the did-haves." He stroked her hair. "Just give them a little while."

He held her until she slept, and stayed there, holding her, all night, getting up only in the morning when someone knocked on the door to the suite. Viv yawned and stretched, watching him pull on some clothes and leave the room. She already felt a thousand percent better than she had the day before, physically and emotionally.

Getting up, she went into the bathroom. She glanced at herself in the mirror, noting that the bruises on her jaw weren't too terrible, and the lip was healing. Outwardly, she looked as if she'd had just a minor mishap, not that she'd been attacked by a rape-and-violence-minded animal.

Inwardly—well, it was time to work on healing inwardly, too. Starting right now.

As she returned to the master bedroom, she stood out of the way to allow Damien to enter. He was carrying a vase with a huge bouquet of pink tulips.

"We're going to have to rent the adjoining room to handle all the flowers."

She almost smiled, the reaction funny after all the tears. "How many of them are from you?"

"No comment."

Though she hadn't left the bedroom, she'd been catching the scent of roses since the day before, and the aroma wasn't merely from the dozen red ones Damien had given her yesterday that were now sitting on the bedside table.

Damien handed her the card.

"They're from my supervisor, Tim, and the rest of the PR staff. That's nice of them."

"Several of the players have sent cards and notes, too. They're all stacked up for you on the table in the other room," Damien said. "I suspect they're feeling some guilt about the part they played in this mess."

"Well, I'd say that's nice, too, except for the fact that they should." If not for the sexist attitude and the stupid bet, Bruno Neeley might never have decided to prove his masculinity by going after her so single-mindedly.

"I agree." He jerked a thumb in the direction of the other room. "Sam and the legal folks went for sunflowers."

Damien had told her about his friendship with Sam yesterday. She'd never interacted much with the lawyer, and wasn't entirely sure she was ready to forgive him for urging Damien to stay away from her.

"Everybody still trying to avoid a lawsuit?" She regretted the jab when she noticed his jaw clench. "I'm sorry."

He slowly turned on his heel, his expression bleak. "You don't still believe that.

Knowing she'd sounded like a queen bitch, she shook her head. "No, I don't. That was awful to say."

"Because it's absolutely not true, Viv," he said, obviously thinking he still needed to convince her.

"I know."

Damien wasn't the type to use shady maneuvers to avoid legal trouble. As he'd said, he could easily pay her off if she decided to be money hungry.

Besides, she trusted him completely. At least, she wanted to. If she allowed herself to believe that he'd only begun dating her to avoid more bad press or legal troubles for the team, she might go crazy. She didn't want it to be true—she wanted to believe that Damien, with all his tenderness and his passion, had begun to feel something for her.

Maybe he wasn't crazy in love with her, maybe he never would be. But he cared. Oh, God, no man could be so shattered at the idea of something bad happening to her, could wash her hair and feed her soup and chocolate pudding, if he didn't care.

"So what do you want to do today?" he asked, picking up a pair of jeans he'd flung on the floor near the bed. She could see he was trying to change the subject, to avoid arguing or saying anything that would upset her. "Are you hungry? Want me to order some breakfast?"

"Pudding and ice cream?"

"Nope." He wagged his index finger, his posture easing. "Healthy stuff from here on out. You're not milking this."

She smiled broadly at that, glad he was giving her crap. He was challenging her to not only feel better, but to also *be* better today. One heartbreakingly lovely day of his tender, loving care and sympathy had been glorious. Now she had to start healing and moving on.

She'd found her smile again—now she would help him find his. "Are you sure I thanked you enough for saving me from George Costanza?"

Damien tilted his head to the side, staring at her with confused eyes. It took him a second before he recognized the name, and then he said, "Uh, you mean George from *Seinfeld*?"

"Yep."

"Oh, no. That doctor was wrong. You do have a concussion." He walked closer, lifting his hand to check her forehead.

She laughed softly. "I mean, didn't that actor play the creepy guy who tried to rape Julia Roberts in *Pretty Woman*?"

He lowered his hand. "Yeah, actually, I believe he did."

"So, billionaire's sleazy employee attacks the woman he's involved with. We're still playing out this movie, aren't we? Only Richard Gere fired the guy. You actually traded Bruno Neeley, and beat the crap out of him." She put her hand on his chest. "My hero."

"If it was George, I wouldn't have required Lex's help to restrain him," he said with a short laugh. "Nor would I have bruises all over my body."

She sucked in a breath. She hadn't seen him totally naked since the incident, and had no idea he'd been so badly hurt.

"I'm all right," he said, reading her mind. "And beating the crap out of that guy was totally worth it."

"Show me?" she whispered, still worried.

"Huh?"

"Show me," she repeated. "Let me take care of you the way you took care of me." She stepped away from him, reaching for the bottom of his T-shirt and pushing it up.

"I'm fine, honestly. Ice and aspirin, I'm all set. You don't have to…"

"I want to," she said, hoping he could read the honest desire in her eyes. But just in case he missed the message, she reached for the sash of her robe and untied it.

"Viv…"

"I'm fine, too," she insisted as she shrugged the robe off her shoulders, letting it fall away. She wore nothing underneath. "Stop worrying about me."

He remained still, staring over her body from head to toe, as if wanting to memorize her, or perhaps just make sure, again, that she truly was okay. He frowned at the sight of a few bruises, but his glower quickly faded as his gaze lingered on her breasts, the nipples dark and taut, and then down her stomach, to the apex of her thighs.

"Say you still want me," she said, feeling exposed, vulnerable, standing here naked while he gazed at her.

He barked a harsh laugh. "Want you? I'm dying for you."

He stepped closer, brushing against her, so she could judge the truth of that. He was rock-hard under his jeans, and Viv went soft and hot with desire.

"I don't want to hurt you," he admitted, not relaxing against her, even when she slid her arms around his neck and pressed her body against his.

"You won't hurt me. You'll help me—you'll make me forget, and you'll give me pleasure." She leaned up to press her lips against his throat, tasting warm, salty skin. "I need you, Damien. And I *want* you."

He slipped his hands around her waist, his resistance melting. His fingertips were warm against her naked skin. With a helpless shrug, he admitted, "I can't stop worrying. Can't stop picturing him dragging you toward that closet."

"Let's both forget together, all right? We'll put all of it behind us and move forward. Help me get over it, won't you?"

She rose on tiptoe and brushed her mouth against his. Damien held himself from her for perhaps the space of a heartbeat. Then, on a deep, hungry groan, he drew her into his arms, pulling her up so their lips could meet for a deep kiss.

Viv sighed happily as their tongues twirled together, hungry and lazy both. There was no fear, no wispy remnant of ugly memories of the other night to interfere with her reaction. There was only Damien—sexy, powerful, tender Damien—wanting her, arousing her, fulfilling her.

The kiss went on and on. He tasted like the morning, delicious and warm. She could breathe nothing but air from his mouth for the rest of her life and be a happy woman.

"Say something to me if I hurt you," he pulled away long enough to say.

"You won't."

She trusted him completely, and went back to pushing his shirt up and out of the way. Hearing his ragged breathing, she knew he was losing any inner battle to stay in control. He was on fire for her; his hands shook as he undid his jeans and shoved them down and off.

She spied a bruise on his chest, and another on his ribs. Saying nothing, she bent to kiss them, treating him with all the tenderness he'd offered her. How could she not? He'd earned these wounds saving her.

He reached down, cupped her chin in his hands and pulled her up until they stood face-to-face. "Don't worry about me," he ordered. "I'd give my right arm for none of that to have happened to you."

She heard the conviction, and believed he was serious. Viv threw her arms around his neck and kissed him again, overwhelmed by the depths and facets of this man.

He didn't have to carry her to the bed. Instead, she pushed him until his legs hit the edge. He collapsed onto his back, bringing her with him. They rolled around in the sheets, kissing, their bare limbs entwining, hands caressing, bodies pressing together in pure, helpless longing.

"You are the most beautiful thing God ever put on this earth," Damien said as he rolled over her and gazed down at her. He bent to kiss her jaw, tasting his way down her throat, pressing his lips in the hollow. His hands were magical, gliding up her sides, and then down her hip.

She moaned when he moved his fingers to one thigh, lifting her leg so he could play with the back of her knee. It was an erogenous spot she'd never even recognized in herself, and Viv whimpered as he slowly—ever so slowly— traced a path up her thigh toward her sex. But he didn't give her the deeper caress she wanted, instead moving right by her damp curls so he could stroke her soft belly.

"Damien, please," she begged.

"Shh," he ordered. "Trust me."

She did, of course, but that didn't mean she didn't want... "Oh, God, yes," she cried as he moved his mouth to her breast. He flicked his tongue against her nipple, wetting it, and then drew the taut peak between his lips to suckle her with exquisitely tender passion. Viv twined her hands in his hair, arching up toward him, loving the sensations he brought forth.

He continued down her body, worshipping her with his mouth and his tongue. She was a live wire of energy, trembling beneath his expert touch. When he reached her sex and his warm lips stroked her clit, she cried out and lost herself to a long, low orgasm. He was kissing her mouth again before the final pulses of it had left her.

He settled between her parted thighs and gazed into her face. "I'll never let anyone hurt you."

"I know," she said, arching toward him in silent invitation.

He sank into her—hot, hard man melting into soft, willing woman. Viv wanted to cry at the perfection of it. He filled her in every possible way, not just the physical. Though, the physical was absolutely fabulous, too.

Damien seemed to catch her building excitement. While he was no less careful with her, he was unable to stop himself from pulling out and thrusting into her, hard, burying himself to the hilt.

"God, yes," she cried, wrapping her legs around his hips and her arms around his shoulders. She kissed him, her tongue thrusting into his mouth as he thrust his cock into her body. She was wrapped around him, joined with him, as much a part of him as she was of herself.

It was magical, utter bliss. And this time when she cried out her ultimate pleasure—a powerful, shattering climax that broke her apart—he came with her, plunging deep once more and filling her with every part of himself.

COLLAPSING TOGETHER IN a heap, they slept for a while. Damien hadn't gotten much rest in the past two nights. He'd been too focused on watching her, making sure she was all right. Now, though, it seemed certain that she was fine and getting better by the moment, he relaxed. He kept her in his arms, not wanting her more than a few inches away, and fell asleep smelling her hair and hearing her soft breaths.

Unfortunately, he didn't awaken the same way.

"Who… Viv?" he mumbled, waking up to the sound of voices. Several voices. Women's voices.

He glanced to the other side of the bed. It was empty. She'd gotten up from their brief nap without waking him.

"Are you trying to say you won't *allow* me to visit my son? Who do you think you are?"

Damien's eyes saucered as that voice hit his eardrums and scratched into his brain. Maybe he was hearing a TV. He *prayed* he was hearing a TV.

"Damien!"

That was no television.

He launched out of bed, wondering who he had wronged in another life to bring his mother here, and to put her in the same room with Viv. If she didn't scare off Viv unintentionally, she'd probably do it just for spite.

"I'll be right out," he called, yanking his jeans off the floor and pulling them on. He scooped his shirt into his fingers and stalked out of the bedroom, his eyes immediately searching for Viv.

He didn't find her right away, because she was surrounded. Literally. Appearing stunned, she was encircled by three women, all of whom he recognized. One was, as he'd feared, his mother. The young redhead on the left was his sister Johanna and on his mother's right was Morgan Duffy, the daughter of his mother's oldest friend. She'd been shoved in his face since he was old enough to understand the words *arranged marriage*.

Christ, this just got better and better.

"What in the hell is going on?" he snapped, pushing between his mother and Johanna, who at least offered him a sheepish wave. "Have you people ever heard of calling?"

"Since when do I have to call to visit the penthouse in one of my own hotels?" his mother snapped.

He bit his tongue, not pointing out that the amount of

stock his father had left her didn't come anywhere close to meaning they were "her" hotels.

Damien went to Viv and put his arm around her waist. She was wearing just a robe, her hair a loose, tangled curtain around her shoulders, and her face was pale and strained. If his family had upset her, set back her recovery, he'd pitch them all down the elevator shaft.

"What happened? Why didn't you wake me?" he asked, his voice low, meant only for her.

"I came to check out the flowers," she mumbled. "They smelled so nice, all the roses. There was a knock at the door."

Huh. He supposed he should be grateful his family hadn't just gotten a manager to let them in to "surprise" him.

"Did you invest in a florist as well as a team of ice-skating hooligans?" his mother asked, her cold expression matched by the icy tone.

Okay, so apparently the news media was all over the story, and had revealed that he was a majority shareholder in the Vanguard. He didn't care that his mother knew, though he hadn't gone out of his way to inform her. Perhaps it had been too much to ask that he have one thing—just one thing—that wasn't subject to the constant meddling, opinions and demands of his family.

He considered it for a moment, and realized he was no longer that guy who only had one thing.

Now he had two.

Because he had Viv. And she was the one thing he couldn't bear to lose.

"Aren't you going to introduce us?" His mother gave Viv another of those glances that both assessed and dismissed. "Although I recognize your little friend from all the media coverage, we hadn't gotten around to introductions."

Viv winced; he could sense the quiver in her body. Jesus, how on earth had his father ever stayed married to his mother? He'd never met a harder person. He'd been aware she had ice in her veins, of course, never having remembered a single moment in his childhood when she'd wiped his tears or tucked him into bed. But she'd gotten worse as she aged, when she'd begun to go through husbands like tissues, all of them breaking her heart. Or whatever she had that masqueraded as a heart.

He'd realized long ago that his mother didn't love him. She might care a bit about his sisters, but definitely not her only son. He'd long suspected it was because his father had loved him so much, and had never tried to hide it. She hadn't been able to stand not being the center of her husband's world.

"Viv, this is my mother, Sylvia Tyson, my sister Johanna Black, and…" He waved toward the woman his mother had been trying to fix him up with for years. "That's Morgan, a friend of my mother's."

Morgan, a tall, willowy brunette whose beauty was matched only by her arrogance, had the audacity to appear betrayed, though he'd never so much as held her hand.

"This is Vivienne Callahan," he announced.

"We know who she is," his mother said. "She's the little tart who has you so tied up in knots you ignore your business and get into public brawls that make you national news."

Viv gasped. Damien growled. He'd never witnessed her being so damn rude to a perfect stranger, and he took a step forward. "Get out."

"It's all right, Damien," Viv said, putting a hand on his arm. She lifted a hand to her face, as if pushing her hair out of her eyes, but he'd swear she was surreptitiously dashing away tears.

"No, it's not. Go, Mother. I'll meet you downstairs in an hour."

Johanna seemed as if she wanted the floor to open up beneath her, Morgan flared her nostrils and his mother's eyes turned that frigid gray that so perfectly matched her personality.

"Thirty minutes," the woman said. She cast a disparaging glance at Viv. "You will allow me to talk to my son? Alone?"

"Of course," Viv said, her mouth trembling only a tiny bit. "Nice to have met you." She immediately left the circle, pushing past Johanna to head into the bedroom.

Damien was about to go after her, but first he took his mother by the arm and propelled her toward the door. "Go. Right now."

She went, taking Morgan and Johanna with her. And Damien followed Viv, torn between fury and concern.

He had a moment's panic when he walked into the bedroom and found it empty, until he noticed the bathroom door was shut tight. He walked over to it, knocked once and tried the knob.

Locked.

"Viv? Are you okay?"

"Yes."

"Please come out."

"I'd rather be alone for a while."

"In the bathroom? Come on, you can talk to me."

The lock clicked, the knob turned, the door opened. He immediately saw the tears in her blue eyes and the way her lips trembled.

Damien pulled her to him, holding her tightly. "I'm so sorry. I did warn you Mother is a dinosaur, didn't I?"

"Dinosaur? Well, she certainly seems cold-blooded enough."

"I have no idea what the hell she's doing here."

"Rescuing you from the clutches of the evil, white-trash slut who's got her hooks in you?"

He took her chin and lifted her face so she had to meet his eye. "Don't ever say that again."

She took a deep breath, exhaled and said, "Sorry."

Damien knew she was a mess, and he wanted nothing more than to crawl into bed with her and spend the whole day there. But he had to deal with his family first, or they'd just come knocking at the door again.

"I want to take a bath," she told him. "While you go…"

"Yeah. I'll go." He brushed a kiss across her lips. "But I'll be back soon. And they won't."

"All right," she said, not smiling, her voice small, her mood strangely subdued. On any other day, Viv wouldn't have let his mother hurt her. She'd have defended herself, been the feisty woman he'd fallen head over heels for. Today, though, had been the wrong day for her to have to deal with this bullshit.

He reached up and brushed a tear from her eye with the tips of his fingers.

"I'm sorry I'm so weepy," she said. "I'm not used to being the damsel-in-distress type."

He slid his thumb across her jaw. "I'll be your white knight once in a while, if you'll let me."

Nodding, she curved her face into his hand and whispered, "That's a deal."

There was more to say. He wanted to tell her how he felt about her, even if he wasn't entirely sure what to say. He could no longer try to pretend he wasn't in love with her, but since he'd never said those words to anyone, or even known what to expect from the whole being-in-love experience, he had to consider it some more.

First, though, he had to get certain people out of his hair. Which was why he reluctantly got cleaned up, left Viv and went downstairs. Calling his mother on her cell, he told her to meet him in one of the restaurants, and was relieved to walk in and find her sitting there alone.

"Where's Johanna?"

"She and Morgan are shopping," his mother said, tilting her head to the side for him to kiss her cheek.

He silently declined that invitation and sat down opposite her. "What are you doing here?"

"Having brunch."

"I meant in Virginia. Why did you come?"

She offered him a conciliatory smile and reached across the table to pat his hand, a completely unnatural gesture for her. "I was worried. I saw the stories on the news."

"I'm fine. I wasn't hurt."

"Not physically."

"Meaning?"

"Well, your reputation certainly was." Her mask of pleasantness fell and she got to what he suspected was the real issue at hand. "Not to mention our stock."

"Excuse me?"

"'CEO of Black Star engaged in violent episode in one of his own hotels.'" She reached for her glass of sparkling water, her heavy gold-and-diamond bracelet clinking against the glass. "What in heaven's name were you thinking?"

"I was thinking that a drunk, dangerous son of a bitch was attacking the woman I love."

His mother dropped her glass. It slid from her fingertips, landing on the pristine white tablecloth, spilling water everywhere. "Don't be ridiculous," she hissed.

"Why is it ridiculous?"

"You can't love her. She's a complete nobody."

"She's everything to me." Although he hadn't entirely decided when he would ask her, or considered how she would respond, he added, "I intend to marry her."

Sylvia lurched in her chair as if slapped. "You can't do that. Damien. You must consider your family, the business—"

"You?"

"Yes." She drew a diamond-bedecked hand to her chest. "You're breaking my heart, wasting yourself on someone who's beneath you. She'd only marry you for the money."

"Like you did with Dad?"

Her hand dropped and his mother's chin went up. "Yes. As I did with your father. And we all know how well that turned out."

Surprised she'd actually admitted it, he shook his head, feeling sorry for his old man, who'd died so young, so un-happy. "Why didn't you just let him go? You made each other miserable."

She sneered. "Not always. We cared about each other once, as you imagine you do this girl. But let me assure you, it will never last." Her lips tightened and her eyes narrowed. "And not just because of her. I actually feel a little sorry for her. *You're* the one who will never be able to make a marriage based on love work."

Damien flinched. "Thanks for the vote of confidence."

She didn't relent, leaning across the table, almost shak-ing as she finally told him what she really thought of him.

"The truth is, Damien, if you care about that girl, you would end it now. Because you will end up breaking her heart. You are just like your father—a lying, deceitful, heartless bastard."

Damien folded his arms over his chest, wanting to in-stead throw his hands over his ears. He didn't give a damn what she said about him, but his father was off-limits. His parents' marriage hadn't been happy, but he'd never fully understood why. And Dad's awful, untimely death should certainly have wiped clean the slate of grievances his mother had carried.

"Don't say those things about him."

"Why not?" she said with a bitter laugh, this woman who'd given birth to him, who'd never shown him a moment's warmth in his entire life. "The apple didn't fall far from the tree. You're incapable of love and fidelity. You are doomed to destroy anyone foolish enough to care about you."

Damien was in shock. The bile directed at him from his own parent was so stunning, he could barely form a response. In the end, all he could mutter was "Why? Why do you hate me?"

She didn't flinch, didn't deny the accusation. No. Instead, her mouth opened then snapped shut, as if she was fighting some internal battle, trying to decide what to say.

Damien realized she was on the verge of admitting something important, something he suspected she'd been keeping from him for years. "Just say it, Mother," he insisted, suddenly weary and wanting this done. "For once in your life, be honest with me."

One more long moment. He couldn't be sure what she was going to do, until she opened her mouth and began to speak.

In the end, she gave him exactly what he'd asked for. The truth.

# 11

***

DAMIEN HAD SAID he would be gone for thirty minutes at most. It had now been two hours, and Viv was climbing the walls.

She'd showered and dressed, assuring herself everything was all right. Surely she wasn't the only woman in the world who'd made a bad first impression on her lover's family. There would be an opportunity to make up for it.

Or, hell, maybe there wouldn't, if his mother really was the cold fish she seemed to be. But still, she'd give it her best shot, at least, if he wanted her to.

He would want her to, wouldn't he?

True, he'd said from day one that he wasn't the love-and-relationship sort. But she'd let herself forget that in recent days. With everything they'd shared—his tenderness, his warmth, his desire for her—surely he didn't still consider her just a brief fling?

Or maybe he did. Maybe his mother convinced Damien that Viv was bad news—the worst thing that could ever happen to him—and he could be trying to figure out how to make a painless getaway.

Whenever she heard a noise, she feared it was a hotel employee coming up with a note demanding she vacate the premises.

"You're being ridiculous," she muttered to herself, trying to find something else to do.

She had food sent up. She called Lulu and filled her in on the whole story of what had happened. She even called her mom, certain her family would want hear her sounding healthy and much more relaxed than she'd been yesterday.

They'd talked about this weekend's anniversary party, which Viv had almost forgotten about in all the excitement. She was scheduled to take a train up to Pennsylvania tomorrow afternoon. Although she hadn't decided for sure, she was considering asking Damien to come with her.

But maybe that was too weird. Damn, she had no idea how to behave. He'd saved her life, he'd taken care of her… did that mean they were serious now? When not one word had been exchanged between them about what this relationship of theirs was all about, aside from sex?

She kept mulling it over until she heard the door to the penthouse opening. Her heart leaped and she sprang to her feet, spinning around, expecting to see Damien.

It wasn't him. Instead, a maid stood there, offering her a weak smile and then gesturing to someone in the hall.

Sylvia walked into the room, handed the woman some cash and then shut the door once the housekeeper had left. Dressed in a designer pantsuit, wearing more jewelry than was technically tasteful for a weekday afternoon, the woman didn't even pretend to smile or act social.

Viv watched her, bracing herself for what she suspected was going to be a very unpleasant scene.

There was a long, uncomfortable silence, and then Damien's mother said, "Are you at least going to ask me to sit down?"

"Of course. Where's Damien?"

"He's in a boardroom downstairs, meeting with the corporate lawyers I brought with me. They're trying to deal with this catastrophe."

"Catastrophe?"

"Yes," Sylvia said, sitting on the sofa. "You, dear." Sylvia peered at Viv's lip, which still had a small scab from the attack. "Tell me, do you take advantage of all the noble men who rescue you from abusive boyfriends?"

"I'm not sure what you've heard, but I was attacked by a former coworker. I had no personal relationship whatsoever with the man."

"The incident at the press conference a few weeks ago would say differently," Sylvia said with a shrug. "You had a lover's quarrel then, too, right? Isn't that why you slapped him?"

Viv couldn't believe how the story was being spun. "Absolutely not. I have no idea who's saying these things, but they are not true."

"Well, whatever the truth, you've certainly managed to drag my family into your sordid nightmare. Do you have any idea how much you've cost us?"

Viv's head was pounding now, a headache slamming into her from out of the blue. "No, I don't."

"Millions, dear," the woman said, the words ground out from between clenched teeth. "After the news about our CEO brawling in the corridor of his own hotel, our stock plummeted."

"Oh, my God," she groaned.

"I hear the sporting world is investigating this situation with the player. He's claiming he was traded because of a love triangle between the three of you."

"That's a lie."

"He's also threatening to sue, claiming Damien attacked him."

"Are you fucking kidding me?"

Whoops. Sylvia obviously didn't appreciate the language and she sneered in distaste.

"How can he possibly sue someone for stopping a crime?"

"Stranger things have happened. Damien could lose control of this team he cares so much about."

That got her attention. "Why?"

"My son doesn't own one hundred percent of the team, naturally. He has investors who aren't happy about this negative press right before the first season. They could push him out."

This couldn't be happening. How was it even possible?

"Bad press is deadly to people in his position, don't you understand? Of course, he'll survive it, we all will. He just has to come home to Florida, get to work and stop, er, putting himself in ugly situations with inappropriate people."

"Meaning me."

She didn't even try to soften the blow. "Yes. Meaning you." Sylvia rose to leave. "If there is an ounce of decency in you, if you care about Damien, do the right thing. Take your sordid drama and get away from him. Frankly, he can't afford it otherwise."

Viv didn't reply. What could she say? This woman—Damien's mother—had just made herself Viv's enemy. The relationship could never be fixed. Never. Which didn't bode well for Viv's future with her son.

After Sylvia left, Viv sat in the living room of the suite, pondering everything that had happened. First, she mourned for Damien—how sad to have grown up with such a vicious bitch for a mother. And then she began to wonder what she could do to make up for all the problems she'd brought into his life.

"Getting out of it might be a start," she whispered.

The idea pained her and brought hot tears to her eyes. She didn't want to lose him, didn't want to end what had become the most important relationship in her life. But she also didn't want to cost him so many things that meant so much to him. His family, the team, even his home in

Florida, which he'd never set foot in as long as Viv and his mother were enemies.

He'd fought for her, taken care of her, made her fall madly in love with him. How could she let him suffer for it?

Before she could decide what to do, her cell phone rang. She picked it up, not surprised to hear his voice.

"Hey, I'm sorry I haven't come back. I got tied up down here."

"Is everything all right?"

He sighed heavily into the phone. "Just a bunch of shit to deal with. My mother dragged half the attorneys in Florida up here with her."

"I'm so sorry, Damien," she whispered, pretending not to know what was going on.

"It's not your fault."

Yes. Yes, it was. At least partially.

"I'm not sure how long I'll be—are you all right alone?"

Viv considered, and suddenly realized she had to get out of here before he arrived. When he was with her, it was too easy to lose herself in his arms, to forget all the difficulties that came with being the pretty but inappropriate woman shacking up in a hotel penthouse with a billionaire.

Julia Roberts might have gotten her happily-ever-after. But she hadn't actually cost Richard Gere his company. And Richard Gere had eventually realized he *did* want love and a happily-ever-after. Damien might be wonderful, tender and supportive, but he hadn't said he loved her. He hadn't given any indication that he'd changed his stance on relationships.

"Listen," she said, "I talked to my mom again. I decided I'm going to catch a train home tonight instead of waiting until tomorrow." He fell silent. She waited, but when he didn't speak, she rushed on. "I mean, you knew I was going home for the anniversary party this weekend. I'll just go a day early to help out."

"Yes, I remember. I—I'd wondered if you wanted me to take you."

She clenched her eyes shut, hearing the shocking note of uncertainty in his voice. When had Damien ever been unsure of anything, before *she* came into his life and screwed things up for him?

Truthfully, she would have loved to bring him home to meet her family, to walk into the party on his arm. But that had been before. Now she realized it was impossible, that she'd merely be dragging him further and further from his real world.

"No, I don't think so." Swallowing, willing herself to be strong, she said, "Look, Damien, after what's happened, well, the truth is, I just want to be with my family. Away from here. Away from…everyone."

A brief hesitation. "From me?"

She didn't deny it. Her heart broke at the idea of hurting him, and she knew she was. But was hurting him emotionally worse than being the cause of his financial trauma? Or, worse, him losing the team, which he'd said was the one thing he'd done for himself in his entire adult life?

"Please try to understand."

He hissed. "Does this have anything to do with my mother?"

Well, his mother had certainly explained what was going on, but Viv wasn't leaving because of Sylvia. She was leaving because it was best for Damien.

Maybe they'd find their way back to each other. Maybe he'd survive this mess and not come out of it blaming her. But for now, the best thing she could do for him was to get out of the way, let the bad publicity die down. She had to hope sanity would prevail and Bruno Neeley would not be able to twist any of this around on Damien and cost him control of the Vanguard.

"No, it doesn't," she said.

"Because she's all kinds of messed up, Viv." He let out a long, low breath. "Some of the things she told me, well, you wouldn't believe it. I'm not sure I do."

"Are you all right?"

"Yeah. I will be, anyway." A harsh laugh. "Probably better than she expected me to."

She heard voices in the background, and then Damien asking for another minute. Things were obviously crazy down there.

"I should go," she said.

"Please don't," he said. "Viv, wait for me. I'll take you to Pennsylvania tomorrow."

She heard the longing in his voice, and the pain. And she almost changed her mind, almost gave in and decided to let the chips—and the companies, and the families—fall where they may.

But she just couldn't do it. Damien didn't deserve to be ruined because he'd had the misfortune of getting involved with a woman who invited, to use his mother's favorite word, *catastrophe.*

"No, Damien. I'm sorry."

"Give me a half hour. I'll come up and we'll talk. Just don't go *yet.*"

She sniffed, starting to cry, sensing her resolve weakening. "Please don't try to talk me out of it." She swallowed, not trying to hide her misery. "I'll miss my train. I have to go, Damien, and I'm begging you to let me."

After another pause, he finally sighed. When he spoke again, he sounded resigned. "When will you be home again?"

"I'm not sure." Her brain was scrambled. "I may request a leave of absence from work."

"You really need that?"

"I really do."

"I'll arrange it."

"Thank you."

He didn't respond for a long moment. The silence was thicker than the band of scar tissue she hoped would someday build around her heart, to seal in all the emotions she had for this wonderful man, and to keep out any painful ones that might threaten to invade in the future.

Finally, to her relief and her great sorrow, he gave in and stopped fighting her. "Promise me you'll take care of yourself."

"I will.

"In fact, let Jed take you to Union Station and put you on the train. Will you do that much for me?"

"All right. Thank you."

Another pause. An ocean of unspoken dreams, and she wondered how this could have become so damn complicated. Then again, she supposed, love always was.

She was about to hang up, wondering if they'd exchanged their last words, when he made a small noise. After it came six whispered words that shattered her heart completely.

"You said you wouldn't leave me."

And the call disconnected.

DAMIEN SPENT THE rest of the day, and much of the next, in a fog of denial. He wasn't just brooding over the incredible story his mother had told him when he'd demanded the truth about why she resented him, but also about Viv's shocking and sudden departure. He'd never been so blindsided in his life—and it had happened twice in the space of a few hours.

"Why did you go?" he mumbled Friday evening as he

poured himself a drink at the penthouse bar, smelling roses and her perfume.

At first, still stunned by the bad news hitting him left, right and center in terms of the business and the team, he'd misunderstood. He'd thought she was only leaving early, but she would expect him to show up the next day. But she hadn't invited him. And when he heard what she was actually saying—the way she made it sound as if she might not be returning—his confusion had deepened.

It had been all he could do not to race up to the penthouse to stop her, but there'd been the strangest tone in her voice. She'd sounded…brittle, hanging by a thin thread. Aware of how close she was to her parents, he could only assume that her second phone call with her mother had instilled a deep hunger in her for their comfort and support.

He had to take her at her word that she wanted time, even though he was incredibly impatient and wanted nothing more than to go up there and be with her. Hell, he hadn't had the chance to reveal to her the amazing truth he'd learned about his life.

Worse, he hadn't had the chance to tell her he loved her.

He did love her. He was certain of it now. Which was, in the end, why he'd been able to let her go.

Because he knew—down to his soul—that he would get her back.

Of all the things his mother might have expected when she'd spilled her guts, it probably hadn't been that her ugly story would have the opposite effect than she'd intended. That was, though, what had happened. When he'd sat down and examined the sad, tarnished truth, he'd realized she'd been wrong. So very wrong.

Damien *was* capable of love, of commitment, of a lifelong devotion. Just as his father had been.

They were both just one-woman men, however. That

lifelong devotion would only ever be directed at a single person.

His father had lost that person.

Damien didn't intend to. He'd witnessed his father endure a lifetime of regrets; Damien wouldn't make the same mistake by letting Viv get away.

"Are you actually going to drink that or are you just going to stare into the glass?" Sam asked, gesturing toward the Scotch Damien was holding in his hand.

Against his better judgment, he'd allowed Sam to come up for a drink that evening. They'd talked about the legal issues, and Sam had insisted that Damien stop worrying about any threats from Bruno Neeley. Especially now that the hotel security tapes had gone to the police, proving beyond any doubt that Bruno had brutally attacked Viv, and Damien had saved her.

Damien hadn't watched the tapes. He didn't suppose he'd ever be able to. Just the memory made his stomach churn.

Aside from the security footage, they had the video that clearly showed what had inspired the slap at the press conference. Sam was confident that Neeley's threats and bluster would go nowhere. There was no risk of Damien being sanctioned by the league, and almost no chance Damien's investors would try to wrest control of the franchise.

He might really have cared about all that a few months ago. Now, he could barely remember to thank his old friend for the hard work he was doing.

"Listen, I wasn't sure how to tell you this, but now that the business stuff's over with, there's something you should be aware of."

Damien swirled his glass, listening to the tinkle of the ice. "Yes?"

"It's about Johanna."

He eyed his friend from across the room. "Are you two…?"

"I'm not sure what's going to happen, but she did come to visit me earlier today."

"I was under the impression she'd left with my…with Sylvia and Morgan."

Sam shook his head. "She said they got to the airport, and your mother confessed to doing something that made her furious, so she left. She had to talk to someone, wasn't sure you'd be in the mood to see any of your family, and came to me."

Interesting. And perhaps a wise choice. He didn't blame Johanna for Sylvia's actions, but his sister had been right there, front row center, during the awful, embarrassing scene with Viv. Johanna could have refused to come crashing in on his life, but she'd always been a bit of a busybody and probably hadn't been able to resist.

"So what did she say?"

Sam studied his own drink, not meeting Damien's eye. "Were you aware that your mother came up here to confront Viv yesterday?"

"Christ, don't remind me. What a scene."

"No," Sam said carefully. "I mean later. While you were in meetings downstairs."

Lowering his glass and slamming it onto the coffee table, Damien stared at his friend. "Tell me that's not true."

"I'm afraid it is. She let it slip to Johanna, about how she'd taken care of the issue with the 'slut trying to sink her claws into you.'"

Damien swiped a hand through his hair, angry, frustrated, even a little hurt that Viv would let his mother drive a wedge between them. Then again, Viv had been in an incredibly vulnerable state. And Sylvia could be…a powerful force.

"I should have guessed," he snarled.

"Yeah, she's not the type to let her son's feelings stop her from doing what she wants."

He could have given Sam the whole story—what he'd learned that had so changed his perspective on his life and his parents—but he was too focused on Viv. "What did she say to her?"

"Johanna seemed to think your mother told Viv you were on the verge of losing the business and the team, and that you were facing lawsuits and financial ruin. All because of your 'disgraceful' relationship with her."

Shock and anger charged through him. Damien leaned forward and swept his glass completely off the table, sending it careening into a wall. It shattered, sending shards of glass, ice and Scotch all over the floor. But he ignored the mess, leaping to his feet and reaching for his phone.

"You okay?" Sam asked, his eyes wide as he surveyed the damage.

"I will be," Damien snapped. "I just have to get ahold of Jed and make some travel arrangements."

Sam put his glass down—carefully—and stood up, reaching for his coat. "So you're going after her?"

"Of course I'm going after her."

Sam nodded, visibly pleased.

"I thought you didn't approve."

"Any idiot can tell you're crazy about her, Damien. And, as you'll remember, considering I dragged your ass through Calculus…I am no idiot." He clapped Damien on the shoulder. "Good luck, my friend. Go get that girl."

Damien extended his hand to shake Sam's and nodded his thanks.

And then went to get that girl.

# 12

KEEPING BUSY WAS the best cure for heartache.

Viv had learned that over the past two days as she'd thrown herself into preparations for her parents' thirty-fifth anniversary party. She'd managed to avoid checking her phone every five minutes, or daydreaming about the man she wished would call. Instead, there were favors to wrap, baked goods to prepare, pictures to put into a slideshow.

Keeping busy was her parents' defense mechanism, too.

Arriving here Thursday evening and noticing their too-bright smiles as they'd greeted her at the train station had been incredibly hard. They'd tried to keep up a happy front, as had she, but the moment her father had moved in for a hug, they'd all started crying.

She'd spent a lot of time talking to them since then, explaining exactly what had happened. They'd of course watched the news coverage—God, everyone at the party would have. But her mom and dad, and her brothers, were the only ones who knew the actual details.

As expected, the men in her family wanted to travel to Virginia, bail Bruno Neeley out of jail and kick his ass straight to the Atlantic Ocean. Fortunately, she'd convinced them that justice would be served, and that Damien had punished him quite thoroughly.

Damien. Oh, his name had brought up even more questions. Her brothers were persistent. But her mom got them to shut up and leave Viv alone about him, as if realizing that the real cause of her sadness and melancholy was him, and not the attack.

"Hey, are you guys almost finished in here? People will be showing up soon," a voice said.

She looked down from the ladder, where she'd been hanging the last of the streamers, and smiled at her brother Joe, who had just walked in carrying another bunch of balloons.

Andy, who'd been working on setting up the computer equipment for the slideshow, stood up and walked over. "Yeah, I'm done. Viv?"

"Finished here," she said, starting to climb down.

Another brother, Neil, appeared from around the corner and grabbed her around the waist, swooping her down. Viv forced a laugh, hoping he hadn't noticed the way she'd stiffened. It would be a long while before she wouldn't react with a quick flash of fear when somebody grabbed her unexpectedly.

"Everything's great, V," Neil said, dropping an arm across her shoulders.

She stared around the banquet room with an assessing eye, agreeing with him. The place was no Black Star—the lodge was decorated more along the lines of hunting-cabin chic than international high fashion. Still, the room was prettily decorated with yellow-and-white streamers and balloons, and tons of fresh mums. A blown-up print of her parents' wedding portrait decorated the gift table, and the cake was an exquisite creation hand-delivered by her cousin, who owned a bakery.

"Guess we'd better put this stuff away and get ready," Joe said, taking the nearly empty streamer spool from her hand. He squeezed her fingers. "It's awesome to have you back, Viv."

She leaned up and kissed his cheek, hearing all the things he wasn't saying. Her brothers might have reacted with storm and bluster, but deep down, they were all worried about her. She knew they wanted nothing more than her happiness.

She hoped someday she'd be able to accommodate them. Happiness seemed a distant commodity right now. Maybe eventually things would get better. Maybe she'd stumble across a news story about Damien's business surging back, his team winning the championship. Perhaps he'd walk through a door as she was coming out, and they'd bump into each other, and start all over again. Fresh this time, no scandals, no stalkers, no risks.

It was worth dreaming about, anyway.

"Hey, Viv, you might want to get out here."

As her brother Aidan stuck his head into the ballroom, she replied, "Why?"

A strange grin appeared on his face. "You have a visitor."

Evan joined him, winking at her other brothers, who'd formed a semicircle behind her. "Yep. He's definitely here for you."

"Who is it?"

Aidan and Evan exchanged a glance, and then Evan said, "Uh, his name is D—"

"Damien?" she whispered, her heart thudding.

Aidan shook his head, and her spirits fell, her silly hopes dashed. "No, that wasn't it. I'm pretty sure it's Danny."

He still wore that goofy grin, and Viv frowned at him. "I'm not familiar with anybody named Danny."

"You know this guy. Or at least, he knows you." He walked over, grabbed her hand and dragged her with him.

"What is going on?" she demanded.

Ignoring her, Aidan continued to pull her forward until they reached the hotel lobby. Stopping, he put his hands on her shoulders and directed her toward the check-in desk.

A man stood there, facing away from her, talking to the clerk, who was smiling at him and batting her eyes.

Viv's heart skipped a beat. Despite the strange clothes—dark, crisp jeans rolled up at the ankle and a white undershirt with what seemed to be a pack of cigarettes rolled up in the sleeve—she recognized that tall form. The thick, dark hair was slicked back, and he had a black leather jacket slung over his shoulder, but oh, God, did that look like…

"Damien?" she whispered.

He must have heard that tiny sound. He turned around slowly. Their stares met and locked.

It was really him. He'd come for her.

He'd put her ahead of his family, his team, his business. His presence here proved that, despite everything he'd said from the day they'd met, Damien Black was definitely good at the relationship thing.

Maybe even the love thing.

Oh, God, did she hope that was so.

Joe gave her a nudge. "Go on."

She took a tentative step closer. There was nothing tentative about Damien's actions, though. He strode toward her, not stopping until he'd pulled her into his arms and caught her mouth in a hot, searing kiss.

She melted into him, stunned, filled with joy, kissing him again and again. Oblivious to everyone around them, including her brothers, who were probably hovering protectively behind her, she wrapped her arms around his neck, pressed hard against him, proclaiming with each hungry kiss how much she'd missed him.

She'd left for what she'd believed were the right reasons, but in this moment, she couldn't remember what those reasons were. When Damien held her, nothing else mattered except him. *Them.*

Finally, a throat-clearing sound intruded. She made herself end the kiss. But she stayed close to him, her arm around his waist, as his was around hers. Addressing her brothers, she said, "Everyone, I'd like you to meet…"

"Wait, lemme guess," Aidan said. His eyes alight with mischief, he stuck out his hand. "Danny Zuko, I presume?"

The comment reminded Viv of Damien's strange outfit. Stepping away, she studied him, top to bottom, and then started to giggle. Because she suspected Aidan was right.

Seeing Damien Black, international businessman, suave billionaire, dressed up as a 50s greaser in a hotel where everyone else was wearing normal clothing, tickled every funny bone in Viv's body. She began to giggle, then to laugh merrily.

"I was under the impression this was a costume party," Damien said, his jaw tight. He stared at her. "Where's the black leather and the chick fro?"

"I said my idiot brother *wanted* us to have a *Grease-*themed costume party. Not that we were stupid enough to actually *do* it." She reached up and slid her fingers through his slicked hair. "Though I must admit, the duck's-ass do suits you."

Others in the lobby—the staff, a few early guests and her obnoxious siblings—all started to chuckle. And within a second, Damien did, too. That handsome face softened, his devastating dimple appeared and he couldn't contain a smile.

Drawing her into his arms again, he murmured, "If you ever tell anyone about this…"

"Are you kidding? The photographer's been snapping away for the last five minutes."

He quickly scanned the lobby, trying to spy said cameraman. Viv took pity and said, "Gotcha."

"You're a vixen, Vivienne Callahan."

"So I've been told."

They kissed again, but this time, when they parted, Damien said, "Can we go somewhere to talk for a few minutes?"

She glanced at her brothers, all of whom wore approving expressions. She imagined they liked a guy who'd make himself look like an idiot for the woman he loved—their sister.

At least…she hoped that's what he was doing here. Coming to admit he loved her. If he did, well, she suspected she could get over all the other issues and just let him.

Promising the others they'd be at the party soon, she led Damien upstairs to the room she'd booked for the night. With its two uncomfortably hard double beds, it was as drastic a departure from the penthouse as was possible.

"I can't believe you came."

He cupped her face in his hands. "I can't believe you left."

Licking her lips, she replied, "I had to."

"For my sake?" He shook his head and tsked. "Do me a favor, would you? Don't ever run away because you think you need to protect me. And God, don't ever do it because Sylvia taunts you into it."

"She didn't taunt me," Viv explained. "I didn't run because I was afraid or because of her name-calling."

He stiffened at that, but she didn't pause to explain.

"She just pointed out how different we are."

"No, we're exactly the same," he insisted. "Bad and

wicked, maybe. But still two people who are perfect together."

"When she mentioned the difficulties you were having because of me, I couldn't stand it. The last thing I would ever want is to cause you problems with your family, your business...the team."

He scraped his lips across hers again. "The only difficulties you cause me are a perpetual hard-on and this strange ache in my chest that could be heartburn or could be crazy, once-in-a-lifetime love."

Viv blinked rapidly, trying to make sure she'd heard correctly. "What?"

"I love you," he said, his voice unwavering, as if reading her mind and seeing what she most wanted to hear. "I really, truly, with all my heart, love you, Viv."

The world grew brighter, bells began to chime in her head. Most importantly, the fear and sadness she'd been carrying around for a week fell away in a rush, leaving her feeling clean, whole and new.

"I didn't believe I was capable of love or commitment."

"I remember," she said. "So what happened?"

"I was wrong," he said simply.

Then he fell silent, waiting for her. Not for a second did she consider denying him. She merely slid her fingers into his hair to pull him close and whispered, "I love you, too, Damien. I have for a lot longer than I've been willing to admit, even to myself. Walking away from you was, believe it or not, an act of that love...even if it was the most painful decision of my life."

"I know," he said. "And I forgive you for it, even if you did leave me a miserable mess for two days."

They kissed again, slowly this time, with warm emotion. Viv put all her love and joy into the kiss, and tasted all the same on his lips. He stroked her body, tenderly and passionately, making her feel cherished and desired.

They embraced for several long moments and then she murmured, "About your family. I will try to get along with them."

"Not necessary," he said with a shrug. "At least, as far as Sylvia goes. She hates your guts."

Viv flinched.

"But that's okay, because she hates mine, too."

She wasn't shocked at the words, but tried to say the right thing. "I'm sure that's not true."

"Oh, yeah, it definitely is."

Damien didn't sound at all dismayed by that. In fact, he seemed almost cheerful.

"What do you mean?"

"I mean, I finally got her to admit how she really feels about me. And why. Are you ready for this?"

She was ready for anything, as long as he was with her.

"She's not my mother."

Viv gasped. Okay, she *hadn't* been ready for that.

Damien held her tightly as she swayed on her feet. "Shocker, right? It turns out my biological mother was my dad's college sweetheart. Dad, being a typical dumb twenty-one-year-old dude, got drunk and cheated on her one night at a party."

Not unusual. Still sad, though.

"She found out, dumped him and disappeared. Nine months later, after my Dad was with Sylvia, he got a letter."

"From your mother?" she asked, fascinated by the story.

He shook his head. His light tone darkened, as did his gleaming eyes. "No, from her roommate. Apparently my real mother was from a pretty conservative family. When they found out she was pregnant, they cut her off. She'd moved to Atlanta and was living with a friend when I was born."

"You were a love child," Viv murmured.

"Sylvia preferred to use the word *bastard*."

"Yeah. She would." *The bitch.* "Why didn't your father marry your mother when he found out about you? If he really loved her, I mean?"

"The roommate wrote the letter to tell Dad about me... and to let him know my mother was dead."

He swallowed visibly. Finding out he had a different mother, one who'd been dead for decades, must have been devastating. Again, Viv mentally kicked herself for running away the other day. She should have been there, waiting for him in the penthouse, ready to share his grief over the truth of his parentage. Instead, she'd left him alone to deal with all of this, as well as her own defection.

Stupid. How could she have been so stupid?

Apparently not noticing her mental self-flagellation, he continued. "She'd had no insurance, no decent prenatal care. There were complications that weren't diagnosed until she was in labor, and they couldn't save her."

Tears welled in her eyes for this latest loss, among the many Damien had endured in his life. Viv cupped his cheek and stroked his face. "I'm so sorry."

He kissed her palm. "So am I. I wish I'd known her. Sylvia had nothing nice to say, but considering my father loved her until the day he died, she must have been pretty special."

His father had been in love all his life with a girl he'd wronged. Perhaps that's why he'd stayed with a cold, uncaring wife. Maybe he'd been punishing himself all along.

"When Sylvia found out, she told Dad she'd marry him and raise me as her own, be a mother to me. But only if he agreed never to reveal to me that she wasn't my mother."

"I can't believe he would say yes to that."

"He didn't. He got her to agree that he'd explain everything me when I was an adult. I wonder if that's a conversation we might have had the weekend of my graduation."

The one his father had tried so hard to get home to.

Tears were spilling from Viv's eyes now as she imagined the years he must have spent, wondering why he'd had to lose his father, and his grandfather, and be left with a parent who didn't seem to give a damn about him.

"I'm so very sorry, Damien."

"Me, too," he said, holding her hands. "But honestly? Sylvia did me a favor. I'd been worried, you see."

"About?"

"About whether I could really ever love anyone. I had never witnessed any evidence of love growing up. Now I understand why—my father was in love with someone else, and his wife could never forgive him for it." He shrugged. "There's nothing wrong with me at all."

"God, of course there isn't!" She slid her arms around his waist holding him tight. "You are one of the most loving people I have ever met."

She should know. She'd been the recipient of that love even before she recognized that it existed.

"So you'll come back with me? Everything's going to be fine with the business, and the team," he said. "I have the best lawyers in the country—Neeley won't get anywhere with his threats, and he's going to be behind bars for many years."

"To hell with him, with everything else," she said, smiling up at him. "Yes, I will most definitely come back with you."

He hesitated, drawing a deep breath, and then asked, "As my fiancée?"

Viv's heart skidded around and her mouth fell open.

Before she could respond, Damien had reached into the pocket of his stiff jeans and pulled out a small velvet box. Flipping it open with his thumb, he revealed an amazing, beautiful ring. An enormous sapphire was at the center, surrounded by smaller sapphires and diamonds.

"We can exchange it for a more traditional one, if you'd prefer." He sounded hoarse. "But diamonds are icy. You are warm and vibrant, colorful. And this reminded me of your eyes."

She held out her hand, unable to speak, watching him slide the ring onto her finger. It fit perfectly—in fact, it was perfect in every way. Exactly what she would have chosen for herself.

"So?" he asked. "Will you marry me?"

"Oh, yes, my love," she whispered, kissing him softly. "I'll definitely marry you."

Then, knowing he loved his vixen, she had to teasingly add, "But only if you wear that costume downstairs to the party. I want my parents to meet you dressed just like that."

He grinned. "Can we tease up your hair and put you in a pair of black leather pants?"

"I'm fresh out."

"Well," he said, reaching for the waistband of her skirt, "you'll just have to put on something else to make it up to me."

"What would that be?"

He unzipped the skirt and pushed it down, stroking her hips as he leaned close and whispered, "Me."

\* \* \* \* \*

*Gage Ringer: Powerful, fierce, unforgettable...
and temporarily sidelined from his MMA career
with an injury. Back home, he has one month
to win over the woman he could never forget...*

*Read on for* New York Times *bestselling author
Lori Foster's*

*HARD KNOCKS*

*The stunning prequel novella for her Ultimate series!*

# HARD KNOCKS

## Lori Foster

# *CHAPTER ONE*

G<small>AGE</small> R<small>INGER</small>, <small>BETTER</small> known as Savage in the fight world, prowled the interior of the rec center. His stride was long, his thoughts dark, but he kept his expression enigmatic to hide his turmoil from onlookers. He didn't want to be here tonight. He'd rather be home, suffering his bad mood alone instead of covering up his regret, forced to pretend it didn't matter. His disappointment was private, damn it, and he didn't want to advertise it to the world. Shit happened.

It had happened to him. So what?

Life went on. There would be other fights, other opportunities. Only a real wimp would sit around bellyaching about what could have been, but wasn't. Not him. Not publicly anyway.

Tonight the rec center would overflow with bodies of all shapes, sizes and ages—all there for different reasons.

Cannon Coulter owned the rec center. It was a part of Cannon's life, a philanthropic endeavor that, no matter how big Cannon got, how well-known he became in the Supreme Battle Championship fight world, would always be important to him.

Armie Jacobson, another fighter who helped run the rec center whenever Cannon had to travel for his career, had planned a long night of fun. Yay.

Not.

At least, not for Gage.

Earlier they'd had a party for the kids too young to stick

around and watch the pay-per-view event that night on the big screen. One of Cannon's sponsors had contributed the massive wall-mounted TV to the center.

So that they wouldn't feel left out, Armie had organized fun activities for the younger kids that had included food, games and some one-on-one play with the fighters who frequented the rec center, using it as a gym.

With the kiddie party now wrapping up, the more mature crowd would soon arrive, mixing and mingling while watching the fights.

The rec center had originally opened with very little. Cannon and some of his friends had volunteered to work with at-risk youths from the neighborhood to give them an outlet. They started with a speed bag, a heavy bag, some mats and a whole lot of donated time and energy.

But as Cannon's success had grown, so too had the rec center. Not only had Cannon added improvements, but his sponsors loved to donate anything and everything that carried their brand so that now the size of the place had doubled, and they had all the equipment they needed to accommodate not only a training camp for skilled fighters, but also dozens of boys, and a smattering of girls, of all ages.

Gage heard a distinctly female laugh and his gaze automatically went to Harper Gates.

So she had arrived.

Without meaning to, he inhaled more deeply, drawing in a calming breath. Yeah, Harper did that to him.

He watched as Harper assisted Armie in opening up folding chairs around the mats. Together they filled up every available speck of floor space. She stepped around a few of the youths who were still underfoot, racing around, wrestling—basically letting off steam with adult supervision, which beat the hell out of them hanging on street corners, susceptible to the thugs who crawled out of the shadows as the sun went down.

Gage caught one boy as he recklessly raced past. He twirled him into the air, then held him upside down. The kid squealed with laughter, making Gage smile, too.

"You're moving awfully fast," Gage told him.

Bragging, the boy said, "I'm the fastest one here!"

"And humble, too," he teased.

The boy blinked big owl eyes at him while grinning, showing two missing teeth. He was six years old, rambunctious and considered the rec center a second home.

"I need you to take it easy, okay? If you're going to roughhouse, keep it on the mats."

"'Kay, Savage."

Gage glanced at a clock on the wall. The younger crowd would be heading out in a few more minutes. Still holding the boy suspended, he asked, "Who's taking you home?"

"My gram is comin' in her van and takin' all of us."

"Good." Luckily the grandmother was reliable, because the parents sure as hell weren't. And no way did Gage want the boys walking home. The rec center was in a decent enough area, but where the boys lived...

The kid laughed as Gage flipped him around and put him back on his feet.

Like a shot, he took off toward Miles, who was already surrounded by boys as he rounded them up.

Grandma would arrive soon. She'd probably appreciate how the kids had been exercised in the guise of play, schooled on control and manners, and fed. The boys always ate like they were starving. But then, Gage remembered being that age and how he could pack it away.

Briefly, his gaze met Harper's, and damn it, he felt it, that charged connection that had always existed between them. She wore a silly smile that, despite his dark mood, made him want to smile, too.

But as they looked at each other, she deliberately wiped the smile away. Pretending she hadn't seen him at all, she got back to work.

Gage grunted. He had no idea what had gotten into her, but in his current frame of mind, better that he just let it go for now.

Very shortly, the most dedicated fight fans would arrive to catch the prelims. By the time the main card started, drawing a few high school seniors, some interested neighbors and the other fighters, there'd be bodies in all the chairs, sprawled on the mats and leaning up against the concrete walls. Equipment had been either moved out of the way or stored for the night.

This was a big deal. One of their own was competing tonight.

The high school guys were looking forward to a special night where they'd get to mingle more with their favorite fighters.

A dozen or more women were anxious to do some mingling of their own.

Armie, the twisted hedonist, had been judicious in handing out the invites: some very hot babes would be in attendance, women who'd already proven their "devotion" to fighters.

Gage couldn't have cared less. If he hadn't been fucked by karma, he'd be there in Japan, too. He didn't feel like celebrating, damn it. He didn't want to expose anyone to his nasty disposition.

The very last thing he wanted was a female groupie invading his space.

Actually, he'd been so caught up in training, he'd been away from female company for some time now. You'd think he'd be anxious to let off steam in the best way known to man.

But whenever he thought of sex…

Harper laughed again, and Gage set his back teeth even while sneaking a peek to see what she found so funny. Armie said something to her, and she swatted at him while smiling widely.

Gage did a little more teeth grinding.

Like most of the fighters, Armie understood Gage's pre-occupation and ignored him. Now if he would just ignore Harper, too, Gage could get back to brooding.

Instead, he was busy thinking of female company—but there was only one woman who crowded his brain.

And for some reason, she seemed irritated with him.

His dark scowl made the stitches above his eye pull and pinch, drawing his thoughts from one problem and back to another.

One stupid mistake, one botched move during practice, and he had an injury that got him kicked out of the competition.

Damn it all, he didn't want to be here tonight, but if he hadn't shown up, he'd have looked sad and pathetic.

"Stop pacing," Harper said from right behind him. "It makes you look sad and pathetic."

Hearing his concern thrown right back at him, Gage's left eye twitched. Leave it to Harper to know his exact thoughts and to use them as provocation. But then, he had to admit, she provoked him so well.…

He'd missed the fights. And he'd missed Harper.

The only upside to heading home had been getting to see her. But since his return three days ago, she'd given him his space—space he wanted, damn it, just maybe not from her. At the very least, she could have *wanted* to see him, instead of treating him like one of the guys.

Relishing a new focus, Gage paused, planning what he'd say to her.

She didn't give him a chance to say anything.

With a hard whop to his ass, she walked on by and sashayed down the hall to the back.

Gage stood there, the sting of her swat ramping up his temper…and something else. Staring after her, he suffered the sizzling clench of emotions that always surfaced whenever Harper got close—which, since he'd returned home with his injury, had been rare.

He'd known her for years—grown up with her, in fact—and had always enjoyed her. Her wit. Her conversation. Her knowledge of mixed martial arts competition.

Her cute bod.

They'd recently taken their friendship to the next level, dating, spending more private time together. He'd enjoyed the closeness…

But he'd yet to enjoy her naked.

Time and circumstances had conspired against him on that one. Just when things had been heating up with Harper, just when it seemed she was ready to say "yes" instead of "not yet," he'd been offered the fight on the main card in Japan. He'd fought with the SBC before. He wasn't a newbie.

But always in the prelims, never on the highly publicized, more important main card. Never with such an anticipated event.

In a whirlwind, he'd gone off to a different camp to train with Cannon, getting swept up in the publicity and interviews that went with a main card bout…

Until, just a few lousy days ago—*so fucking close*—he'd miscalculated in practice and sustained a deep cut from his sparring partner's elbow.

A cut very near his eye that required fifteen stitches.

It made him sick to think of how quickly he'd been pronounced medically ineligible. Before he'd even caught his breath the SBC had picked his replacement.

That lucky bastard was now in Japan, ready to compete.

And Gage was left in Ohio. Instead of fighting for recognition, he fought his demons—*and got tweaked by Harper.*

He went after her, calling down the empty hallway, "I am not pathetic."

From inside a storage room, he heard her loud "Ha!" of disagreement.

Needing a target for his turbulent emotions and deciding Harper was perfect—in every way—he strode into the room.

And promptly froze.

Bent at the waist, Harper had her sexy ass in the air while she pulled disposable cups off the bottom shelf.

His heart skipped a beat. Damn, she was so hot. Except for bad timing, he'd be more familiar with that particular, *very perfect* part of her anatomy.

Not sleeping with her was yet another missed opportunity, one that plagued him more now that he didn't have the draining distraction of an upcoming fight. His heart started punching a little too hard. Anger at his circumstances began to morph into red-hot lust as he considered the possibilities.

But then, whenever he thought of Harper, lust was the least confusing of his emotions.

Now that he was home, he'd hoped to pick up where they'd left off. Only Harper had antagonism mixed with her other more welcoming signals, so he had to proceed with caution.

"What are you doing?" he asked, because that sounded better than saying, *"Damn, girl, I love your ass."*

Still in that tantalizing position, she peeked back at him, her brown hair swinging around her face, her enormous blue eyes direct. With her head down that way, blood rushed to her face and made her freckles more noticeable.

There were nights he couldn't sleep for wondering about all the places she might have freckles. Many times he'd imagined stripping those clothes off her, piece by piece, so he could investigate all her more secret places.

Like him, she was a conservative dresser. Despite working at a secondhand boutique clothing store she always looked casual and comfortable. Her jeans and T-shirts gave an overview of sweet curves, but he'd love to get lost in the details if he could ever get her naked.

She straightened with two big boxes in her hands. "Armie had small juice containers out for the kids, but of course adults are going to want something different to drink. Same with the snacks. So I'm changing up the food spread."

Due to her schedule at the boutique, Harper had been unable to attend the party with the youngsters, but she'd sent in snacks ahead of time. She had a knack for creating healthy treats that looked fun and got gobbled up. Some of the options had looked really tasty, but if she wanted to switch them out, he could at least help her.

She glanced at the slim watch on her wrist. "Lots to do before everyone shows up for the prelims."

Since pride kept him at the rec center anyway...

"What can I do to help?"

Her smile came slow and teasing. "All kinds of things, actually. Or—wait—do you mean with the setup?"

"I… What?" Was that a come-on? He couldn't tell for sure—nothing new with Harper. Clearly she'd been pissed at him about something, but now, at her provocative words, his dick perked up with hopes of reconciliation.

Snickering, she walked up to him, gave him a hip bump, then headed out of the room. "Come on, big boy. You can give me a hand with the folding tables."

As confusion warred with disgruntlement, he trailed after her. "All right, fine." Then he thought to remind her, "But I'm not pathetic."

Turning to face him, she walked backward. "Hit home with that one, did I?"

"No." *Yes.*

"I can help you to fake it if you want."

Despite the offhand way she tossed that out, it still sounded suggestive as hell. "Watch where you're going." Gage reached out, caught her arm and kept her from tripping over the edge of a mat.

Now that he had ahold of her, he decided to hang on. Where his fingers wrapped around her arm just above her elbow, she was soft and sleek and he couldn't stop his thumb from playing over the warm silk of her skin.

"Thanks," she said a little breathlessly, facing forward again and treading on.

"So." Though he walked right beside her, Gage couldn't resist leaning back a bit to watch the sway of her behind. "How would we fake it? Not that I need to fake shit, but you've got me curious."

Laughing, she leaned into him, smiled up at him, and damn it, he wanted her. *Bad.*

Always had, probably always would.

He'd had his chance before he left for the new camp. Even with the demands of training, he'd wanted her while he was away. Now he was back and the wanting boiled over.

Her head perfectly reached his shoulder. He stood six-three, nine inches taller than her, and he outweighed her by more than a hundred pounds.

But for a slim woman, she packed one hell of a punch.

"Harper," he chided. She was the only person he knew who seemed to take maniacal delight in tormenting him.

Rolling her eyes, she said, "You are such a grouch when you're being pathetic." She stepped away to arrange the cups on a long table placed up against the wall. "Everyone feels terrible for you. And why not? We all know you'd have won. Maybe even with a first-round knockout."

Did she really believe that? Or was she just placating him? "Darvey isn't a slouch." Gage wouldn't want an easy fight. What the hell would that prove?

"No," she agreed, "but you'd have creamed him."

"That was the plan." So many times he'd played it out in his head, the strategy he'd use, how he'd push the fight, how his cardio would carry him through if it went all three rounds. Darvey wasn't known for his gas tank. He liked to use submissions, manipulating an arm or leg joint to get his opponent to tap before something broke. His plan was always to end things fast. But Gage knew how to defend against submissions, how to make it *his* fight, not anyone else's.

"Sucks that you have to sit this one out," Harper continued. "But since you do, I know you'd rather be brimming with confidence, instead of moping around like a sad sack."

Folding his arms over his chest, he glared down at her. "I don't mope."

She eyed his biceps, inhaled slowly, blew the breath out even slower.

"Harper."

Brows raised, she brought those big blue eyes up to focus on his face. "What?"

He dropped his arms and stepped closer, crowding her, getting near enough to breathe in her unique scent. "How do you figure we'd fake things?"

"Oh, yeah." She glanced to one side, then the other. "People are looking at us."

"Yeah?" Currently the only people in the gym were the guys helping to set it up for the party. Armie, Stack, Denver, a few others. "So?"

"So…" She licked her lips, hesitated only a second, then came up against him. In a slow tease, her hands crawled up and over his chest. Fitted against him, she went on tiptoe, giving him a full-body rub.

Without even thinking about it, Gage caught her waist, keeping her right there. Confusion at this abrupt turnaround of hers stopped him from doing what came naturally.

Didn't bother her, though.

With her gaze locked on his, she curled her hands around his neck, drew him down to meet her halfway and put that soft, lush, taunting mouth against his.

Hell, yeah.

Her lips played over his, teasing, again provoking. They shared breath. Her thighs shifted against his. Her cool fingers moved over his nape and then into his hair. The kiss stayed light, slow and excruciating.

Until he took over.

Tilting his head, he fit his mouth more firmly against her, nudged her lips apart, licked in, deeper, hotter…

"Get a room already."

Gasping at the interruption, Harper pulled away. Embarrassed, she pressed her face against his chest before rearing back and glaring at Armie.

Gage just watched her. He didn't care what his dipshit friends said.

But he'd love to know what Harper was up to.

"Don't give me that look," Armie told her. "We have high school boys coming over tonight."

"The biggest kids are already here!"

"Now, I know you don't mean me," Armie continued, always up for ribbing her. "You're the one having a tantrum."

Gage stood there while they fussed at each other. Harper was like that with all the guys. She helped out, gave as good as she got, and treated them all like pesky brothers that she both adored and endured.

Except for Gage.

From the get-go she'd been different with him. Not shy, because seriously, Harper didn't have a shy bone in her hot little body. But maybe more demonstrative. Or rather, demonstrative in a different way.

He didn't think she'd smack any of the other fighters on the ass.

But he wasn't stupid. Encouraged or not, he knew guys were guys, period. They'd tease her, respect her boundaries, but every damn one of them had probably thought about sleeping with her.

For damn sure, they'd all pictured her naked.

Those vivid visuals were part of a man's basic DNA. Attractive babe equaled fantasies. While Harper hustled around the rec center helping out in a dozen different ways, she'd probably been mentally stripped a million times.

Hell, even while she sniped back and forth with Armie, Gage pictured her buck-ass, wondering how it'd feel to kiss her like that again, but without the barrier of clothes in the way.

"You need a swift kick to your butt," Harper declared.

"From you?" Armie laughed.

Fighting a smile, she said, "Don't think I won't."

"You wanna go?" Armie egged her on, using his fingertips to call her forward. "C'mon then, little girl. Let's see what you've got."

For a second there, Harper looked ready to accept, so Gage interceded. "Children, play nice."

"Armie doesn't like *nice*." She curled her lip in a taunt. "He likes *kinky*."

In reply, Armie took a bow.

True enough, if ever a man liked a little freak thrown into the mix, it was Armie. He'd once been dropped off by a motorcycle-driving chick dressed in leather pants and a low-cut vest, her arms circled with snake tattoos. She'd sported more piercings than Gage could count—a dozen or so in her ears, a few in her eyebrows, lip, nose. The whole day, Armie had limped around as if the woman had ridden him raw. He'd also smiled a lot, proof that whatever had happened, he'd enjoyed himself.

Unlike Gage, Armie saw no reason to skip sex, ever. Not even prior to a fight. The only women he turned down were the ones, as Harper had said, that were too nice.

"Come on." She took Gage's hand and started dragging him toward the back.

"Hey, don't leave my storage closet smelling like sex," Armie called after them. "If you're going to knock boots, take it elsewhere!"

Harper flipped him the bird, but she was grinning. "He is so outrageous."

"That's the pot calling the kettle black." Just where was she leading him?

"Eh, maybe." She winked up at him. "But I just act outrageous. I have a feeling it's a mind-set for Armie."

Ignoring what Armie had said, she dragged him back into the storage closet—and shut the door.

Gage stood there watching her, thinking things he shouldn't and getting hard because of it. Heart beating slow and steady, he asked, "Now what?"

## CHAPTER TWO

COULD A MAN look sexier? No. Dumb question. Harper sighed. At twenty-five, she knew what she wanted. Whether or not she could have it, that was the big question.

Or rather, could she have it for the long haul.

"Is that for me?" She nodded at the rise in his jeans.

Without changing expressions, Gage nodded. "Yeah." And then, "After that kiss, you have to ask?"

Sweet. "So you like my plan?"

Looking far too serious, his mellow brown gaze held hers. "If your plan is to turn me on, yeah, I like it."

As part of her plan, she forced a laugh. She had to keep Gage from knowing how badly he'd broken her heart.

Talk about pathetic.

Gage was two years older, which, while they'd been in school, had made him the older, awesome star athlete and popular guy that *every* girl had wanted. Her included.

Back then, she hadn't stood a chance. He'd dated prom queen, cheerleader, class president material, not collect-for-the-homeless Goody Two-shoes material.

So she'd wrapped herself in her pride and whenever they'd crossed paths, she'd treated him like any other jock—meaning she'd been nice but uninterested.

And damn him, he'd been A-OK with that, the big jerk.

They lived in the same small neighborhood. Not like Warfield, Ohio, left a lot of room for anonymity. Everyone knew everyone, especially those who went through school together.

It wasn't until they both started hanging out in the rec center, her to help out, him to train, that he seemed to really tune in to her. Course, she hadn't been real subtle with him, so not noticing her would have required a deliberate snub.

She was comfortable with guys. Actually, she was comfortable with everyone. Her best friend claimed she was one of those nauseatingly happy people who enjoyed life a little too much. But whatever. She believed in making the most of every day.

That is, when big, badass alpha fighters cooperated.

Unfortunately, Gage didn't. Not always.

Not that long ago they'd been dating, getting closer. Getting steamier.

She'd fallen a little more in love with him every day.

She adored his quiet confidence. His motivation and dedication. The gentle way he treated the little kids who hung out at the center, how he coached the older boys who revered him, and the respect he got—and gave—to other fighters.

She especially loved his big, rock-solid body. Just thinking about it made her all twitchy in private places.

Things had seemed to be progressing nicely.

Until the SBC called and put him on the main card for freaking other-side-of-the-world Japan, and boom, just like that, it seemed she'd lost all the ground she'd gained. Three months before the fight, Gage had packed up and moved to Harmony, Kentucky, to join Cannon in a different camp where he could hone his considerable skills with a fresh set of experienced fighters.

He'd kissed her goodbye first, but making any promises about what to expect on his return hadn't been on his mind. Nope. He'd been one big obsessed puppy, his thoughts only on fighting and winning.

Maybe he'd figured that once he won, his life would get too busy for her to fit into it.

And maybe, she reminded herself, she was jumping ahead at Mach speed. They hadn't even slept together yet.

But that was something she could remedy.

Never, not in a million years, would she have wished the injury on him. He'd fought, and won, for the SBC before. But never on the main card. Knowing what that big chance had meant to him, she'd been devastated on his behalf.

Yet she'd also still been hurt that the entire time he was gone, he hadn't called. For all she knew, he hadn't even thought about her. Ignoring him had seemed her best bet—until she realized she couldn't. Loving him made that impossible.

And so she decided not to waste an opportunity.

Gage leaned against the wall. "I give up. How long are you going to stand there staring at me?"

"I like looking at you, that's all." She turned her back on him before she blew the game too soon. "You're terrific eye candy."

He went so silent, she could hear the ticking of the wall clock. "What are you up to, Harper?"

"No good." She grinned back at him. "Definitely, one hundred percent no good." Locating napkins and paper plates on the shelf, she put them into an empty box. Searching more shelves, she asked, "Do you see the coffeemaker anywhere?"

His big hands settled on her waist. "Forget the coffeemaker," he murmured from right behind her. Leaning down, he kissed the side of her neck. "Let's talk about these no-good plans of yours."

Wow, oh, wow. She could feel his erection against her

tush and it was so tantalizing she had to fight not to wiggle. "Okay."

He nuzzled against her, his soft breath in her ear, his hands sliding around to her belly. Such incredibly large hands that covered so much ground. The thumb of his right hand nudged the bottom of her breast. The pinkie on his left hovered just over the fly of her jeans.

Temptation was a terrible thing, eating away at her common sense and obscuring the larger purpose.

He opened his mouth on her throat and she felt his tongue on her skin. When he took a soft, wet love bite, she forgot she had knees. Her legs just sort of went rubbery.

To keep her upright, he hugged her tighter and rested his chin on top of her head. "Tell me what we're doing, honey."

Took her a second to catch her breath. "You don't know?" She twisted to face him, one hand knotted in his shirt to hang on, just in case. "Because, seriously, Gage, you seemed to know exactly what you were doing."

His smile went lazy—and more relaxed than it had been since he'd found out he wouldn't fight. He slipped a hand into her hair, cupping the back of her head, rubbing a little. "I know I was making myself horny. I know you were liking it. I'm just not sure why we're doing this here and now."

"Oh." She dropped against him so she could suck in some air. "Yeah." Unfortunately, every breath filled her head with the hot scent of his powerful body. "Mmm, you are so delicious."

A strained laugh rumbled in his chest. "Harper."

"Right." To give herself some room to think, she stepped back from him. So that he'd know this wasn't just about sex, she admitted, "I care about you. You know that."

Those gorgeous brown eyes narrowed on her face. "Ditto."

That kicked her heart into such a fast rhythm, she almost gasped. *He cared about her.* "And I know you, Gage. Probably better than you think."

His smile softened, and he said all dark and sensuous-like, "Ditto again, honey."

Damn the man, even his murmurs made her hot and bothered. "Yeah, so…" Collecting her thoughts wasn't easy, not with a big hunk of sexiness right there in front of her, within reach, ready and waiting. "I know you're hammered over the lost opportunity."

"The opportunity to have sex with you?"

Her jaw loosened at his misunderstanding. "No, I meant…" Hoping sex was still an option, she cleared her throat. "I meant the fight."

"Yeah." He stared at her mouth. "That, too."

Had he somehow moved closer without her knowing it? Her back now rested against the shelving and Gage stood only an inch from touching her. "So…" she said again. "It's understandable that you'd be stomping around in a bad mood."

He chided her with a shake of his head. "I was not stomp-ing."

"Close enough." Damn it, now she couldn't stop staring at his mouth. "But I know you want to blow it off like you're not that upset."

"I'm not *upset*." He scoffed over her word choice. "I'm disappointed. A little pissed off." His feet touched hers. "I take it you have something in mind?"

She shifted without thinking about it, and suddenly he moved one foot between hers. His hard muscled thigh pressed at the apex of her legs and every thought she had, every bit of her concentration, went to where they touched.

Casual as you please, he braced a hand on the shelf be-side her head.

Gage was so good at this, at stalking an opponent, at gaining the advantage before anyone realized his intent.

But she wasn't his opponent. Keeping that in mind, she gathered her thoughts, shored up her backbone and made a proposal. "I think we should fool around." Before he could reply to that one way or the other, she added, "Out there. Where they can all see." *And hopefully you'll like that enough to want to continue in private.*

He lifted one brow, the corner of his mouth quirking. "And you called Armie kinky."

Heat rushed into her face. "No, I don't mean anything really explicit." But that was a lie, so she amended, "Well, I mean, I do. But not with an audience."

Again his eyes narrowed—and his other hand lifted to the shelving. He effectively confined her, not that she wanted freedom. With him so close, she had to tip her head back to look up at him. Her heart tried to punch out of her chest, and the sweetest little ache coiled inside her.

"I'm with you so far," he whispered, and leaned down to kiss the corner of her mouth.

"I figured, you know…" How did he expect her to think while he did that? "We could act all cozy, like you had other things on your mind. Then no one would know how distressed you are over missing the fight."

"First off, I'm not acting." His forehead touched hers. "Second, I am *not* distressed. Stop making me sound so damned weak."

Not acting? What did that mean? She licked her lips—and he noticed. "I know you're not weak." Wasn't that her point? "So…you don't like my plan?"

"I like it fine." His mouth brushed her temple, his tongue touched the inside of her ear—*Wow, that curled her toes!*—then he nibbled his way along her jaw, under her chin. "Playing with you will make for a long night."

"Yes." A long night where she'd have a chance to show him how perfect they were for each other. And if he didn't see things the same as she did, they could still end up sharing a very special evening together. If she didn't have him forever, she'd at least have that memory to carry her through.

But before she settled for only a memory, she hoped to—

A sharp rap on the door made her jump.

Gage just groaned.

Through the closed door, Armie asked, "You two naked?"

Puffing up with resentment at the intrusion, Harper started around Gage.

Before she got far, he caught her. Softly, he said, "Don't encourage him," before walking to the door and opening it. "What do you want, Armie?"

"Refreshments for everyone." Armie peeked around him, ran his gaze over Harper, and frowned. "Damn, fully clothed. And here I was all geared up for a peep show."

Harper threw a roll of paper towels at him.

When Armie ducked, they went right past him and out into the hall.

Stack said, "Hey!"

And they all grinned.

Getting back to business, she finished filling the box with prepackaged cookies, chips and pretzels, then shoved it all into Armie's arms, making him stumble back a foot.

He just laughed at her, the jerk.

"Where did you hide the coffeemaker?" Harper asked, trying to sound normal instead of primed.

"I'll get it." Armie looked at each of them. "Plan to join us anytime soon?"

Unruffled by the interruption, Gage said, "Be right there."

"Not to be a spoilsport, but a group of the high school

boys have arrived, so, seriously, you might want to put a lid on the hanky-panky for a bit."

"People are here already?" She'd thought she had an hour yet. "They're early."

Armie shrugged. "Everyone is excited to watch Cannon fight again." He clapped Gage on the shoulder. "Sucks you're not out there, man."

"Next time," Gage said easily with no inflection at all.

Harper couldn't help but glance at him with sympathy.

"If you insist on molesting him," Armie said, "better get on with it real quick."

She reached for him, but he ducked out laughing.

She watched Armie go down the hall.

Gage studied her. "You going to molest me, honey?"

Did he want her to? Because, seriously, she'd be willing. "Let's see how it goes."

His eyes widened a little over that.

She dragged out a case of cola. Gage shook off his surprise and took it from her, and together they headed back out.

A half hour later they had everything set up. The colas were in the cooler under ice, sandwiches had been cut and laid out. A variety of chips filled one entire table. More people arrived. The boys, ranging in ages from fifteen to eighteen, were hyped up, talking loudly and gobbling down the food in record time. The women spent their time sidling up to the guys.

The guys spent their time enjoying it.

"Is there more food in the back room?"

Harper smiled at Stack Hannigan, one of the few fighters who hadn't yet staked out a woman. "Yeah, but I can get it as soon as I finish tidying up here." Every ten minutes she needed to reorganize the food. Once the fights started, things would settle down, but until then it was pure chaos.

Stack tugged on a lock of her hair. "No worries, doll. Be right back." And off he went.

Harper watched him walk away, as always enjoying the show. Long-legged with a rangy stride, Stack looked impressive whether he was coming or going—as all of them did.

In some ways, the guys were all different.

Stack's blond hair was darker and straighter than Armie's. Denver's brown hair was so long he often contained it in a ponytail. Cannon's was pitch-black with a little curl on the ends.

She preferred Gage's trimmed brown hair, and she absolutely loved his golden-brown eyes.

All of the fighters were good-looking. Solid, muscular, capable. But where Stack, Armie and Cannon were light heavyweights, her Gage was a big boy, a shredded heavyweight with fists the size of hams. They were all friends, but with different fighting styles and different levels of expertise.

When Stack returned with another platter of food, he had two high school wrestlers beside him, talking a mile a minute. She loved seeing how the older boys emulated the fighters, learning discipline, self-control and confidence.

With the younger kids, it sometimes broke her heart to see how desperate they were for attention. And then when one or more of the guys made a kid feel special, her heart expanded so much it choked her.

"You're not on your period, are you?" Armie asked from beside her.

Using the back of her hand to quickly dash away a tear, Harper asked him, "What are you talking about?"

"You're all fired up one minute, hot and bothered the next, now standing here glassy-eyed." Leaning down to better see her, he searched her face and scowled. "What the hell, woman? Are you *crying?*"

She slugged him in the shoulder—which meant she hurt her hand more than she hurt him. Softly, because it wasn't a teasing subject, she said, "I was thinking how nice this is for the younger boys."

"Yeah." He tugged at his ear and his smile went crooked. "Makes me weepy sometimes, too."

Harper laughed at that. "You are so full of it."

He grinned with her, then leveled her by saying, "How come you're letting those other gals climb all over Gage?"

She jerked around so fast she threw herself off balance. Trapped by the reception desk, Gage stood there while two women fawned over him. Harper felt mean. More than mean. "What is he doing now?"

"Greeting people, that's all. Not that the ladies aren't giving it the old college try." He leaned closer, his voice low. "I approve of your methods, by the way."

"Meaning what?"

"Guys have to man up and all that. Be tough. But I know he'd rather be in the arena than here with us."

Than here—with her. She sighed.

Armie tweaked her chin. "Don't be like that."

"Like what?"

"All 'poor little me, I'm not a priority.' You're smarter than that, Harper. You know he's worked years for this."

She did know it, and that's why it hurt so much. If it wasn't so important to him, she might stand a chance.

"Oh, gawd," Armie drawled, managing to look both disgusted and mocking. "You're deeper down in the dumps than he is." He tipped up her chin. "You know, it took a hell of a lot of discipline for him to walk away from everyone, including you, so he could train with another camp."

She gave him a droll look rife with skepticism.

Armie wasn't finished. "It's not like he said goodbye to you and then indulged any other women. Nope. It was celibacy all the way."

"That's a myth." She knew because she'd looked it up. "Guys do not have to do without in order to compete."

"Without sex, no. Without distractions, yeah. And you, Harper Gates, are one hell of a distraction."

Was she? She just couldn't tell.

Armie leaned in closer, keeping his voice low. "The thing is, if you were serving it up regular-like, it'd probably be okay."

She shoved him. "Armie!" Her face went hot. Did everyone know her damn business? Had Gage talked? Complained?

Holding up his hands in surrender, Armie said, "It's true. Sex, especially good sex with someone important, works wonders for clearing the mind of turmoil. But when the lady is holding out—"

She locked her jaw. "Just where did you get this info?"

That made him laugh. "No one told me, if that's what you're thinking. Anyone with eyes can see that you two haven't sealed the deal yet."

Curious, eyes narrowed in skepticism, she asked, "How?"

"For one thing, the way Gage looks at you, like he's waiting to unwrap a special present."

More heat surfaced, coloring not only her face, but her throat and chest, too.

"Anyway," Armie said, after taking in her blush with a brow raised in interest, "you want to wait, he cares enough not to push, so he did without. It's admirable, not a reason to drag around like your puppy died or something. Not every guy has that much heart." He held out his arms. "Why do you think I only do local fighting?"

"You have the heart," Harper defended. But she added,

"I have no idea what motivates you, I just know it must be something big."

Pleased by her reasoning, he admitted, "You could be right." Before she could jump on that, he continued. "My point is that Gage is a fighter all the way. He'll be a champion one day. That means he has to make certain sacrifices, some at really inconvenient times."

Oddly enough, she felt better about things, and decided to tease him back a little. "So I was a sacrifice?"

"Giving up sex is always a sacrifice." He slung an arm around her shoulders and hauled her into his side. "Especially the sex you haven't had yet."

"Armie!" She enjoyed his insights, but he was so cavalier about it, so bold, she couldn't help but continue blushing.

"Now, Harper, you know…" Suddenly Armie went quiet. "Damn, for such a calm bastard, he has the deadliest stare."

Harper looked up to find Gage scrutinizing them. And he did look rather hot under the collar. Even as the two attractive women did their best to regain his attention, Gage stayed focused on her.

She tried smiling at him. He just transferred his piercing gaze to Armie.

"You could go save him from them," Harper suggested.

"Sorry, honey, not my type."

"What?" she asked as if she didn't already know. "The lack of a Mohawk bothers you?"

He laughed, surprised her with a loud kiss right on her mouth and a firm swat on her butt, then he sauntered away.

# CHAPTER THREE

GAGE LOOKED READY to self-combust, so Harper headed over to him. He tracked her progress, and even when she reached him, he still looked far too intent and serious.

"Hey," she said.

"Hey, yourself."

She eyed the other ladies. "See those guys over there?" She pointed to where Denver and Stack loitered by the food, stuffing their faces. "They're shy, but they're really hoping you'll come by to say hi."

It didn't take much more than that for the women to depart.

Gage reached out and tucked her hair behind her ear. "Now why didn't I think of that?"

"Maybe you were enjoying the admiration a little too much."

"No." He touched her cheek, trailed his fingertips down to her chin. "You and Armie had your heads together long enough. Care to share what you two talked about?"

She shrugged. "You."

"Huh." His hand curved around her nape, pulling her in. "That's why he kissed you and played patty-cake with your ass?"

She couldn't be this close to him without touching. Her hands opened on his chest, smoothing over the prominent muscles. What his chest did for a T-shirt should be illegal. "Now, Gage, I know you're not jealous."

His other hand covered hers, flattening her palm over his heart. "Do I have reason to be?"

"Over *Armie?*" She gave a very unladylike snort. "Get real."

He continued to study her.

Sighing, she said, "If you want to know—"

"I do."

Why not tell him? she thought. It'd be interesting to see his reaction. "Actually, it's kind of funny. See, Armie was encouraging me to have sex with you."

Gage's expression went still, first with a hint of surprise, then with the heat of annoyance. "What the hell does it have to do with him?"

No way could she admit that Armie thought they were both sad sacks. "Nothing. You know Armie."

"Yeah." He scowled darker. "I know him."

Laughing, she rolled her eyes. "He's lacking discretion, says whatever he thinks and enjoys butting in." She snuggled in closer to him, leaning on him. Loving him. "He wants you happy."

"I'm happy, damn it."

She didn't bother telling him how *un*happy he sounded just then. "And he wants me happy."

Smoothing a hand down her back, pressing her closer still, he asked, "Sex will make you happy?"

Instead of saying, *I love you so much, sex with you would make me ecstatic,* she quipped, "It'd sure be better than a stinging butt, which is all Armie offered."

"Want me to kiss it and make it better?"

She opened her mouth, but nothing came out.

With a small smile of satisfaction, Gage palmed her cheek, gently caressing. "I'll take that as a yes."

She gave a short nod.

He used his hand on her butt to snug her in closer. "Armie kissed you, too."

Making a face, she told him, "Believe me, the swat was far more memorable."

"Good thing for Armie."

So he *was* jealous?

"Hey," Stack called over to them. "We're ready to get things started. Kill the overhead lights, will you?"

Still looking down at her, Gage slowly nodded. "Sure thing." Taking Harper with him, he went to the front desk and retrieved the barrel key for the locking switches.

The big TV, along with a security lamp in the hallway, would provide all the light they needed. When Gage inserted the key and turned it, the overhead florescent lights clicked off. Given that they stood well away from the others, heavy shadows enveloped them.

Rather than head over to the crowd, Gage aligned her body with his in a tantalizing way. His hand returned to her bottom, ensuring she stayed pressed to him. "Maybe," he whispered, "I can be more memorable."

As he moved his hand lower on her behind—his long fingers seeking inward—she went on tiptoe and squeaked, "*Definitely.*"

Smiling, he took her mouth in a consuming kiss. Combined with the way those talented fingers did such incredible things to her, rational thought proved impossible.

Finally, easing up with smaller kisses and teasing nibbles, he whispered, "We can't do this here."

Her fingers curled in against him, barely making a dent in his rock-solid muscles. "I know," she groaned.

He stroked restless hands up and down her back. "Want to grab a seat with me?"

He asked the question almost as if a big *or* hung at the end. Like… *Or should we just leave? Or should we find an empty room?*

*Or would you prefer to go anywhere private so we can both get naked and finish what we started?*

She waited, hopeful, but when he said nothing more, she blew out a disappointed breath. "Sure."

And of course she felt like a jerk.

He and Cannon were close friends. Everyone knew he wanted to watch the fights. Despite his own disappointment over medical ineligibility, he was excited for Cannon's competition.

Her eyes were adjusting and she could see Gage better now, the way he searched her face, how he…waited.

For her to understand? Was Armie right? Maybe more than anything she needed to show him that she not only loved him, but she loved his sport, that she supported him and was as excited by his success as he was.

"Yes, let's sit." She took his hand. "Toward the back, though, so we can sneak away later if we decide to." Eyes flaring at that naughty promise, he didn't budge.

"Sneak away to where?"

"The way I feel right now, any empty room might do." Hiding her smile, Harper stretched up to give him a very simple kiss. "That is, between fights. We don't want to miss anything."

His hand tightened on hers, and she couldn't help thinking that maybe Armie's suggestion had merit after all.

GAGE GOT SO caught up in the prefights that he almost—*almost*—forgot about Harper's endless foreplay. Damn, she had him primed. Her closeness, the warmth of her body, the sweet scent of her hair and the warmer scent of her skin, were enough to make him edgy with need. But every so often her hand drifted to his thigh, lingered, stroked. Each time he held his breath, unsure how far she'd go.

How far he wanted her to go.

So far, all he knew was that it wasn't far enough.

Once, she'd run her hand up his back, just sort of feeling him, her fingers spread as she traced muscles, his shoulder blades, down his spine...

If he gave his dick permission, it would stand at attention right now. But he concentrated on keeping control of things—himself and, when possible, Harper, too.

It wasn't easy. Though she appeared to be as into the fights as everyone else, she still had very busy hands.

It wasn't just the sexual teasing that got to him. It was emotional, too. He hated that he wasn't in Japan with Cannon, walking to the cage for his own big battle. He'd had prelim fights; he'd built his name and recognition.

He'd finally gotten that main event—and it pissed him off more than he wanted to admit that he was left sitting behind.

But sitting behind with Harper sure made it easier. Especially when he seemed so attuned to her.

If her mood shifted, he freaking felt it, deep down inside himself. At one point she hugged his arm, her head on his shoulder, and something about the embrace had felt so damn melancholy that he'd wanted to lift her into his lap and hold her close and make some heavy-duty spur-of-the-moment promises.

Holding her wouldn't have been a big deal; Miles had a chick in his lap. Denver, too.

With Harper, though, it'd be different. Everyone knew a hookup when they saw one, and no way did Gage want others to see her that way. Harper was like family at the rec center. She was part of the inner circle. He would never do anything to belittle her importance.

Beyond that, he wanted more than a hookup. He cared about her well beyond getting laid a single time, well beyond any mere friendship.

Still, as soon as possible, he planned to get her alone and, God willing, get her under him.

Or over him.

However she liked it, as long as he got her. Not just for tonight, but for a whole lot more.

Everyone grimaced when the last prelim fight ended with a grappling match—that turned into an arm bar. The dominant fighter trapped the arm, extended it to the breaking point while the other guy tried everything he could to free himself.

Squeezed up close to his side, peeking through her fingers, Harper pleaded, "Tap, tap, tap," all but begging his opponent to admit defeat before he suffered more damage. And when he did, she cheered with everyone else. "Good fight. Wow. That was intense."

It was so cute how involved she got while watching, that Gage had to tip up her chin so he could kiss her.

Her enthusiasm for the fight waned as she melted against him, saying, "Mmm…"

He smiled against her mouth. "You're making me a little nuts."

"Look who's talking." She glanced around with exaggerated drama. "If only we were alone."

Hoping she meant it, he used his thumb to brush her bottom lip. "We can be." His place. Her place. Either worked for him. "It'll be late when the fights end, but—"

"I really have to wait that long?"

Yep, she meant it. Her blue eyes were heavy, her face flushed. She breathed deeper. He glanced down at her breasts and saw her nipples were tight against the material of her T-shirt.

Okay, much more of that and he wouldn't be able to keep it under wraps.

A roar sounded around them and they both looked up

to see Cannon on the screen. Gage couldn't help but grin. Yeah, he wanted to be there, too, but at the same time, he was so damn proud of Cannon.

In such a short time, Cannon had become one of the most beloved fighters in the sport. The fans adored him. His peers respected him. And the Powers That Be saw him as a big draw moneymaker. After he won tonight, Gage predicted that Cannon would be fighting for the belt.

He'd win it, too.

They showed footage of Cannon before the fight, his knit hat pulled low on his head, bundled under a big sweatshirt. Keeping his muscles warm.

He looked as calm and determined as ever while answering questions.

Harper squeezed his hand and when she spoke, Gage realized it was with nervousness.

"He'll do okay."

Touched by her concern, he smiled. "I'd put money on it."

She nodded, but didn't look away from the screen. "He's been something of a phenomenon, hasn't he?"

"With Cannon, making an impact comes naturally."

"After he wins this one," she mused, "they'll start hyping him for a title shot."

Since her thoughts mirrored his own, he hugged her. Her uncanny insight never ceased to amaze him. Then again, she was a regular at the rec center, interacted often with fighters and enjoyed the sport. It made sense that she'd have the same understanding as him.

"Cannon's earned it." Few guys took as many fights as he did, sometimes on really short notice. If a fighter got sick—or suffered an injury, as Gage had—Cannon was there, always ready, always in shape, always kicking ass. They called him the Saint, and no wonder.

Gage glanced around at the young men who, just a few years ago, would have been hanging on the street corner looking for trouble. Now they had some direction in their lives, the attention they craved, decent role models and a good way to expend energy. But the rec center was just a small part of Cannon's goodwill.

Whenever he got back to town, he continued his efforts to protect the neighborhood. Gage had enjoyed joining their group, going on night strolls to police the corruption, to let thugs know that others were looking out for the hardworking owners of local family businesses. Actual physical conflicts were rare; overall, it was enough to show that someone was paying attention.

It didn't hurt that Cannon was friends with a tough-as-nails police lieutenant and two detectives. And then there was his buddy at the local bar, a place where Cannon used to work before he got his big break in the SBC fight organization. The owner of the bar had more contacts than the entire police department. He influenced a lot of the other businesses with his stance for integrity.

Yeah, Cannon had some colorful, capable acquaintances—which included a diverse group of MMA fighters.

Saint suited him—not that Cannon liked the moniker. It wasn't nearly as harsh as Gage's own fight name.

Thinking about that brought his attention back to Harper. She watched the TV so he saw her in profile, her long lashes, her turned up nose, her firm chin.

That soft, sexy mouth.

He liked the freckles on her cheekbones. He liked everything about her—how she looked, who she was, the way she treated others.

He smoothed Harper's hair and said, "Most women like to call me Savage."

She snorted. "It's a stupid nickname."

Pretending great insult, he leaned away. "It's a fight name, not a nickname. And it's badass."

She disagreed. "There's nothing savage about you. You should have been named Methodical or Accurate or something."

Grinning, he shook his head. "Thanks, but no thanks."

"Well," she muttered, "you're not savage. That's all I'm saying."

He'd gotten the name early on when, despite absorbing several severe blows from a more experienced fighter, he'd kept going. In the end, he'd beaten the guy with some heavy ground and pound, mostly because he'd still been fresh when the other man gassed out.

The commentator had shouted, *He's a damn savage*, and the description stuck.

To keep himself from thinking about just how savage Harper made him—with lust—he asked, "Want something to eat?"

She wrinkled her nose. "After those past few fights? Bleh."

Two of the prelim fights were bloody messes, one because of a busted nose, but the other due to a cut similar to what Gage had. Head wounds bled like a mother. During a fight, as long as the fighter wasn't hurt that badly, they wouldn't stop things over a little spilled blood. Luckily for the contender, the cut was off to the side and so the blood didn't run into his eyes.

For Gage, it hadn't mattered. If only the cut hadn't been so deep. If it hadn't needed stitches. If it would have been somewhere other than right over his eye. If—

Harper's hand trailed over his thigh again. "So, *Savage*," she teased, and damned if she didn't get close to his fly. "Want to help me bring out more drinks before the main event starts?"

Anything to keep him from ruminating on lost opportunities, which he was pretty sure had been Harper's intent.

"Why not?" He stood and hauled her up with him.

They had to go past Armie who stood with two very edgy women and several teenagers, munching on popcorn and comparing biceps.

Armie winked at Harper.

She smiled at him. "We'll only be a minute."

The idiot clutched his chest. "You've just destroyed all my illusions and damaged Savage's reputation beyond repair."

Gage rolled his eyes, more than willing to ignore Armie's nonsense, but he didn't get far before one of the boys asked him about his cut. Next thing he knew, he was surrounded by wide eyes and ripe curiosity. Because it was a good opportunity to show the boys how to handle disappointment, he lingered, letting them ask one question after another.

Harper didn't complain. If anything, she watched him with something that looked a lot like pride. Not exactly what he wanted from her at this particular moment, but it felt good all the same.

He didn't realize she'd gone about getting the drinks without him until Armie relieved her of two large cartons of soft drinks. Together they began putting the cans in the cooler over ice. They laughed together, and even though it looked innocent enough, it made Gage tense with—

"You two hooking up finally?"

Thoughts disrupted, Gage turned to Denver. Hard to believe he hadn't noticed the approach of a two-hundred-and-twenty-pound man. "What?"

"You and Harper," Denver said, while perusing the food that remained. "Finally going to make it official?"

"Make what official?"

"That you're an item." Denver chose half a cold cut sandwich and devoured the majority of it in one bite.

Gage's gaze sought Harper out again. Whatever Armie said to her got him a shove in return. Armie pulled an exaggerated fighter's stance, fists up, as if he thought he'd have to defend himself.

Harper pretended a low shot, Armie dropped his hands to cover the family jewels, and she smacked him on top of the head.

The way the two of them carried on, almost like siblings, made Gage feel left out.

Were he and Harper an item? He knew how he felt, but Harper could be such a mystery.

Denver shouldered him to the side so he could grab some cake. "Gotta say, man, I hope so. She was so glum while you were away, it depressed the hell out of everyone."

Hard to imagine a woman as vibrant as Harper ever down in the dumps. When he'd left for the camp in Kentucky, she'd understood, wishing him luck, telling him how thrilled she was for him.

But since his return a few days ago, things had been off. He hadn't immediately sought her out, determined to get his head together first. He didn't want pity from anyone, but the way he'd felt had been pretty damned pitiful. He'd waffled between rage at the circumstances and mind-numbing regret. No way did he want others to suffer him like that, most especially Harper.

He knew he'd see her at the rec center and had half expected her to gush over him, to fret over his injury, to sympathize.

She hadn't done any of that. Mostly she'd treated him the same as she did the rest of the guys, leaving him confused and wallowing in his own misery.

Until tonight.

Tonight she was all about making him insane with the need to get her alone and naked.

"You listening to me, Gage?"

Rarely did another fighter call him by his given name. That Denver did so now almost felt like a reprimand from his mom. "Yeah, *Denver*, I'm listening."

"Good." Denver folded massive arms over his massive chest, puffing up like a turkey. "So what's it to be?"

If Denver expected a challenge, too bad. Gage again sought out Harper with his gaze. "She was really miserable?"

Denver deflated enough to slap him on the back. "Yeah. It was awful. Made me sad as shit, I don't mind telling you."

"What was she miserable about?"

"Dude, are you that fucking obtuse?"

Stack stepped into the conversation. "Hell, yeah, he is." Then changing the subject, Stack asked, "Did Rissy go to Japan with Cannon?"

Denver answered, saying, "Yeah, he took her and her roommate along."

Merissa, better known as Rissy, was Cannon's little sis. A roommate was news to Gage, though. "If you have ideas about his sister, you're an idiot."

Stack drew back. "No. Hell, no. Damn man, don't start rumors."

Everyone knew Cannon as a nice guy. More than nice. But he was crazy-particular when it came to Merissa. For that reason, the guys all looked past her, through her or when forced to it, with nothing more than respect. "Who's the roommate?"

"Sweet Cherry Pie," Denver rumbled low and with feeling.

Stack grinned at him.

Gage totally missed the joke. "What?"

"Cherry Payton," Denver said, and damn if he didn't almost sigh. "Long blond hair, big chocolate-brown eyes, extra fine body…"

"Another one bites the dust," Stack said with a laugh.

"Another one?"

"Obtuse," Denver lamented.

Stack nodded toward Harper. "You being the first, dumb ass."

"We all expect you to make her feel better about things."

Confusion kicked his temper up a notch. "What *things?*"

Slapping a hand over his heart, Stack said, "How you feel."

Striking a similar pose, Denver leaned into Stack. "What you want."

Heads together, they intoned, *"Love."*

"You're both morons." But damn it, he realized that he did love her. Probably had for a long time. How could he not? Priorities could be a bitch and he hated the idea that he'd maybe made Harper unhappy by not understanding his feelings sooner.

He chewed his upper lip while wondering how to correct things.

"Honesty," Stack advised him. "Tell her how the schedule goes, what to expect and leave the rest up to her."

"Harper's smart," Denver agreed. "She'll understand."

It irked Gage big-time to have everyone butting into his personal business. "Don't you guys have something better to do than harass me?"

"I have some*one* better to do," Stack told him, nodding toward one of the women who'd hit on Gage earlier. "Butting in to your business was just my goodwill gesture of the day." And with that he sauntered off.

Denver leaned back on the table of food. "We all like Harper, you know."

Gage was starting to think they liked her a little too much. "Yeah, I get that."

"So quit dicking around, will you?" He grabbed up another sandwich and he, too, joined a woman.

Gage stewed for half a minute, turned—and almost ran into Harper.

## CHAPTER FOUR

GAGE CAUGHT HER ARMS, steadying them both. "Why does everyone keep sneaking up on me?"

She brushed off his hands. "If you hadn't been ogling the single ladies, maybe you'd be more aware."

She absolutely had to know better than to think that, but just in case… "How could I notice any other woman with you around?"

She eyed him. "Do you notice other women when I'm not around?"

Damn, he thought, did she really *not* know how much he cared? Worse, had she been sad while he was away?

The possibility chewed on his conscience. "No, I don't." He drew her up to kiss her sweetly, and then, because this was Harper, not so sweetly.

To give her back a little, he shared his own complaint. "You spend way too much time horsing around with Armie."

Shrugging, she reached for a few chips. "I was trying not to crowd you."

"What does that mean?"

While munching, she gestured around the interior of the rec center. "This is a fight night. You're hanging with your buds. When I see you guys talking, I don't want to horn in."

Whoa. Those were some serious misconceptions. To help clear things up, he cupped her face. "You can't."

"Can't what?"

"Horn in. Ever."

Brows pinching in disgruntlement, she shoved away from him. "I just told you I wouldn't."

He hauled her right back. "I'm not saying you shouldn't, honey, I'm saying you can't because there's never a bad time for you to talk to me. Remember that, okay?"

Astonished, she blinked up at him, and he wanted to declare himself right then. Luckily the first fight on the main card started and everyone went back to their seats, saving him from rushing her.

This time, Gage had a hard time concentrating. He saw the fight, he cheered, but more of his attention veered to Harper, to how quiet she was now.

Thinking about him?

The fight ended in the first round with a knockout.

Instead of reacting with everyone else, Harper turned her face up to his. As if no time had passed at all, she said, "That's not entirely true."

Damn, but it was getting more difficult by the second to keep his hands off her. He contented himself by opening his hand on her waist, stroking up to her ribs then down to her hip. "What's that?"

"There are plenty of times when I can't intrude."

She was still stewing about that? "No."

Like a thundercloud, she darkened. Turning to more fully face him, she said low, *"Yes."* Before he could correct her, she insisted, "But I want you to know that I understand."

Apparently she didn't. "How so?"

Leaning around him, she glanced at one and all to ensure there were no eavesdroppers. As if uncertain, she puckered her brows while trying to find the right words. "I know when you're in training—"

"I'm pretty much always in training."

She looked like she wanted to smack him. "There's training and then there's *training*."

True enough. "You mean when I go away to another camp."

"That, and when you're close to a fight."

Should he tell her how much he'd enjoy coming home to her—every night, not just between fights? Would she ever be willing to travel with him? Or to wait for him when she couldn't?

He had a feeling Harper would fit seamlessly into his life no matter what he had going on.

Being as honest as he could, Gage nodded. "There will be times when my thoughts are distracted, when I have to focus on other stuff. But that doesn't mean I don't care. It sure as hell doesn't mean you have to keep your distance."

The next fight started and though a few muted conversations continued, most in attendance kept their comments limited to the competition. Beside him, Harper fell silent. Gage could almost feel her struggling to sort out everything he'd said.

Again, he found himself studying her profile; not just her face, but her body, too. Her breasts weren't large, but they fit her frame, especially with her small waist and the sexy flare of her hips. She kept her long legs crossed, one foot nervously rocking. She drew in several deep breaths. A pulse tripped in her throat.

By the second the sexual tension between them grew.

The end of the night started to feel like too many hours away. They had at least three more fights on the main card. Cannon's fight would be last. It wasn't a title fight, but it'd still go five rounds.

The current match went all three rounds and came down to a split decision. Gage no longer cared; hell, he'd missed more of the fight than he'd seen.

Around him, voices rose in good-natured debate about how the judges had gotten it right or wrong.

"What do you think?" Gage asked Harper.

She shrugged. "Depends on how the judges scored things. The guy from Brazil really pushed the fight, but the other one landed more blows. Still, he didn't cause that much damage, and the Brazilian got those two takedowns—"

Gage put a finger to her mouth. "I meant about us."

Her wide-eyed gaze swung to his. "Oh." She gulped, considered him, then whispered, "I like it."

"It?"

"There being an 'us.'"

Yeah, he liked it, too, maybe more than he'd realized before now. "I missed you while I was away."

She scoffed. "You were way too busy for that."

"I worked hard, no denying it. But it wasn't 24/7. I found myself alone with my thoughts far too often."

She forced a smile. "I'm sure at those times you were obsessed about the SBC, about the competition, about winning."

"All that—plus you." When it came to priorities, she was at the top. He'd just made too many assumptions for her to realize it.

She looked tortured for a moment before her hand knotted in his shirt and she pulled him closer. With pained accusation, she said, "You didn't call."

Hot with regret, Gage covered her hand with his own. "I was trying to focus." Saying it out loud, he felt like an ass.

But Harper nodded. "That's what I'm saying. There will be times when I need to stay out of your way so I don't mess with that focus."

He hated the idea of her avoiding him.

Almost as much as he hated the thought of ever leaving her again. Yet that was a reality. He was a fighter; he would go to other camps to train, travel around the country, around the world.

He'd go where the SBC sent him.

"You have to know, Gage. I'd never get in your way, not on purpose."

He almost groaned.

"I'm serious! I know how important your career is and I know what a nuisance it can be to—"

Suddenly starved for the taste of her, for the feel of her, Gage took her mouth in a firm kiss.

But that wasn't enough, so he turned his head and nibbled her bottom lip until she opened. When he licked inside her warm, damp mouth, her breath hitched. Mindful of where they were, he nonetheless had a hell of time tempering his lust.

Damn it.

The next fight started. Cannon would be after that.

In a sudden desperate rush, Gage left his chair, pulling her up and along with him as he headed toward the dimly lit hallway. He couldn't wait a second more. But for what he had to say, had to explain, he needed the relative privacy of a back room.

Luckily she'd seated them at the end of the back row. In only a few steps, and without a lot of attention, he had them on their way.

Tripping along with him, Harper whispered, *"Gage."*

"There are high school boys out there," he told her. He glanced in the storage room, but no, that was too close to the main room and the activity of the group.

"I know. So?"

He brought her up and alongside him so he could slip an arm around her. "So they don't need to see me losing my head over you."

She stopped suddenly, which forced him to stop.

Looking far too shy for the ballsy woman he knew her to be, she whispered, "Are you?"

This time he understood her question. "Losing my head over you?" Gently, he said, "No."

Her shoulders bunched as if she might slug him.

Damn, but he adored her. "I lost it a long time ago. I just forgot to tell you."

Suspicious, she narrowed her eyes. "What does that mean exactly?"

Not about to declare himself in a freaking hallway, he took her hands and started backing up toward the office. "Come along with me and I'll explain everything." This particular talk was long overdue.

She didn't resist, but she did say, "The fight you should have been in is next. And Cannon will be fighting soon after that."

"I know." At the moment, seeing the fight he'd missed was the furthest thing from his mind. As to Cannon, well, he'd be in a lot of fights. This wasn't his first, wouldn't be his last. If all went well, Gage would get her commitment to spend the night, and more, before Cannon entered the cage. "The thing is, I need you."

She searched his face. "Need me...how?"

*In every way imaginable.* "Let me show you."

Her gaze went over his body. "Sounds to me like you're talking about sex."

Did lust taint his brain, or did she sound hopeful? They reached the office door and he tried the handle. Locked, of course. Trying not to think about how the night would end, he said, "Seriously, Harper, much as I love that idea, we're at the rec center."

"So?"

Damn, she knew how to throw him. He sucked in air and forged on. "I thought we'd talk." Digging in his pocket, he found the keys he'd picked up earlier when he shut off the lights.

Sarcasm added a wicked light to her beautiful blue eyes. "Talk? That's what you want to do? Seriously?"

"Yeah. See, I need to explain a few things to you and it's better done in private." The door opened and he drew her in.

Typical of Harper, she took the initiative, shutting and locking the door, then grabbing him. "We're alone." Her mouth brushed his chin, his jaw, his throat. "Say what you need to say."

"I love you."

She went so still, it felt like he held a statue. Ignoring her lack of a response, Gage cupped her face. "I love you, Harper Gates. Have for a while now. I'm sorry I didn't realize it sooner. I'm especially sorry I didn't figure it out before I took off for Kentucky."

Confused, but also defending him, she whispered, "You were excited about the opportunity."

She made him sound like a kid, when at the moment he felt very much like a man. "True." Slowly, he leaned into her, pinning her up against the door, arranging her so that they fit together perfectly. She was so slight, so soft and feminine—when she wasn't giving him or one of the other fighters hell. "I thought it'd be best for me to concentrate only on the upcoming fight, but that was asinine."

"No," she said, again defending him. "It made sense."

"Loving you makes sense." He took her mouth, and never wanted to stop kissing her. Hot and deep. Soft and sweet. With Harper it didn't matter. However she kissed him, it blew his mind and pushed all his buttons.

He brushed damp kisses over to the side of her neck, up to her ear.

On a soft wail, Harper said, "How can you love me? We haven't even had sex yet."

"Believe me, I know." He covered her breast with his hand, gently kneading her, loving the weight of her, how her nipple tightened. He wanted to see her, wanted to take her in his mouth. "We can change that later tonight."

"I'll never last that long." She stretched up along his body, both hands tangled in his hair, anchoring him so she could feast off his mouth.

No way would he argue with her.

Everything went hot and urgent between them.

He coasted a hand down her side, caught her thigh and lifted her leg up alongside his. Nudging in against her, knowing he could take her this way, right here, against the door, pushed him over the edge.

Not what he would have planned for their first time, but with Harper so insistent, he couldn't find the brain cells to offer up an alternative.

"Are you sure?" he asked, while praying that she was.

"Yes. Now, Gage." She moved against him. "Right now."

HARPER GRABBED FOR his T-shirt and shoved it up so she could get her hands on his hot flesh, so she could explore all those amazing muscles. Unlike some of the guys, he didn't shave his chest and she loved—*loved, loved, loved*—his body hair.

God, how could any man be so perfect?

She got the shirt above his pecs and leaned in to brush her nose over his chest hair, to deeply inhale his incredible scent. It filled her head, making her dazed with need.

When she took a soft love bite, he shuddered. "Take it easy."

No, she wouldn't.

"We have to slow down or I'm a goner."

But she couldn't. Never in her life had she known she'd miss someone as much as she'd missed him when he'd left. Now he was back, and whether he really loved her or was just caught up in the moment, she'd worry about it later.

She needed him. All of him.

She cupped him through his jeans and heard him groan. He was thick and hard and throbbing.

He sucked in a breath. "Harper, baby, seriously, we have to slow down." Taking her wrist, he lifted her hand away. "You need to catch up a little."

"I'm there already." She'd been there since first deciding on her course of action for the night.

"Not quite." Gage carried both her hands to his shoulders before kissing her senseless, giving her his tongue, drawing hers into his mouth.

She couldn't get enough air into her starving lungs but didn't care. Against her belly she felt his heavy erection, and she wanted to touch him again, to explore him in more detail.

He caught the hem of her T-shirt, drawing it up and over her head. Barely a heartbeat passed before he flipped open the front closure on her bra and the cups parted.

Taking her mouth again, he groaned as his big hands gently molded over her, his thumbs teasing her nipples until she couldn't stop squirming. She wasn't one of the overly stacked groupies who dogged his heels, but she didn't dislike her body, either.

She'd always considered herself not big, but big enough.

Now, with his enormous hands on her, she felt delicate— even more so when he scooped an arm under her behind and easily lifted her up so he could draw one nipple into his hot mouth.

Harper wrapped her legs around his waist, her arms

around his neck. He took his time, drawing on her for what felt like forever, until she couldn't keep still, couldn't contain the soft cries of desperate need.

From one breast to the other, he tasted, teased, sucked, nibbled.

"Gage..." Even saying his name took an effort. "Please."

"Please what?" he asked, all full of masculine satisfaction and a fighter's control. He licked her, circling, teasing. "Please more?"

*"Yes."*

Back on her feet, she dropped against the door. He opened her jeans and a second later shoved them, and her panties, down to her knees.

Anticipation kept her still, kept her breath rushing and her heart pounding. But he just stood there, sucking air and waiting for God knew what.

"Gage?" she whispered with uncertainty.

One hand flattened on the wall beside her head, but he kept his arm locked out, his body from touching hers. "I should take you to my place," he rasped, sounding tortured. "I should take you someplace with more time, more privacy, more—"

Panic tried to set in. "Don't you even *think* about stopping now." No way could he leave her like this.

His mouth touched her cheek, the corner of her lips, her jaw, her temple. "No, I won't. I can't."

A loud roar sounded from the main part of the room. Knowing what that meant, that Cannon's fight was about to start, guilt nearly leveled Harper. "I forgot," she admitted miserably.

"Doesn't matter," he assured her.

But of course it did. He was here to watch Cannon compete, to join in with his fight community to celebrate a close friend.

She was here to show him she wouldn't interfere and yet, that's exactly what she'd done. "We could—"

"No, baby." Need made his short laugh gravelly. "Believe me when I say that I *can't*."

"Oh." Her heart started punching again—with excitement. "We'll miss the fight."

"We'll catch the highlights later. Together." He stroked her hair with his free hand, over her shoulder, down the side of her body.

"You're sure?"

Against her mouth, he whispered, "Give or take a bed for convenience, I'm right where I want to be." His kiss scorched her, and he added, "With you."

*Aww.* Hearing him say it was nice, but knowing he meant it multiplied everything she felt, and suddenly she couldn't wait. She took his hand and guided it across her body.

And between her legs.

They both groaned.

At first he just cupped her, his palm hot, his hand covering so much of her. They breathed together, taut with expectation.

"It seems like I've wanted you forever," he murmured at the same time as his fingers searched over her, touching carefully. His forehead to hers, he added, "Mmm. You're wet."

Speaking wasn't easy, but he deserved the truth. "Because I *have* wanted you forever."

"I'm glad, Harper." His fingers parted her swollen lips, stroked gently over her, delved. "Widen your legs a little more."

That husky, take-charge, turned-on tone nearly put her over the edge. Holding on to his shoulders, her face tucked into his throat, she widened her stance. Using two fingers, he glided over her, once, twice, testing her readiness—and he pressed both fingers deep.

Legs stiffening, Harper braced against the door.

"Stay with me," Gage said before kissing her throat.

She felt his teeth on her skin, his hot breath, those oh-so-talented fingers.

"Damn, you feel good. Tight and wet and perfect." He worked her, using his hand to get her close to climax. "Relax just a little."

"Can't." Her fingernails bit into his shoulders. "Oh, God."

"If we were on a bed," he growled against her throat, "I could get to your nipples. But you're so short—"

"I'm not," she gasped, unsure whether she'd be able to take that much excitement. "You're just so damn big."

"Soon as you come for me," he promised, "I'll show you how big I am."

Such a braggart. Of course, she'd already had a good idea, given she often saw him in nothing more than athletic shorts. And she'd already had her hands on him. Not long enough to do all the exploring she wanted to do, but enough to—

He brought his thumb up to her clitoris, and she clenched all over.

"Nice," he told her. "I can feel you getting closer."

*Shut up, Gage.* She thought it but didn't say it, because words right now, at this particular moment, would be far too difficult.

He cupped her breast and, in keeping with the accelerated tempo of the fingers between her legs, he tugged at her nipple.

The first shimmer of approaching release took her to her tiptoes. *"Gage."*

"I've got you."

The next wave, stronger, hotter, made her groan in harsh pleasure.

"I love you, Harper."

Luckily, at that propitious moment, something happened in the fight because everyone shouted and cheered—and that helped to drown out the harsh groans of Harper's release.

# CHAPTER FIVE

GAGE BADLY WANTED to turn on lights, to strip Harper naked and then shuck out of his own clothes. He wanted to touch her all over, taste her everywhere, count her every freckle while feeling her against him, skin on skin, with no barriers.

Even with her T-shirt shoved up above her breasts and her jeans down around her knees, holding Harper in his arms was nice. Her scent had intensified, her body now a warm, very soft weight limp against him. He kept one hand tangled in her hair, the other cupping her sexy ass.

He let her rest while she caught her breath.

If he'd found a better time and place for this, he could stretch her out on a bed, or the floor or a table—didn't matter as long as he could look at every inch of her, kiss her all over.

Devour her slowly, at his leisure.

But they were in an office, at the rec center, with a small crowd of fighters and fans only a hallway away.

He kissed her temple, hugged her protectively.

His cock throbbed against her belly. He badly wanted to be inside her, driving them both toward joint release.

But this, having Harper sated and cuddling so sweetly... yeah, that was pretty damn special.

"Mmm," she murmured. "I lost my bones somewhere."

"I have one you can borrow."

He felt her grin against his throat, then her full-body

rub as she wiggled against him. "Yes," she teased. "Yes, you do."

"I like hearing you come, Harper." With small pecks, he nudged up her face so he could get to her mouth. "Whatever you do, you do it well."

That made her laugh, so the kiss was a little silly, tickling.

She drew in a deep breath, shored up her muscles, and somewhat stood on her own. "The fight is still going on?"

"Sounds like."

"So all that excitement before—"

"You coming?"

She bit his chest, inciting his lust even more. "No, I meant with everyone screaming."

"Probably a near submission. Cannon is good on the ground, good with submissions." Good with every facet of fighting. "But let's not talk about Cannon right now."

"You really don't mind missing his fight?"

"Jesus, woman, I'm about to bust my jeans. Cannon is the furthest thing from my mind."

Happy with his answer, she said, "Okay, then, let's talk about you." She nibbled her way up to his throat. "There is just so much of you to enjoy."

"You could start here," he said, taking one of her small, soft hands down to press against his fly.

"I think I will." With her forehead to his sternum, she watched her hands as she opened the snap to his jeans, slowly eased down the zipper. "I wish we had more light in here."

Because that mirrored his earlier thought, he nodded. "You can just sort of feel your way around."

"Is that what you did?" Using both hands, she held him, so no way could he reply. She stroked his length, squeezed him. "You are so hard."

"Yup." He couldn't manage anything more detailed than that.

"You have a condom?"

"Wallet."

Still touching him, she clarified, "You have a condom in your wallet?"

"Yup."

She tipped her face up to see him, and he could hear the humor in her voice. "A little turned on?"

"A *lot* turned on." He covered her hand with his own and got her started on a stroking rhythm he loved. *"Damn."*

Harper whispered, "Kiss me."

And he did, taking her mouth hard, twining his tongue with hers, making himself crazy by again exploring her, the silky skin of her bottom, the dampness between her thighs, her firm breasts and stiffened nipples.

Harper released him just long enough to say, "Shirt off, big boy." She tried shoving it up, but Gage took over, reaching over his back for a fistful of cotton and jerking the material away. Anticipating her hands, her mouth, on his hot skin, he dropped the shirt.

She didn't disappoint. Hooking her fingers in the waistband of his jeans, she shoved down the denim and his boxers, too, then started feeling him all over. His shoulders to his hips. His pecs to his abs. She grazed her palms over his nipples, then went back to his now throbbing cock.

"You are so impressive in so many ways."

He tried to think up a witty reply, but with her small, soft hands on him, he could barely breathe, much less banter.

"I've thought about something so many times…" And with no more warning than that, she sank to her knees.

*Oh, God.* Gage locked his muscles, one hand settling on top of her head.

Holding him tight, Harper skimmed her lips over the sensitive head, licked down the length of his shaft.

Never one for half measures, she drew her tongue back up and slid her mouth over him.

A harsh groan reverberated out of his chest. "Harper."

Her clever tongue swirled over and around him—and she took him deep again.

Too much. Way too much. He clasped her shoulder. "Sorry, honey, but I can't take it."

She continued anyway.

"Harper," he warned.

She reached around him, clasping his ass as if she thought she could control him.

But control of any kind quickly spiraled away. Later, he thought to himself, he'd enjoy doing this again, letting her have her way, giving her all the time she wanted.

Just not now, not when he so desperately wanted to be inside her.

"Sorry, honey." He caught her under the arms and lifted her to her feet, then set her away from him while he gasped for breath. As soon as he could, he dug out his wallet and fumbled for the condom.

Sounding breathless and hot, she whispered, "You taste so good."

*He'd never last.* "Shh." He rolled on the condom with trembling hands. Stepping up to her in a rush, he stripped away her shirt and bra, shoved her jeans lower. "Hold on to me."

Hooking her right knee with his elbow, he lifted her leg, opening her as much as he could with her jeans still on, his still on. He moved closer still, kissing her until they were both on the ragged edge.

"Now," Harper demanded.

He nudged against her, found his way, and sank deep in one strong thrust.

More cheers sounded in the outer room, but neither of them paid much attention. Already rocking against her, Gage admitted, "I'm not going to last."

She matched the rhythm he set. "I don't need you to... *Gage!*"

Kissing her, he muffled her loud cries as she came, holding him tight, squeezing him tighter, her entire body shimmering in hot release. Seconds later he pinned her to the door, pressed his face into her throat, and let himself go.

For several minutes he was deaf and blind to everything except the feel of Harper in his arms where she belonged.

Little aftershocks continued to tease her intimate muscles, and since he remained joined with her, he felt each one. Their heartbeats danced together.

Gradually he became aware of people talking in the outer room. They sounded happy and satisfied, telling him the fight had ended.

Harper came to the same realization. "Oh, no. We missed everything?"

"Not everything." After a nudge against her to remind what they hadn't missed, he disengaged their bodies. Slowly he eased her leg down, staying close to support her—which was sort of a joke, given how shaky he felt, too.

"Do you think Cannon won?"

"I know he did."

Her fingers moved over his face, up to the corner of his eye near his stitches. "You're sure?"

"Absolutely." He brought her hand to his mouth and kissed her palm. "I was sure even before the fight started."

Letting out a long breath, she dropped her head. "I'm sorry we missed it."

"I don't have any regrets."

She thought about that for a second, then worried aloud, "They'll all know what we were doing."

"Yeah." There was barely enough light to see, but he located paper in the printer, stole a sheet, and used it to wrap up the spent condom. He pitched it into the metal waste can.

"I hope they didn't hear us."

Gage tucked himself away and zipped his jeans. "Even if they did—"

She groaned over the possibility. "No, no, no."

Pulling her back into his arms, he teased, "They won't ask for too many details."

Her fisted hands pressed against his chest. "I swear, if Armie says a single word, I'll—"

Gage kissed her. Then touched her breasts. And her belly. And lower.

"Gage," she whispered, all broken up. "We can't. Not now."

"Not here," he agreed, while paying homage to her perfect behind. "Come home with me."

"Okay."

He'd told her that he loved her. She hadn't yet said how she felt. But while she was being agreeable... "I'll fight again in two months."

Gasping with accusation, she glared at him. "You knew you'd fight again—"

"Of course I will." He snorted. "I got injured. I didn't quit."

"Yeah, I know. But..." Her confusion washed over him. "I didn't realize things were already set. Why didn't you tell me?"

"Didn't come up." He kissed the end of her nose. "And honestly, I was too busy raging about the fight I'd miss to talk about the next one."

He felt her stillness. "You're not raging anymore?"

"Mellow as a newborn kitten," he promised. "Thank you for that."

Thinking things through, she ran her hands up his chest to his collarbone. "Where?"

"Canada."

Gage felt her putting her shoulders back, straightening her spine, shoring herself up. "So when you leave again—"

Before she could finish that thought, he took her mouth, stepping her back into the door again, unable to keep his hands off her ass. When he came up for air, he said, "If you can, I'd love it if you came with me."

She was still all soft and sweet from his kiss. "To Canada?"

"To wherever I go, whenever I go. For training. For fighting." He tucked her hair behind her ear, gave her a soft and quick kiss. "For today and tomorrow and the year after that."

Her eyes widened and her lips parted. "Gage?"

"I told you I love you. Did you think I made it up?"

In a heartbeat, excitement stripped away the uncertainty and she threw herself against him, squeezing tight. With her shirt still gone, her jeans still down, it was an awesome embrace.

A knock sounded on the door, and Armie called, "Just about everyone is gone if you two want to wrap it up."

"He loves me," Harper told him.

Armie laughed. "Well, duh, doofus. Everyone could see that plain as day."

Gage cupped her head in his hands, but spoke to Armie. "Any predictions on how she feels about me?"

"Wow." The door jumped, meaning Armie had probably just propped his shoulder against it. "Hasn't told you yet, huh?"

"No."

"Cruel, Harper," he chastised her. "Really cruel. And here I thought you were one of those *nice* girls."

Lips quivering, eyes big and liquid, she stared up at him. "I love you," she whispered.

"Me or Gage?" Armie asked with facetious good humor.

Harper kicked the door hard with her heel, and Armie said, "Ow, damn it. Fine. I'm leaving. But Gage, you have the keys so I can't lock up until—"

"Five minutes."

"And there go my illusions again."

The quiet settled around them. They watched each other. Gage did some touching, too. But what the hell, Harper was mostly naked, looking at him with a wealth of emotion.

"I should get dressed."

"You should tell me again that you love me."

"I do. *So much*," Harper added with feeling. "I have for such a long time."

Nice. "The things you do to me…" He fumbled around along the wall beside the door and finally located the light switch.

She flinched away at first, but Harper wasn't shy. God knew she had no reason to be.

Putting her shoulders back, her chin up, she let him look. And what a sight she made with her jeans down below her knees and her shirt gone. He cupped her right breast and saw a light sprinkling of freckles decorating her fair skin.

"Let's go," he whispered. "I want to take you home and look for more freckles."

That made her snicker. As she pulled up her jeans, she said, "I don't really have that many."

"Don't ruin it for me. I'll find out for myself."

By the time they left the room, only Armie, Stack and Denver were still hanging around.

With his arm around Harper, Gage asked, "You guys didn't hook up?"

"Meeting her in an hour," Stack said.

"She's pulling her car around," Denver told him.

Armie shrugged toward the front door. "Those two are waiting for me."

Two? Everyone glanced at the front door where a couple of women hugged up to each other. One blonde, one raven-haired.

"Why does she have a whip in her belt?" Harper asked.

"I'm not sure," Armie murmured as he, too, watched the women. "But I'm intrigued."

"Are they fondling each other?" Gage asked.

"Could be." Armie drew his gaze back to Harper and Gage, then grinned shamelessly. "But I don't mind being the voyeuristic third wheel."

The guys all grinned with amusement. They were well used to Armie's excesses.

A little shocked, Harper shook her head. "One of these days a nice girl will make an honest man of you. That is, if some crazy woman doesn't do you in first."

"At least I'd die happy." Leaning against the table, arms folded over his chest, Armie studied them both. "So. You curious about how your match went?"

"Wasn't my match," Gage said.

"Should have been. And just so you know, Darvey annihilated your replacement."

"How many rounds?"

"Two. Referee stoppage."

Gage nodded as if it didn't matter all that much. Darvey had gotten off easy because Gage knew he'd have won the match.

Then Armie dropped a bombshell. "Cannon damn near lost."

Because he'd been expecting something very different, Gage blinked. "No way."

Armie blew out a breath. "He was all but gone from a vicious kick to the ribs."

"Ouch." Gage winced just thinking of it. If the kick nearly took Cannon out, it must have been a liver kick, and those hurt like a mother, stole your wind and made breathing—or fighting—impossible.

Stack picked up the story. "But you know Cannon. On his way down he threw one last punch—"

"And knocked Moeller out cold," Denver finished with enthusiasm. "It was truly something to see. Everyone was on their feet, not only here but at the event. The commentators went nuts. It was crazy."

"Everyone waited to see who would get back on his feet first," Stack finished.

And obviously that was Cannon. Gage half smiled. Every fighter knew flukes happened. Given a fluke injury had taken him out of the competition, he knew it better than most. "I'm glad he pulled it off."

"That he did," Armie said. "And if you don't mind locking up, I think I'll go pull off a few submissions of my own."

Harper scowled in disapproval, then flapped her hand, sending him on his way.

A minute later, Denver and Stack took off, too.

Left alone finally, Gage put his arm around Harper. "Ready to go home?"

"My place or yours?"

"Where doesn't matter—as long as you're with me."

She gave him a look that said *"Awww!"* and hugged him

tight. Still squeezed up close, she whispered with worry, "I can't believe Cannon almost lost."

Gage smoothed his hand down her back. "Don't worry about it. We fighters know how to turn bad situations to our advantage."

"We?" She leaned back in his arms to see him. "How's that?"

"For Cannon, the near miss will only hype up the crowd for his next fight." He bent to kiss the end of her freckled nose. "As for me, I might have missed a competition, but I got the girl. There'll be other fights, but honest to God, Harper, there's only one *you*. All in all, I'd say I'm the big winner tonight."

"I'd say you're *mine*." With a trembling, emotional smile, Harper touched his face, then his shoulders, and his chest. As her hand dipped lower, she whispered, "And that means we're both winners. Tonight, tomorrow and always."

\* \* \* \* \*

*Want more sizzling romance from*
New York Times *bestselling author Lori Foster?*
*Pick up every title in her Ultimate series:*

*HARD KNOCKS*
*NO LIMITS*
*HOLDING STRONG*
*TOUGH LOVE*

*Available now from HQN Books!*

COMING NEXT MONTH FROM

HARLEQUIN *Blaze*

Available September 15, 2015

### #863 TEASING HER SEAL
*Uniformly Hot!*
by Anne Marsh
SEAL team leader Gray Jackson needs to convince Laney Parker to leave an island resort before she gets hurt—and before his cover is blown. But as his mission heats up, so do their nights...

### #864 IF SHE DARES
by Tanya Michaels
Still timid months after being robbed at gunpoint, Riley Kendrick wants to rediscover her fun, daring side, and Jack Reed, her sexy new neighbor, has some wicked ideas about how to help.

### #865 NAKED THRILL
*The Wrong Bed*
by Jill Monroe
They wake up in bed together. Naked. And with no memory. So Tony and Hayden follow a trail of clues to piece together what—or *who*—they did on the craziest night of their lives.

### #866 KISS AND MAKEUP
by Taryn Leigh Taylor
Falling into bed with a sexy guy she met on a plane is impulsive even for Chloe. But when Ben's client catches them together, she does something even more impulsive: she pretends to be his wife!

YOU CAN FIND MORE INFORMATION ON UPCOMING HARLEQUIN® TITLES, FREE EXCERPTS AND MORE AT WWW.HARLEQUIN.COM.

HBCNM0915

# REQUEST YOUR FREE BOOKS!
## 2 FREE NOVELS PLUS 2 FREE GIFTS!

**HARLEQUIN®**

*Blaze*

### red-hot reads!

---

**YES!** Please send me 2 FREE Harlequin® Blaze® novels and my 2 FREE gifts (gifts are worth about $10). After receiving them, if I don't wish to receive any more books, I can return the shipping statement marked "cancel." If I don't cancel, I will receive 4 brand-new novels every month and be billed just $4.74 per book in the U.S. or $5.21 per book in Canada. That's a savings of at least 14% off the cover price. It's quite a bargain. Shipping and handling is just 50¢ per book in the U.S. and 75¢ per book in Canada.* I understand that accepting the 2 free books and gifts places me under no obligation to buy anything. I can always return a shipment and cancel at any time. Even if I never buy another book, the two free books and gifts are mine to keep forever.

150/350 HDN GH2D

Name _____ (PLEASE PRINT) _____

Address _____ Apt. #

City _____ State/Prov. _____ Zip/Postal Code

Signature (if under 18, a parent or guardian must sign)

---

Mail to the **Reader Service:**
**IN U.S.A.:** P.O. Box 1867, Buffalo, NY  14240-1867
**IN CANADA:** P.O. Box 609, Fort Erie, Ontario  L2A 5X3

**Want to try two free books from another line?**
**Call 1-800-873-8635 or visit www.ReaderService.com.**

* Terms and prices subject to change without notice. Prices do not include applicable taxes. Sales tax applicable in N.Y. Canadian residents will be charged applicable taxes. Offer not valid in Quebec. This offer is limited to one order per household. Not valid for current subscribers to Harlequin Blaze books. All orders subject to credit approval. Credit or debit balances in a customer's account(s) may be offset by any other outstanding balance owed by or to the customer. Please allow 4 to 6 weeks for delivery. Offer available while quantities last.

**Your Privacy**—The Reader Service is committed to protecting your privacy. Our Privacy Policy is available online at www.ReaderService.com or upon request from the Reader Service.

We make a portion of our mailing list available to reputable third parties that offer products we believe may interest you. If you prefer that we not exchange your name with third parties, or if you wish to clarify or modify your communication preferences, please visit us at www.ReaderService.com/consumerchoice or write to us at Reader Service Preference Service, P.O. Box 9062, Buffalo, NY 14240-9062. Include your complete name and address.

HBI5

**Limited time offer!**

# $1.⁰⁰ OFF

## TOUGH LOVE

*New York Times* Bestselling Author
## LORI FOSTER

She's playing hard to get...to win the
MMA fighter of her ultimate fantasies.

*Available August 25, 2015,
wherever books are sold.*

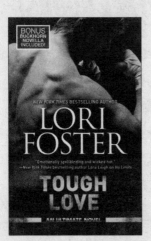

**HQN**™

---

## $1.⁰⁰ OFF
the purchase price of
**TOUGH LOVE by Lori Foster.**

Offer valid from August 25, 2015, to September 30, 2015.
Redeemable at participating retail outlets. Not redeemable at Barnes & Noble.
Limit one coupon per purchase. Valid in the U.S.A. and Canada only.

52612796

**Canadian Retailers:** Harlequin Enterprises Limited will pay the face value of this coupon plus 10.25¢ if submitted by customer for this product only. Any other use constitutes fraud. Coupon is nonassignable. Void if taxed, prohibited or restricted by law. Consumer must pay any government taxes. Void if copied. Inmar Promotional Services ("IPS") customers submit coupons and proof of sales to Harlequin Enterprises Limited, P.O. Box 3000, Saint John, NB E2L 4L3, Canada. Non-IPS retailer—for reimbursement submit coupons and proof of sales directly to Harlequin Enterprises Limited, Retail Marketing Department, 225 Duncan Mill Rd., Don Mills, Ontario M3B 3K9, Canada.

5 65373 00076 2    (8100)0 12073

**U.S. Retailers:** Harlequin Enterprises Limited will pay the face value of this coupon plus 8¢ if submitted by customer for this product only. Any other use constitutes fraud. Coupon is nonassignable. Void if taxed, prohibited or restricted by law. Consumer must pay any government taxes. Void if copied. For reimbursement submit coupons and proof of sales directly to Harlequin Enterprises Limited, P.O. Box 880478, El Paso, TX 88588-0478, U.S.A. Cash value 1/100 cents.

® and TM are trademarks owned and used by the trademark owner and/or its licensee.

© 2015 Harlequin Enterprises Limited

PHLF0915COUP

# HARLEQUIN

# *Blaze*

### Red-Hot Reads

*A hot shade of lipstick calls for a hot, sexy guy...*

Falling into bed with a sexy guy she met on a plane is impulsive even for Chloe. But when Ben's client catches them together, she does something even more impulsive: she pretends to be his wife!

FINALIST
SO YOU THINK YOU CAN WRITE

✂

---

# SAVE $1.00

on the purchase of KISS AND MAKEUP by Taryn Leigh Taylor {available Sept. 15, 2015} or any other Harlequin® Blaze® book.

Redeemable at participating outlets in the U.S. and Canada only. Not redeemable at Barnes & Noble stores. Limit one coupon per customer.

52612884

**Canadian Retailers:** Harlequin Enterprises Limited will pay the face value of this coupon plus 10.25¢ if submitted by customer for this product only. Any other use constitutes fraud. Coupon is nonassignable. Void if taxed, prohibited or restricted by law. Consumer must pay any government taxes. Void if copied. Inmar Promotional Services ("IPS") customers submit coupons and proof of sales to Harlequin Enterprises Limited, P.O. Box 3000, Saint John, NB E2L 4L3, Canada. Non-IPS retailer—for reimbursement submit coupons and proof of sales directly to Harlequin Enterprises Limited, Retail Marketing Department, 225 Duncan Mill Rd., Don Mills, Ontario M3B 3K9, Canada.

**U.S. Retailers:** Harlequin Enterprises Limited will pay the face value of this coupon plus 8¢ if submitted by customer for this product only. Any other use constitutes fraud. Coupon is nonassignable. Void if taxed, prohibited or restricted by law. Consumer must pay any government taxes. Void if copied. For reimbursement submit coupons and proof of sales directly to Harlequin Enterprises Limited, P.O. Box 880478, El Paso, TX 88588-0478, U.S.A. Cash value 1/100 cents.

5 65373 00076 2   (8100)0 12081

**COUPON EXPIRES DEC. 15, 2015**
Available wherever books are sold, including most bookstores, supermarkets, drugstores and discount stores.
**www.Harlequin.com**

® and ™ are trademarks owned and used by the trademark owner and/or its licensee.
© 2015 Harlequin Enterprises Limited

HBCOUP0915

Turn your love of reading into rewards you'll love with

# Harlequin My Rewards

**Join for FREE today at
www.HarlequinMyRewards.com**

Earn **FREE BOOKS** of your choice.

Experience **EXCLUSIVE OFFERS** and contests.

Enjoy **BOOK RECOMMENDATIONS**
selected just for you.

**PLUS!** Sign up now
and get **500** points
right away!

Earn
**FREE**
REWARDS
HarlequinMyRewards.com
Join
Today!

MYR16R